DUALITY

The Fractured Soul Saga: Book One

Ametra S. Rayford

Cover typography and layout by Arrayed Formats™

This book is a work of fiction. Names, characters, places, and incidents are either products of the author's imagination or are inspired by actual events and used fictitiously. Any resemblance to actual persons, living or dead, is intentional and presented as fictionalized for the purposes of this story.

ISBN: 978-1-737-01480-5

Published by Arrayed Formats™

Dedication

For my mother

Prologue

She crouched as she forced her body deep inside the crowded closet. She wiped tears from her cheeks and shuddered as her fingertips grazed the clots of blood and flesh stuck to her skin. Gritting her teeth, she swallowed as bile rose in her throat.

An ear-splitting scream rang out. Guttural gurgles answered, twisting into something like laughter. She heard panting and the wet slap of bare feet scurrying down the hallway toward her. Her eyes flicked upward to the doorknob. She grasped the knob and held it in place with all her strength. As it rattled in her hands, she heard frustration and terror.

"Please!" a female voice cried. "I know you're in there! I heard you come this way. Let me in! Why is this happening?"

She closed her eyes, pressing her forehead against the cool wooden door as she tightened her grip. She did not know why this was happening. She should not have been there...

"PLEASE!" the voice on the other side of the door screamed. "You can't just stay in there and let this happen to me! Why won't you... NO!"

Pleas turned to choking.

Bones broke.

A high-pitched giggle followed, then the unmistakable sounds of flesh tearing and being devoured.

The victim's whimpering turned into a raspy keening... then nothing.

The stench of blood thickened in the closet. The sounds of sloppy consumption filled her ears while slippery blood crept beneath the crack of the closet door.

Minutes passed after the smacking ceased.

She caught a glimpse of a hulking shadow beneath the door.

She heard its purring as if content with the meal.

That was it. The others were gone.

She remained still, wondering how long she would have to wait, hoping her friend hadn't made it aware that someone was still left. Her grip on the doorknob trembled, but held fast.

A flickering shadow beneath the door locked her in place.

The door burst apart.

She screamed as it snatched her into the hallway.

Chapter One

"Now that must have been a wild weekend."

The young woman started, blinking into focus the clear blue gaze of the young man sitting across from her. He had an angular face, wide at the forehead, with chiseled cheekbones tapering to a delicate, squared jawline. Clean-shaven with thick black hair and sculpted eyebrows, a single dimple studded his right cheek and enhanced a bright smile. His heather-blue button-down shirt was starched to perfection, as were his black slacks. The polished gleam of his black shoes made it more obvious that he wasn't wearing socks.

"I'm sorry?" she said at last, finding her voice.

He chuckled, his dimple returning. "You looked so distracted. Ah, never mind. It was a poor joke and not likely worth repeating," he explained, running a manicured hand through the lushness of his hair, offering a glimpse of what looked like an awfully expensive watch.

Though well-dressed in a burgundy sheath that complemented the caramel undertones of her smooth, light brown skin, she still felt slightly underdressed in comparison.

"You're here to interview?" the young man said enthusiastically.

"At twelve-thirty," she said softly, pausing as he peeked at his watch and then whistled.

"Early bird, huh?" he asked. "You still have about an hour."

"I do," she confirmed with a nod. "And I am."

"Who's your pick, Blake or Matheson?" When she arched a dark brow and did not respond, he shrugged. "Come on. It's not exactly a secret. Everyone knows who's hiring in this building."

"I'm not sure what you mean," she answered.

"Edmund Blake runs one of the largest advertising firms in the city," the young man said. "Well, outside the city, anyway. He's headquartered about an hour away. But, this building houses the office of the hottest new firm downtown—run by Gabriel Matheson. Heard of him?" She responded with a blank expression. "Anyway, they're merging."

"And, you know this... how?"

"Like I said, it's not exactly a secret." He sat back in his chair, looking pleased with himself. "You should know it, too, if you're planning to interview well."

"I'll interview well," she said with confidence.

The thick lashes of her hazel eyes swept past him to follow a young woman in a worn black suit, rushing to catch an elevator before it closed. When she didn't make it, her gaze returned to the young man with a twinkle. He was watching her with interest.

"What is it you're interviewing for?" he asked.

"Junior Executive Assistant."

The blue eyes widened. "You're young for that."

"Hardly," she smiled.

"You're... what... twenty-two? Twenty-three?" he said. She shifted her gaze to her manicure, the smile not leaving her face. "The juniors aren't exactly junior, if you get what I mean."

"I'm sure I'll manage," she assured him.

"Could be cutthroat," he warned. "I'm sure that not everyone's coming along on that merger."

"I'll manage," she repeated.

He dimpled again. "Manage by what—sitting here?"

"Don't knock it," she chided. "I enjoy moments like this."

His brow furrowed, somehow making his chiseled features seem more attractive. "Moments like what?"

"People watching," she responded. "Getting to know my surroundings, the comings and goings of others."

She noted the arch of his dark brow as he glanced around the reception area, through the glass doors, and at the rush of people outside. He then looked back at her with a puzzled expression. She could not help chuckling.

"It's an acquired taste," she admitted.

"And this is what you plan to do for the next hour?" he queried.

"And what I've done for the hour before now," she said.

"How is this helping you to prepare for your interview? Usually people have flash cards, speeches to rehearse, that sort of thing."

"This is all I need for the interview," she replied, patting the black leather satchel resting in her lap.

He smiled again, something that seemed easy for him, as he leaned forward in the sturdy, upholstered gray chair and steepled his fingertips beneath his nose.

"What have you learned?"

"From watching?" she asked, straightening a bit when he nodded. "I've seen dozens of people come through those doors, and nearly all of them do the same thing—either right before they enter or immediately after."

"And what's that?"

"They change everything—expression, posture, demeanor. They put on a second face to get ready for the day ahead." She watched as he blinked. "What do you do when you have to talk with someone—particularly a person you don't entirely care to be around?"

"I brace myself," he answered after a moment. "I prepare for the situation before facing it."

She nodded. "Yes, you adopt certain personality traits—become that snake oil salesman, if you will—just so that you can get through it. That's what these people do. Watch."

"Hmm?" he asked.

"Watch the door," she said. "Watch those coming in. See for yourself."

The young man turned around in his seat. A man carrying a black briefcase and wearing an expensive dark blue suit was getting out of a cab parked at the curb. He walked toward the building, straightening his tie, and stopped before opening one of the doors. He took a deep breath, pulled his shoulders back, affected a smile, and stepped inside.

The smile was still plastered across his lips as he moved through the lobby to approach the bank of elevators, nodding to different people along the way. He continued smiling until the elevator arrived. He stepped in, and the doors closed behind him.

"You're sitting in the reception area of the building that houses the city's fastest-growing advertising company... home of the busiest and brightest...

and you're grading the denizens on their posture and facial expressions?" the dark-haired man said when he turned back to look at the woman.

"Grading?" she giggled. "I'm not the administrator."

"Proctor, then?"

She smirked. "You noticed," she said. "You saw exactly what I mean. You don't want to concede the point."

"There was a point?" he asked, reddening. "You're here, too, you know. Did you assume another demeanor before coming in?"

"Like I said," she laughed, "nearly everyone does." Though not a lock of her berry-kissed black hair had escaped from its side-swept chignon, she reached up to give it a gentle pat, the smirk still playing on her lips. "I'm hardly exceptional."

"Somehow, I doubt that." The dimple returned. "It's definitely an interesting concept. But, why are you interested?"

"In?"

"In the comings and goings of those in the lobby," he wanted to know. She smiled without answering, and he chuckled. "We should discuss it during lunch."

He grabbed the black briefcase from its resting place beside the chair and got to his feet, the blue gaze examining her with interest.

"What?" she snorted.

"Lunch," he said again.

"I've an interview in forty-five minutes," she said, her almond-shaped hazel eyes wide. "I can't go to lunch with you."

"Correction: you've had your interview," he grinned before extending a hand. "Gabriel Matheson. Looks like we'll be working together."

"Xiomara Grant," came the response. "And, you're not Edmund Blake."

"So?" Gabriel challenged.

"To answer your earlier question, he's my pick. He's who I'm to interview with."

"Formality," Gabriel said with a wave of his hand. "Like I told you, Blake's firm is being absorbed by mine. I have as much of a say in who gets hired. Probably more, really, and I'm currently interviewing for another assistant of my own—so this meeting was fortuitous."

"We haven't talked salary or benefits," Xiomara reminded him.

"Another formality," he said. "I'll even add another ten percent to what Blake would likely have offered you, since I know how he thinks."

Xiomara got to her feet and at last shook the proffered hand. "This is… highly unusual," she said.

"I'm an unusual man," he said, still smiling. "Something you'll learn and appreciate in time."

Xiomara arched a brow as Gabriel's blue eyes took her in. In black leather pumps with three-inch heels, she was taller than Gabriel by several inches, something he seemed to make a note of in that sweeping look.

"If I may say so, Mr. Matheson—"

"Gabriel," he corrected, amused.

"If I may say so, Gabriel," Xiomara tried again, "this is the most unorthodox interview I've ever taken part in."

"Good!" he said, pleased, as they began walking. "Once we get to my office, we'll go over things a bit more while we have lunch. What do you like? I have a portfolio of menus showcasing some of the most wonderful local fare: sushi, Japanese-French fusion, Neo-Mexican…"

"Cuisine befitting the busiest and brightest?"

Gabriel stopped walking and turned to look at her. "Not interested?"

"In Japanese-French fusion?" Xiomara smirked.

"All right, then." Gabriel held the door open that separated the main reception area from the offices on the ground floor. They moved along the carpeted hallway until they reached another set of double doors, above which winked the gold lettering showing that they had arrived at Matheson Media. As they entered, he smiled over at her. "Ladies Choice: What would you like for lunch?"

"Hummus," she responded, "some lovely falafel… maybe a bite of kafta…"

They stopped again, this time at the door at the end of the hall. A gold-lettered plaque reading 'Gabriel Q. Matheson' glittered against the dark cherry wood. She considered his expression.

"Mediterranean food," she offered. He blinked. "Does that have a spot in your portfolio?" Gabriel reddened. "There's a family-owned place a few blocks from here."

"Great!" he said, reaching into his pocket and pulling out his iPhone. "What's it called? I can have some delivered." The silence that followed compelled him to look up from the bright display and into the amusement reflected in her hazel eyes. "What?"

"They're a small place," she told him. "They don't deliver."

"Well, how are we supposed to get lunch?" he asked, frowning.

"We could go there, sit at a table, and order," Xiomara said in a gentle tone. "After about fifteen minutes, they'll bring everything out." Gabriel's frown deepened.

"You're making fun of me," he accused.

"Maybe a bit," she conceded, with a playful wrinkling of her nose as she smiled.

"Ah, Gabriel!"

The duo turned to see a broad smile stretched across the tanned face of the man approaching them. Despite the advantage of the three-inch heels she wore, Xiomara was still at least a few inches shorter than the newcomer, and Gabriel's slight build made him look childlike in comparison.

"Good morning, Edmund," Gabriel greeted, shaking the older man's hand. Xiomara, fascinated, watched Gabriel's delicate hand disappear inside the other man's paw. "I'd like you to meet Xiomara Grant. Xiomara, this is Edmund Blake."

"Grant?" Blake said, his brow furrowing as he took Xiomara's hand and offered a firm shake. "Xiomara Grant? You and I have an interview in less than an hour, I believe."

"I took care of it," Gabriel said with a wave of his hand. "We were going to discuss specifics during lunch now that I've made her an offer."

"Is that right?" Blake said, his cognac-brown eyes shifting from Xiomara to Gabriel and back. "And how did you come to meet young Gabriel here?"

"He was in the lobby, and we struck up a conversation," she answered. "I didn't know who he was at first, though. He said something about needing to hire an assistant of his own as well?"

"Did he now?" Blake said, his face an unreadable mask as the smile locked in place. "How fortuitous for him to have encountered you."

"Same as he said, more or less."

10

"Indeed." Blake's eyes shifted to take Gabriel in. "We should talk, Gabriel."

"Mr. Blake," Xiomara interjected, "if there's a problem or if you think it's best for us to proceed with our interview as scheduled…"

"No, that isn't it," Blake replied, looking at Xiomara once more. She could not help noticing that his expression, when directed at her, seemed almost warm. That did not seem to be the case when he focused on Gabriel. "I've looked over your background and the samples of your work for other employers, and I'm immensely pleased. I know that the interview would have been nothing more than a formality, and I would have hired you myself. You are an exceptionally talented young woman."

"Then what's the problem?" Gabriel asked. This time, Blake did not look at Gabriel. He instead kept his gaze locked on Xiomara.

"I'm glad to welcome you to the team, Miss Grant," Blake said with an encouraging nod. "I want very much for you to enjoy a lovely lunch with young Gabriel here. Once you return, I'll have someone bring you in to get you up to speed; and, of course, you'll need to talk with Valerie in Human Resources to get all the annoying paperwork out of the way."

"Of course, Mr. Blake," Xiomara said. "Thank you very much."

"It would appear that we both have Gabriel to thank," he responded, his gaze landing upon the younger man again. "How fortuitous, indeed."

Xiomara watched as Blake ambled down the hallway and went into an office on the right.

"You can put your bag down and I'll get us an Uber," Gabriel said from behind her. She turned to see that he was looking down at his phone as he opened the door to his office and stepped in. He then paused and looked back at Xiomara, who was still standing in the hallway. "Now what?"

"You have as much say in who gets hired?" she said. "Probably more?"

Gabriel shrugged. "He didn't overturn the decision, did he? Besides, he'd already hired you even before you showed up." The dimple resurfaced. "I guess you didn't need to practice after all." Xiomara arched a brow at him, and he held up his phone. "Uber?"

Chapter Two

"Not bad at all for your first day, as unconventional as it was," Gabriel remarked several hours later as he and Xiomara stepped into the summer evening. They faced each other outside the building.

Her hair, initially styled for a brief interview, was long since freed from confinement and hung in loose waves below her shoulders.

"That it was," Xiomara agreed.

"It's a wonder we could get anything done, with Blake keeping you holed away in his office for most of the afternoon."

Xiomara grinned. "Still upset about that, are you?"

"I'm not sure why he needed to speak with you alone," Gabriel said, shrugging slender shoulders. "My afternoon was clear. I could have attended."

"Considering that I'll be working for him, I'd say he was justified," she said.

"What did he want to talk with you about?"

"As he said: paperwork, salary negotiations…"

"You and I talked about salary already," Gabriel said.

"No, what you did was tack a percentage onto some imagined figure," Xiomara corrected. "By the way, it would seem that your intention to hire another assistant might come as quite the surprise to the one you already have."

Gabriel flushed. "I'll need more assistants once this merger is done," he said. "You'll be helping me with my projects at some point." Xiomara scoffed, then looked away with a slight shake of her head. "What else is bothering you?"

She took her time, choosing her words with care.

"Those people in the reception area," she said. "I saw the same three when we left for lunch, when we came back, and I'd swear we just walked by one of them."

"What about them?" Xiomara raised both brows at him, and he looked at her with wide eyes. "What, Xiomara?"

"Did Mr. Blake have other interviews today?" she asked.

"Of course he did," Gabriel said. "Surely you didn't think you were the only one—not to work *here*. He even interviewed others before you."

"And you weren't going to say anything?"

"To whom?" he asked, puzzled.

"To them!" she exclaimed. "You left them there! Even after the decision was made to hire me, you never once had your assistant dismiss any of the people sticking around and hoping their interview would still take place— something I'm sure Mr. Blake trusted you to take care of."

"Well, I couldn't very well do that, could I?" Gabriel asked, dimple on display. "I might've ended up needing one of them if things backfired with you. You could've ended up being one of those Alex Jones fans, or something vile like that."

Xiomara sighed and shook her head, her hazel gaze drifting to the city lights against a darkening sky.

"You don't agree with my methods," Gabriel surmised.

"Of course I don't," she responded without looking at him.

"You knew that there'd be others," he said. "So, you knew that someone would get left out."

"Not like that. I wouldn't have thought about that. But, I guess it's the way things are done now."

"That almost sounds like a rebuke," he remarked.

"Merely an observation," she clarified.

"A pastime you won't have as much time for, now that you're on my team."

"*That* sounded like a rebuke," Xiomara said, tilting her head as her gaze returned to Gabriel.

They looked at one another—crystal blue meeting warm hazel—with nothing said for a moment. At last, Gabriel found himself unable to maintain the stare as a flush crept up from his neck and colored his cheeks.

"Come have a drink with me," he offered at last.

"It's getting late," Xiomara challenged.

"It's barely seven," he protested.

"Exactly."

"There's a place up the street. We don't even have to get an Uber."

"I'd rather not. Thanks, though."

"You're that upset about those people in the lobby? Really?"

"That's not the only reason."

"It's the one I'm concerned with," Gabriel confessed.

"Now you show concern?" Xiomara countered with a smirk.

Gabriel laughed, though there was little mirth in it. "I don't get you," he admitted. "From the moment I spotted you in the waiting area until now, you've carried yourself as someone without a care in the world. You sat there... people watching... not rehearsing, not fretting over your hair and makeup, not fiddling with your bag or checking your watch every seven minutes.

"I told you who I am, and you didn't so much as blink. Mind you, the fact that you did not already know who I am is baffling. I... I thrust you into a meeting this afternoon, making you take my assistant's place at the last minute to help me with a presentation Ruby could barely understand..."

"Right under Mr. Blake's nose," Xiomara commented.

"Right under Blake's nose!" Gabriel agreed with a smile. "Ruby stayed late for weeks to help with that project, and you stepped right in like it was nothing."

"Poor Ruby," she sighed. "And, I highly doubt that she didn't understand the presentation if she worked on it for as long as you say. It was very well put together."

"And you think that's because of Ruby?" Gabriel asked. "All I know is that you've made quite the impression, and you've yet to break a sweat or seem out of sorts... until I ask you to have a simple drink with me."

"I'm hardly sweating," she commented.

"You see? There you go again. So many would give their right arm for a drink with Gabriel Quentin Matheson..."

"Like any of those sycophants you deserted in reception?"

"I'm trying to apologize!" Gabriel insisted.

"There's no need," Xiomara said, shrugging.

"Well, you could've fooled me." He studied her. "It's like dealing with my mother. Automatic guilt trip everywhere I turn."

Xiomara laughed. "Your mother? Really?"

14

"You know what I mean," Gabriel countered. "Or you would if you'd come out with me."

"I respectfully decline—again. It's been an eventful day, and if I'm to be ready for tomorrow, I need to get home."

Gabriel nodded. "Can I get you an Uber?"

"I don't live that far away," Xiomara responded. "I can walk, thank you."

"You live within walking distance?" he queried, with brows raised. "I'm not sure I could manage that even on my salary! How much is Blake paying you?"

She laughed again and then turned away, lifting a hand in farewell as she walked. "Have a good evening, Gabriel!" she called, the evening breeze rippling her hair over her shoulders.

"Sycophants," she heard him snort behind her as she departed.

Chapter Three

The living room was large, anchored by a sectional sofa with beige microfiber seating atop a chocolate leather base.

Decorative pillows in alternating shades of terracotta, tan, and mocha accented the sofa, and an immense cocktail ottoman sat in front of it.

A large estate rug in complementary colors lay across the gleaming hardwood floor. Though there was no other furniture, several well-placed brass wall sconces bathed the room in soft, warm light.

Xiomara sat on the floor, far from the ottoman, legs crossed before her in the lotus position. Her long lashes rested against her cheeks, and her hands curved palm-down against her knees. Her breathing was steady and soft. She appeared to be asleep despite her straight back and unbowed head.

The knock did not startle her. Instead, she sighed and opened her eyes. She rose to her feet without using her hands, then approached and opened the door. A massive arrangement of flowers all but dwarfed the person holding it.

"Ex-oh-mera Grant?" piped a voice.

"As you like," Xiomara drawled, accepting the extravagant bouquet.

"Have a good evening, ma'am," the young lady said, turning away from the barn-style door and heading back to the antiquated elevator.

Xiomara considered the flowers, closing the door with a backward kick of her right heel. She moved through the spacious loft into the kitchen, placing the flowers and their heavy, gold-swirled crystal vase on the silver-flecked black quartz countertop.

Spying a card nestled near the center of the arrangement, she grabbed and opened it, brows raised as she read the neat script.

Alas—left to my own devices without a sycophant in sight. 825 W. Trace Terrace, if you feel thirsty.

Xiomara exited the kitchen, turned off the light, and tossed the card into the nearby silver trash can before walking to the panel near the front door. She twisted the knob, dimming the living room lights until they went out. Xiomara continued down the hallway, went into her bedroom, and closed the door.

Chapter Four

Xiomara had already finished organizing several of her belongings in her spacious new office when Gabriel first passed the open door. He doubled back to linger in the doorway. Seeing him through a gap in her hair, she leaned forward to reach for a binder. She did nothing to betray her awareness of his presence. It was only after his polite knock on the door frame that she looked up.

"Good morning, Gabriel," she offered.

"Good morning to you," he countered, still lingering. "Get an early start this morning? It's not even eight o'clock."

"I did," Xiomara said as she opened the binder. "I wanted to be ready to assist Mr. Blake this morning with his itinerary, so I came in to get set up first."

She closed the binder, placing it on her desk before giving Gabriel her full attention. As expected, his charcoal-gray slacks were creased razor-sharp, and a pink shirt complemented the flush in his cheeks. Gabriel's bright eyes swept the room before landing on Xiomara again.

"Nice to see you getting settled in," he remarked. "We also have an interior designer on staff if you wanted to order anything to, you know, spruce things up."

"I think I'm sufficiently spruced, thank you," Xiomara smirked. "But, I'll keep it in mind."

She watched as Gabriel's eyes danced over the space. Aside from silver-framed representations of her credentials on the wall, the office was devoid of any personal touches, apart from a series of photographs. While there were no close-ups of people on display, a variety of picturesque landscapes from cities around the world brought life to the room, including panoramic shots of landmarks.

"Bit of a travel bug, are you?" he remarked.

"Something like that," Xiomara answered, turning to place the remaining binders on a shelf on the bookcase, aligning their spines flush with one another. "My passport's seen some action."

"Have any favorite places?" Gabriel asked.

"Hmm," Xiomara considered with a tilt of her head, "Santorini, Barcelona, Prague..."

"You've been to all those places?"

"Twice to Barcelona." She turned and pointed at one of the larger pictures showing the Cathedral of Santa Eulalia. Gabriel moved closer to look at it and the others.

"I don't even recognize some of these places," he admitted.

"I do a fair bit of hiking on my trips. I enjoy capturing what I find along the trails."

Gabriel chuckled as he turned to her. "No wonder you seem to enjoy walking everywhere," he commented. "Walking in the city must seem like nothing when compared to an unmarked trail."

"You should try it," Xiomara said.

"When's your next vacation?" Gabriel challenged.

Xiomara laughed. "Thank you, by the way."

"For?" he asked, though his face flushed again.

"The flowers," she answered. "They're exquisite."

"I'm glad you like them... though they didn't seem to accomplish what I hoped," Gabriel said, walking back toward the door.

"You didn't hope to provide a colorful and sweet-smelling welcome to a new employee?" Xiomara asked lightly.

"I hoped to enjoy your company," Gabriel said.

A tall, curvaceous blonde with eyes resembling dull green glass joined him in the doorway. Wearing a somewhat expensive, expertly tailored suede wrap dress in an unflattering shade of brown, Mary Jane clogs covered her tiny feet.

"Good morning, Mr. Matheson," she murmured, shifting from one thick ankle to the other. "I thought I heard your voice. I'm happy to put fresh coffee on, but I haven't yet ordered your breakfast. I wasn't expecting you yet. You're early."

She then glanced at Xiomara as if it were her fault. Xiomara, noting the glance, smiled and then turned back to her binders.

"That's fine, Ruby," Gabriel responded. "When you go across the street to the bakery, get a few dozen assorted for the main conference room... and maybe something specific for Ms. Grant?"

"Ms. Grant has had her breakfast," Xiomara said before turning to face Ruby. "Thank you, though." Ruby reddened and shuffled away. Xiomara shook her head and flicked her gaze toward Gabriel again, chuckling. "I think you owe *her* some flowers, particularly after what you put her through yesterday. She can barely look at me now since you set me up to take credit for her work."

"This isn't the first time that you've incorrectly assumed that the work was hers," Gabriel commented. "In any case, she'll get over it. Ruby's loyal."

"Loyalty doesn't translate to being a doormat," Xiomara cautioned.

"Think I'm treating her like a sycophant, huh?" he said.

"Oh!" Xiomara said in pretend shock. "Someone has a new favorite word."

"You never let me explain that, by the way," Gabriel accused.

"As I said yesterday, there's no need," Xiomara answered.

"I could have explained it over drinks last night."

"There was no need for that, either."

"So, I guess that your busy day of coddling Blake won't have any room for lunch with me, then?" he asked in a light tone.

Xiomara bristled as her eyes narrowed.

"Frankly, I don't understand why you bother," she said.

"With?"

"With any attempt at apology or amends," Xiomara said. "You do well for a while, then make a remark that negates all of it. You must be awfully fond of the taste of toes, judging from the way you insist upon sticking your foot in your mouth."

"This is ridiculous!" Gabriel said through clenched teeth.

"At last, we agree," she returned before studying him again. "What exactly is your issue with Mr. Blake, anyway?"

"Who says I have an issue?"

"Nothing about you, from the moment we met yesterday, has given me any sign that you have a modicum of respect for the man whose company is about to merge with yours."

"Respect?" Gabriel scoffed.

"Never mind," Xiomara said with a shake of her head, sitting at her desk. "That response tells me all I need to know."

"I didn't even say anything!"

"You said plenty," she countered. "And no need to send me any flowers once you figure it out." She paused and looked at him again. "How did you get my address, anyway?" This time, even Gabriel's ears turned red. "Mr. Matheson, for shame..."

"It's not like I'm coming on to you or anything," he said in a casual tone.

"Oh, I know," Xiomara answered as she leafed through one of her manuals and then glanced at the computer screen.

He started at that. "What do you mean you know?" he accused.

Xiomara looked up at him, mirth twinkling in her eyes. Her gaze then shifted as she noticed Ruby ambling by, laden with pastry boxes, as she shuffled along.

"Your breakfast is here," Xiomara said. Gabriel's glance followed Ruby's departing form and then returned to Xiomara. She beamed at him. "I'll see you at the meeting later?"

Gabriel nodded without comment and left Xiomara's office to, she assumed, head for his own.

Chapter Five

Xiomara bolted upright in bed, stifling a scream. Covered in sweat, her hair damp and clinging, she looked at the illuminated clock on the bedside table. It was a few minutes past midnight, and she had been asleep for an hour.

She climbed out of bed with a sigh, going into the adjoining bathroom. Looking into the mirror, she studied her reflection for a moment. There she stood: five-foot-ten in bare feet, clad in a soft—though somewhat damp—pink tank top and matching pajama bottoms scattered with gray dots.

Her dark hair, with its burgundy undertones, fell in a limp tangle past her shoulders. She was not pleased to see that her skin, usually warm with a natural glow, seemed drained of color, revealing gentle gray smudges beneath her almond-shaped hazel eyes.

Xiomara reached for the medicine cabinet to retrieve what she needed. She nibbled her bottom lip, lifting the cap of the red-topped bottle of witch hazel infused with a bit of rose water and aloe before squeezing a few drops onto one cotton crescent, then another. Satisfied, she replaced the cap and returned the bottle to the cabinet.

Leaning toward the mirror, Xiomara pressed a crescent into place beneath each eye, covering the smudges, before returning to the bedroom to select a fresh pair of pajamas.

An hour later, after showering and changing, she padded down the hallway toward the spare room, pulling on a red robe. She had washed her hair, separating it into two braids that hung over her shoulders. The cotton crescents lay discarded in the trash.

The rest of the apartment was immaculate.

Most of the contents of the spare room were in boxes stacked with care along the far wall. Among the unpacked items was a sturdy mahogany desk, on which sat an open laptop. A charcoal-gray, backless balance ball chair was tucked beneath it. A rectangular wooden box sat to the left of the laptop.

Xiomara lingered in the well-lit hallway before entering the room and approaching the desk. She drew out the balance ball chair and took a seat. After steadying herself, she reached toward the box and opened it to reveal a wire-bound 11x14 sketchpad. She lifted it from the box, revealing a kit containing dozens of oil-based pencils in myriad colors.

Flipping through the pad, her hazel eyes dancing over at least a dozen detailed drawings, Xiomara stopped, focusing on one while frowning in concentration.

It was a sketch of a man from the shoulders up. The rendering of his clothing was unfinished, and most of the drawing was still in outline form. The only thing clear—to the point of leaping from the page—was a pair of penetrating and direct hazel eyes set in the outline of a face framed by lifelike hair drawn in shades of gold with streaks of silver woven through it. Xiomara studied the drawing for a few minutes, her brow still furrowed, and shook her head as if to clear it.

"Who are you?" she whispered to the page. "Why do I keep seeing you? I don't understand what this means."

She narrowed her eyes at the drawing, trying to recall something from the dream that might help. The details had already faded, leaving her once again with the same unsettling fear the nightmare always carried.

Xiomara sighed, looking again into the hazel eyes before slapping the sketchpad closed and tossing it back into the wooden case. She then got up from the chair and exited the room without a backward glance.

Chapter Six

"Thank you so much for helping me set up. I can't believe how the morning has gotten away from me."

Xiomara moved through the conference room, her burgundy suede wrap dress whispering as she walked. She wore her hair pulled back into a low bun, and she flitted about in knee-high brown leather boots with hand-tooled accents around the ankles.

Ruby, her blonde hair falling in soft waves below her shoulders, mirrored her as she placed colorful portfolios on the table opposite where Xiomara was working. She wore a tailored navy-blue piqué knit dress that flattered her curves without being too ostentatious and moved about in low-heeled pumps.

"Doesn't seem like you needed much help at all," Ruby murmured in response. "As always, you have a firm grasp on everything."

Xiomara paused and looked up. "Is that what you think?" she asked.

"I know how much Mr. Matheson counts on you—and Mr. Blake does, too," Ruby said, shrugging.

"Ruby," Xiomara began with care, "I know we didn't start out in the best way."

"That wasn't because of you. That was Mr. Matheson's doing." The truth of the statement startled Xiomara, and she dropped the portfolios onto the table. "I know he tried to stir things up when he replaced me with you in that meeting your first day here, and in other meetings over the last few weeks."

"And that was okay with you?"

"No, it wasn't okay," Ruby admitted. "But, these are his meetings and his presentations, despite the amount of work I put into them. Nothing here belongs to me—not yet—and so I have no say."

Xiomara considered the other woman before nodding. She then leaned against the table and arched a brow.

"You're an astute woman, Ruby," she said, "and I will not insult your intelligence. I imagine you've already guessed that there's more to your being here than me needing your help to set up for the meeting."

"Like I said," Ruby said in the calm tone Xiomara had grown used to, "you always have a firm grasp on everything. So, why am I here?"

"That's my question to you, Ruby," Xiomara countered. "Why are you here? Gabriel routinely underestimates your abilities, and you don't have any semblance of the voice or presence you've earned. Fetching doughnuts, arranging lunches... I know that there's more to you than that—much more—and yet you allow Gabriel to portray you as someone who barely understands the presentations you had as much of a hand in as he did."

"Mr. Matheson is very talented," Ruby said. "I've learned a lot from him."

"Not because he planned it that way, but because you're a sponge, Ruby. I'm sure you've learned a great deal just by watching. You also seem to go out of your way to be inconspicuous. Why? Why are you an assistant rather than an executive?"

"This from the woman who seems to have strolled in from the ether and changed the dynamics of the Matheson-Blake merger," Ruby commented before, at long last, smiling. The simple shift in expression illuminated Ruby's face, and Xiomara could not help smiling as well.

"Changed the dynamics?" Xiomara asked.

"Both men are fighting harder now, it seems. This merger has started to mean more to each of them, though for different reasons."

"What does it mean for you, Ruby?"

Ruby paused for a moment, reaching down to straighten a folder.

"I want to head a team of my own," she murmured, not looking up as the smile faded. "I want to pick my projects and create my legacy. There's still more for me to learn, there always is, but you're right. I'm not about pastries and menus. I'm hoping that there'll be some benefit in this merger for me—a means to advance—something I haven't yet achieved as an employee of Matheson Media."

"If you know you can't advance here," Xiomara began, "why do you stay?"

"Because this is the fastest-growing firm in this region," Ruby said, looking up again with determination infusing light into her dull green eyes. "Mr. Matheson can't control everything on his own as we grow. Soon, he's going to have to delegate, and I want in. I have a right to be included. Isn't that why you're here, to get a place on the ground floor of what Matheson Media will become?"

Xiomara chuckled and retrieved the fallen portfolios. "Remember, I didn't interview to become a part of Matheson Media," she said. "I was hired to serve the interests of Mr. Blake."

Ruby studied her. "But, EJB Advertising is being absorbed," she pointed out. "What will you do once Blake has moved on?"

Xiomara laughed again as she cradled the extra portfolios. "Maybe I'll work for you," she commented.

Ruby shook her blonde head. "Not if Mr. Matheson has any say."

"Then let's pretend that he doesn't," Xiomara answered, still smiling. "I'm glad that we got to talk, though. I hope you see that I'm not your enemy, Ruby."

"I see that," Ruby said, nodding. "You don't seem to have any goal other than helping Mr. Blake to succeed, even on his way out. Can't say that I understand it, because you're obviously highly skilled and you also have Mr. Matheson's ear. Yet, you're genuinely not clamoring for a spot. Doesn't make you an enemy, it just makes you... puzzling."

"It's looking pretty good in here, ladies," Gabriel said as he strolled in. He locked a blushing Ruby in his blue gaze. "Why don't you go on ahead and pick up our usual order from the bakery so that everything can be ready for the meeting?"

"I was about to take care of that myself," Xiomara interjected as Ruby opened her mouth to speak. Ruby's expression went from slight embarrassment to complete awe. "Ruby was so kind to come help me finish the setup since I was behind this morning. The least I can do is go grab our order while Ruby checks over the PowerPoint presentation once more."

"I would really rather that you..." Gabriel began.

"Nothing to it!" Xiomara said with enthusiasm, walking toward the door carrying the remaining reading materials. "I won't be long." She looked at Ruby with a bright smile. "Thanks so much again for bailing me out, Ruby. I won't forget it."

As Gabriel stared at Ruby, Xiomara winked at her counterpart before rushing from the room.

Chapter Seven

"I'm having dinner with some friends tonight," Gabriel said to Xiomara after the conference room emptied following the afternoon meeting. "I was wondering if you'd like to... come along." Xiomara looked at him and arched an eyebrow. "You'd enjoy yourself, and I think you'd like my friends. Diana is the chef of a lovely restaurant close to here, and that's where we'll be dining. Joran and I grew up together. He's a musician and usually travels a lot with his group, but he's in town for the next several weeks on a local tour."

"Sounds like an interesting evening," Xiomara said. "Where and what time?"

"That's too bad," Gabriel said automatically, tossing papers at random into a nearby wastebasket. "I really thought this might..." He paused and then looked up. Surprised blue eyes met amused hazel ones. "What?"

"Where should I meet you and at what time?" Xiomara said, measuring her words.

"Here," Gabriel said, surprise still clear on his face. "We'll be leaving from here. I have some late calls to make, but then we can head over to the restaurant. It closes at nine and is about a ten-minute Uber ride. I hope that isn't too late for you to eat."

"It'll be fine," Xiomara said. "I have some work to do for Mr. Blake and can snack on something light in the meantime."

"Good, very good!" he said, as a warm smile spread across his face. "I'm glad you're coming. I'll stop by your office when it's time to leave."

"See you then," Xiomara offered, returning to her task of tidying the conference room.

The restaurant, La Bonne Vie, was a cozy space nestled on the corner of a downtown intersection that was still busy even during the late evening. Gabriel held the door open for Xiomara as they entered, and it did not take long for her eyes to adjust to the dim lighting as she scanned her surroundings.

It was an intimate setting, with seating for thirty in tight quarters. The room was rectangular, with the bar, kitchen, and service area along the left side, and button-tufted booth seating along the right wall. Blue-striped white linen covered the tables, complementing the delicate chairs with low backs set opposite the booths.

Two starched and pressed bussers were cleaning a section of tables with synchronized speed: dirtied plates and glasses removed, candles snuffed, soiled linen discarded, fresh linen placed and smoothed, and seating returned to rightful order. One of them glanced up after Gabriel and Xiomara walked in and hurried into what was presumably the kitchen.

"Looks like the alarm has been sounded," Xiomara smirked, as a willowy whirlwind in white burst from the direction of the departed busser.

She stood five-foot-eleven in white leather ballet-style flats, impossibly skinny white jeans, a long-sleeved white chef's coat, and a white half-apron tied around her narrow waist. She was all angles: a pointed chin, a pointed nose, and Elven ears. She had platinum hair shaved low on both sides, but longer on top and swirled into a pompadour the fifties would have been proud to claim.

There were six small silver hoops climbing each ear, anchored by diamond studs the size of peanuts. Her flat gray eyes flicked over Xiomara, but when her focus shifted to Gabriel, the hint of a smile spread already thin lips even thinner.

"Finally!" she shrilled. "Gabriel, I didn't think you were going to show up!"

"We're actually early, Diana," he remarked, glancing around the space. "How were things tonight?"

"Not bad," she sighed. "Could always be better, which is what I wanted to talk with you about."

Gabriel cleared his throat. "Diana Watley-Sinclair, this is Xiomara Grant," he said, indicating Xiomara with the grand sweep of his arm.

"Xiomara, this is Diana—a great friend, our hostess, and the owner of this lovely establishment."

"Thank you for having me," Xiomara offered, noting that Diana's alarming eyes were now swallowing her whole: from her trendy, messy bun to the twinkling rhinestone accents on her black velvet pumps.

"Ah," Diana said, her lashes sweeping toward Gabriel before returning once again to Xiomara. "I should check on the courses."

"Always pleasant, isn't she?" came a voice from behind the duo as Diana swept away. Xiomara turned, looking up into the weary green eyes of a young man who had slipped in behind them.

He was well over six feet tall; with a lanky yet strong build and a tangle of golden curls—some of which had fallen into his smiling face. He wore a simple dark green T-shirt that complemented his eyes, and loose-fitting, faded black jeans. Carelessly buckled black leather boots completed the look.

"Careful," Gabriel said with a roll of his eyes. "She's back there making us dinner. She might poison it if she hears you talking about her."

"She might poison it anyway," the young man countered, before smiling at Xiomara again and extending a hand. "Joran," he offered, "Joran Talbert."

Xiomara put her hand in his, noting the roughness of the palm and fingertips. His hand was warm, though, and the grip firm, though not unpleasant.

"Xiomara Grant," she returned.

"I know," he smiled again. "Gabriel told us he'd be dragging you to this shindig. Nice to finally meet you."

Xiomara paused before squinting up at him. "Joran Talbert from Tourists of Dreams?" she asked.

Joran reddened a bit. "Gabriel actually mentioned that?"

"Not exactly," Xiomara said with a gentle shake of her head. "He told me you're a musician, but it wasn't until now that I recognized you. Not to sound like an annoying fan, but I am a great admirer of your work."

"I highly doubt that you could be annoying," Joran said, focusing on his boots. "But, thank you. I appreciate it."

"You're very welcome," she said with a smile.

Xiomara noticed Gabriel had edged away from Joran and was now fiddling around at the bar. She wondered if it was because there was a difference in height between the two of almost six inches, as with Edmund Blake. Even at five-foot-ten, Xiomara felt dwarfed by Joran.

"I'm sure we can sit wherever we want," Joran told her. "Do you have a preference?"

"None," she answered, walking with him to a table, where he waited until she settled into the booth before easing into the chair across from her. The back of the chair extended only inches above his waistline, and Xiomara watched him try to get comfortable as he treated her to a lopsided grin.

"I told Diana to get some real chairs in here," he explained. "She's under the misguided impression that all of her patrons are Lilliputian."

"It's not like you're a patron, though, Joran," Gabriel informed him, coming to the table with two bottles of wine and sitting beside Xiomara in the booth. "I don't think you've ever paid for a meal here."

"And, I wouldn't!" Joran said with glee, eyeing the wine. "Over $500 a head for a thirteen-course meal of barely-there bites? And she covers half the courses in cat spit, to boot!"

"Philistine!" Diana hissed; two delicate wine glasses hooked into each of her hands as she approached the table. "You don't understand art or fine dining."

"I understand that neither has come within ten feet of this place," Joran retorted, grabbing two of the glasses from Diana, placing one in front of Xiomara and keeping the other in his hand. "And, I'll thank you to keep the cat spit off of my plate this time."

"It's called foam," Diana said between clenched teeth, placing the remaining two glasses.

"My cat, Abby, produces a substance more visually appealing than your so-called foam," Joran snorted.

"Your ex-wife's cat, Abby," Diana remarked icily, turning on her heels and returning to the kitchen.

Xiomara's gaze went from Joran's face, from which the smile had melted, to Gabriel, who appeared fixed on the bottle of wine he was holding. When she looked at Joran again, it surprised her to find that he was looking at her.

"Welcome to our happy little group," he drawled.

"So, what's this all about, Diana?" Gabriel asked later, after the group sampled eight courses that represented the best selections of land, sea, and air.

The most recent offering, Wagyu tartare, was covered in a dollop of Joran's much-loved foam—this time in a shocking shade of pink. Not a fan of raw meat, no matter how expensive the cut, Xiomara scanned the offering for anything she could eat—even eyeing the vibrant microgreens with some suspicion. When at last she settled back into her chair, touching nothing, her eyes met Joran's, whose look spoke volumes.

Gabriel, having no such trepidation, had already dug into the minuscule massacre. Diana beamed with undisguised pleasure in her colorless eyes.

"I have an announcement to make," she heralded, her upturned nose in the air. "I wanted to share it with you since you're so dear and so supportive."

"Bullshit!" Joran coughed under his breath. Diana focused on Gabriel and leaned toward him across the table.

"I've been selected to appear in a culinary competition!" she clapped her hands together, her large, frightening, and straight white teeth on full display. To Xiomara, she looked as though her mouth housed a full pack of Chiclets gum.

Joran, who had been flicking at the deflated foam with a fork, looked up. "You're going to be on a cooking show?" he asked.

Diana froze, turning in her seat to look at Joran beside her, and placed a skeletal hand on a non-existent hip.

"Not a cooking show," she refuted in an acidic tone. "That's plebeian. This is much more elegant; much more elevated. This is highly suited to my skill level, and we're already done with preproduction. Shooting begins next week."

Joran turned to look at Xiomara and crossed his eyes. When Diana looked from Joran to Xiomara with a murderous expression, Xiomara matched the look with one of her own. Diana was the first to break the stare.

"Gabriel," Diana went on, shifting her attention back to its desired target, "this is important to me, darling. I'll need your help. We're on a twelve-week shooting schedule, so there's not much time."

"You cook, Gabriel?" Xiomara asked with a smile.

In the silence that followed, Xiomara wondered what was wrong with the question she had asked as the smile slid from her face. Joran drained the serving of wine he had picked up after he had finished playing with his food, keeping his gaze locked on the empty glass.

"This is why you invited us here tonight?" Gabriel said with a chuckle.

"It's why she invited *you*," Joran mumbled, though Xiomara had no trouble hearing him.

"It's why I invited *you*," Diana said, nonplussed. "I hoped that we could discuss it and set something up."

"This isn't exactly the best time, Diana," Gabriel said in an undertone.

"How was I to know?" she protested. "I did not know that..." She tossed a gray gaze in Xiomara's direction before settling on Gabriel once more.

"I told you yesterday that I'd be bringing Xiomara," Gabriel said.

"You also told me how she makes a habit of saying no every time you ask her to do anything!" Diana retorted; a bony hand clasped to her chest as she shuddered. "Imagine my utter shock when she turned up tonight!"

Gabriel's face reddened to his hairline, and he stared down at the smear of congealing blood inside his otherwise-empty dish.

"Okay, then!" Xiomara said sweetly, removing the cloth napkin from her lap and folding it lengthwise before draping it over the travesty of beef. "This has been quite an engrossing experience, but I'm sure you understand why I can't stay."

Xiomara reached down to retrieve the leather satchel that rested on the floor between hers and Gabriel's places at the table, and it surprised her when his hand fell on hers. Gabriel's skin differed from Joran's: cool and unbelievably soft. Though his grasp was strong, he had very tapered fingers that seemed almost feminine.

"You *can* stay," he countered, silencing Diana with a look when she opened her mouth to speak again. "After all, Diana spent so much time preparing these courses, and she has at least another half dozen treats for us— don't you, Diana? This other stuff will wait."

Diana reddened; the first bit of color to infuse her person for the entire evening, got up from the table without another word, and returned to the kitchen.

Chapter Eight

"Well, I don't know about you, but I'm starving!" Joran announced as he and Xiomara exited the restaurant. Xiomara looked up at him and said nothing. "If, after tonight, you decide to speak to any of us ever again, you'll learn that unspeakable rudeness is a rite of passage with Diana. She gets under everyone's skin... repeatedly... like a wiry old tick."

"Like with you earlier, and the remark about your ex-wife?" Xiomara asked. Joran laughed uneasily.

"Exactly that," he admitted. "I am recently divorced, you see, and Diana considers herself to be the standard for the lengths one will endure to hold on to a marriage that has long atrophied, died, and mummified."

"That woman is married?" Xiomara couldn't help asking.

"Truly boggles the mind," Joran agreed. They both looked through the window at what appeared to be a heated exchange between Gabriel and Diana, though they could not hear it. Joran then turned to Xiomara. "We should go," he said. "This could take a while, and neither of them would think anything of leaving us out here to wait."

"It's okay," Xiomara said, adjusting the strap of the satchel at her shoulder. "I can see my way from here."

"Wait," Joran said, "at least let me get you a cab or something."

"It's fine. I can manage. Thanks, though."

"Gabriel would probably have my neck in a sling if I let you wander off alone."

Xiomara shook her head and turned to leave. "The same Gabriel who thinks nothing of leaving us out here to wait?" Joran laughed as Xiomara strolled along, pausing for a moment to turn back with a smile. "Pleasure to meet you!" she called before continuing.

"Same here!" Joran returned, and Xiomara had no trouble hearing him when he repeated it in a lowered tone.

33

"Where'd you run off to?" Gabriel demanded a short time later.

Xiomara took the cell phone from her ear, stared at it, and then returned it.

"I didn't run anywhere, Gabriel," she said, examining the selection of fresh fruit in a dark red bowl on the island in her kitchen. "I walked home."

"You walked all the way home?"

"You say that as though I live in a neighboring state," Xiomara answered.

"Without telling me?"

"I needed to tell you?"

"I was going to make sure you got home okay," he said.

"There was no need," Xiomara answered. "I managed beautifully."

"You don't think leaving like that seemed rather... abrupt?" he asked.

"I didn't exactly feel welcome anyway, Gabriel," Xiomara reminded him. "So, I'm sure you'll forgive the lack of pleasantries... which you seemed to do throughout dinner, anyway."

"Look, I'm sorry about Diana," Gabriel said.

"I should say the same to you. She's your friend." She heard Gabriel's chuckle as she bit into a large plum taken from the bowl.

"Diana might seem like a bit much at times," he conceded, "but, she's not all bad once you get to know her. I know she seems a bit... high-strung..."

"Oh, high-strung," Xiomara said. "Is that how we're referring to outright rudeness?"

"She is, admittedly, somewhat defensive..." Gabriel began.

"She is, admittedly, somewhat possessive..." Xiomara corrected.

"...but, she's a talented chef beneath it all," Gabriel finished. "She catered a gathering I took part in a few years back. That's how we met."

"Has cat spit been in style so long?" Xiomara asked with a laugh.

"Now, you sound like Joran," he commented. "I heard part of your conversation with him, by the way."

"Oh?" she said.

"I didn't realize you were such a fan that you already knew who he was."

Xiomara hooted. "Oh, I see. You're still butthurt about the day we met, and I didn't recognize you."

"I'm merely commenting on how the two of you seemed to hit it off."

"That's what you wanted, isn't it?" she asked. "It's why you brought me to dinner?"

"You hit it off with him much more so than with Diana."

"Gee, I wonder why," Xiomara said.

For several seconds, the silence was punctuated by the crisp sounds of stone fruit consumption.

"Xiomara?" Gabriel said at last.

"Hmm?"

"Did Joran walk you home?"

This time Xiomara guffawed, pulled the phone away to look at it, and pressed the END button.

Chapter Nine

Xiomara remained in the conference room as it emptied, packing some items into a small plastic storage bin and tossing others into a nearby wastebasket. A shadow stretched across the table in front of her, and she turned to find Gabriel lounging in the doorway.

"Forget something?" she asked, returning to her task.

"What are you doing for lunch?"

She arched an eyebrow. "Excuse me?"

"*Lurnch*," he said in an exaggerated tone, rubbing his stomach in wide, extravagant circles to complete the effect.

"Mr. Blake has another meeting later this afternoon," Xiomara said. "I plan to eat in my office and finish the prep for it."

"Boring," Gabriel sighed.

"Don't you have some work you should be doing?"

"Perks of running this company," he responded. "I create my own. I can also rearrange the itineraries of others in my employ, so I say you're free for lunch."

"Interesting, considering that I don't work for you," Xiomara observed.

"I will sign the papers soon enough," he said, dimpling. "Good thing I helped you get hired. You'll be part of the winning team once I acquire you."

Xiomara, who had been placing a small stack of presentation portfolios into the storage bin, turned to look at Gabriel. He was looking back with an open challenge on his face.

"You acquire capital," she said in an even tone. "You acquire *things*. You do not acquire people, and you certainly will never acquire me!"

"Don't be so testy," Gabriel said with a casual shrug. "It was a figure of speech."

"One you'd do better to rethink before repeating," Xiomara warned.

"I'm just trying to get to know you, Xiomara," Gabriel said. "You act as though I'm committing a crime."

"The crime is in the approach and likely the intent," Xiomara said. "Besides, I'd be happy to mingle with you and all the others working here—at a company-sanctioned event."

"You didn't have trouble accepting the invitation to dinner with Joran and Diana," Gabriel pointed out.

"Note that it entailed the inclusion of Joran and Diana, though the latter is an obstacle I'll consider much more carefully."

"Ah, Gabriel!"

Edmund Blake, announcing his presence with a resounding clap to the younger man's shoulder, joined Gabriel in the doorway. Xiomara smirked as Gabriel's knees buckled, then returned to the collection of portfolios as the conversation continued behind her.

"Somehow, I thought I'd find you here," Blake went on. "And, a good thing, too."

"Is it?" Gabriel said, sounding surly.

"Yes, of course!" Blake pressed. "I wanted to chat with you. How about some lunch?"

"Excuse me?"

"*Lurnch*," Xiomara said without turning around, mocking Gabriel's tone from earlier. There was no need to check. She was quite certain that Gabriel was staring at her hard enough to set her aflame.

"I had Ruby set it up," Blake went on. "I hope you like Asian fusion!"

"I've actually got some calls scheduled for today," Gabriel hedged.

"Nonsense!" Blake insisted. "I've already checked, and those aren't until later this afternoon. Your calendar's free until about two-thirty!" Xiomara turned around, storage bin in hand, feasting on the buffet of misery etched on Gabriel's scowling face. Blake's watery brown gaze shifted to her. "Ah, Xiomara! You can leave that—there's no rush to do it now. But, hang tight here for a bit before you see to your own lunch. I'd like to have a word with you once I get Gabriel nice and settled. Gabriel?"

Xiomara flashed a bright smile as a somewhat deflated Gabriel trailed along beside Blake, further down the hallway. She did not have long to wait before her boss returned, closing the door behind him with a solemn expression.

"Mr. Blake?" Xiomara said, confused as she placed the storage bin atop the table. This was not the same jovial individual who had departed the room moments before.

Blake looked at her, ran a hand over his shining bald head, and then shrugged.

"Xiomara, I'd like to speak plainly," he began.

"Of course, Mr. Blake," she answered. "Have I done something wrong?"

"No, no—nothing like that," he said with a wave of his hand. "It isn't you. It's Matheson." Xiomara blinked, intrigued by the almost derisive way in which Gabriel's name tumbled from his lips, and said nothing more. "Gabriel has a... certain reputation, and not just in his business dealings... and I..." He glanced over at the closed door and lowered his voice. "You are doing a stellar job, and I know you have a bright future ahead of you." He glanced at the door again. "Brighter if you listen to me carefully because there is something you should know.

"Gabriel specifically requested that you become part of the administrative staff once this merger is completed," Blake revealed. "The stipulation made it into the most recent version of the contract. It's buried in so much drivel that it would be easy to miss, but I noticed it. And there's no reason for it—none—because we already stipulated that room would be made for any recent hires once our efforts combine. In fact, that's why we're still hiring people—with plans to bring you all along to aid in the joint effort.

"But, this clause means you would become his employee. You would be directly under the Matheson name, and no longer an employee of EJB Advertising. He hasn't made the provision to transition anyone else—none of the new or existing employees of EJB."

"What does it mean?" Xiomara asked. "What are you trying to tell me, Mr. Blake?"

"Be careful," he said. "Gabriel is methodical in the way he handles things. His business acumen is chilling, and I can't help but feel that he's that way in *all* aspects of his life." He looked at her with bushy brows raised. "Please don't mistake my trepidation as a lack of confidence in the way you carry yourself, or in your skill set..."

"But, you think that Gabriel's interest lies in something else?"

"I don't think it, Xiomara. He has an acute interest in preserving your standing within the company and, just as now, seems to make himself a constant presence wherever he knows you will be. Look after yourself." Xiomara watched, fascinated, as Edmund Blake straightened his shoulders and the familiar smile spread across his face. "Take a long lunch, would you?" he said amiably, as if their previous conversation had not taken place. "Gabriel will be well-occupied in your absence... whether or not he likes it. I'm sure that the presentation is fine, and you won't need to spend any more time on it. Go someplace nice and put it on my account."

Xiomara could not help being impressed as he approached the door and let himself out of the conference room. She was still reflecting on her conversation with Mr. Blake when Ruby entered.

"I thought you might still be in here," Ruby said. "I'm glad I caught you."

"Oh?" Xiomara said. "What's up?"

"There's someone in reception asking for you. A Joran Talbert?"

"Joran?" Xiomara repeated in surprise. "Asking for me?"

"Well, he was initially looking for Mr. Matheson, but I explained that someone had pulled him into a meeting, so he asked if you were available. Are you?"

"I am," Xiomara said. "I can show him to my office, though, Ruby. Thank you."

"Then I'll take those portfolios and put them away," Ruby offered, walking over to grab the storage bin from the table. "Will you two be having lunch? I can pick something up while I'm out grabbing the order for Mr. Matheson's meeting with Mr. Blake."

"Not sure, really," Xiomara said as the two of them exited the conference room. "No need for you to delay on my account, though I appreciate the offer."

"Sure thing," Ruby said. "Call me if you change your mind within the next twenty minutes. Back soon!"

Xiomara continued along the hallway to the reception area as Ruby went across the hall. She found Joran leaning against the wall, a plastic shopping bag dangling from one hand, apparently deciding that standing was a better bet than trying to settle into a chair. As Xiomara approached, he straightened and pushed a handful of curls from his face, treating her to a warm smile.

"You're a surprise," she said, also smiling.

"Hopefully a pleasant one," he said as he followed her along the hallway and into her office. "There's a music store nearby that I've been buying my strings from since I was a kid. Thought I'd stop over since I was in the area."

"Gabriel mentioned a local tour?" Xiomara asked, sitting behind her desk, as Joran settled on the plush sofa.

"It's the longest stretch of the national tour since all three members of Tourists of Dreams are local boys," he grinned. Though he was smiling, he looked exhausted. "Wouldn't do to cheat the homestead."

"I'd imagine not," she said with a laugh, and then paused, unable to help herself. "Joran? Are you all right?"

He started at that before shrugging. "No," he answered, and then chuckled. "Do you realize that you're the only one of our little group to ever ask me that?"

"Is that what I've become?" Xiomara asked, unable to resist a chuckle of her own. "Part of your little group?"

"Ah, it's probably not fair to lump you in with the other two," Joran admitted. "You seem very different from them."

"Because of my aversion to cat spit on bruschetta?" Xiomara said, chortling, to which Joran responded with laughter. "Would you like something to drink or snack on?"

"All the above!" Joran said with enthusiasm, still laughing.

"Skipped lunch?" Xiomara asked, moving to extract a bottle of water from the mini-fridge near the corner before going back to her desk to grab a small bag of white cheddar popcorn from the drawer, both of which Joran accepted.

"Nope, there's a dinner at Diana's later," he said, ripping open the bag. "I'm doing my best to be prepared."

"Again?" Xiomara asked, sitting behind her desk and wiggling the wireless mouse to rouse her computer from slumber. "I've got more snacks. You're welcome to them."

"I'll save some for you," Joran said. "You're invited."

Xiomara glanced up at him from the glow of her screen. "I am not," she said.

"Sure, you are!" he insisted, tossing a fluffy bit of popcorn into the air and catching it in his mouth with a hearty crunch.

"I saw Gabriel not twenty minutes ago. He said nothing about any dinner!"

"I'd bet our dear Gabriel is waiting until the last minute to tell you to minimize the chances you'll say no."

"I can still say no," Xiomara said. "Last week's dinner was bad enough. Aside from the glaring fact that Diana obviously wants me nowhere near her…"

"Or Gabriel," Joran offered, draining half the contents of the bottle of water in three great gulps.

"Or Gabriel," Xiomara repeated. "Why should I bother?"

At that moment, Gabriel entered, pausing as he noticed Joran comfortably installed on the brown leather sofa. Joran, with the bottle of water still at his lips, waved at the newcomer with his pinky. Gabriel looked at Xiomara, who was now sitting back in her chair with her fingers interlaced over her abdomen and her brows raised.

"Meeting over already?" Xiomara asked with an edge to her voice.

"No," Gabriel said. "When Ruby stopped by on her way to pick up our lunch, she said that Joran was here to see me."

"Was," Joran offered. "But, you're busy."

"I'm told there's a dinner tonight," Xiomara commented. Gabriel looked over at Joran again, who appeared focused on the contents of the bag of popcorn.

"Good news travels fast," Gabriel said, still watching as Joran flipped the bag to read the information on the back.

"Not exactly good news, Gabriel," Xiomara informed him, and he looked at her again.

"Diana is harmless," he replied. "We've talked about this."

"That's hardly the point," Xiomara stressed.

"I've even asked her to make something a little less…"

"…pretentious," Joran crooned to the bag.

"Time-consuming," Gabriel said loudly before returning to his normal tone. "Perhaps without all of that pressure, you'll find her to be less…"

"…venomous," Joran whispered to the water bottle.

"I'd like you to join us," Gabriel went on. "Give it a chance. I hope that you'll find it interesting—both the food and the conversation."

"Oh, there'll be actual conversation this time?" Xiomara mused.

"And actual food?" Joran wanted to know. "Because if not we'll need more popcorn."

"As I was telling Joran earlier," Xiomara interjected before Gabriel could answer, "Diana doesn't want me anywhere near her, and I'm fairly certain that the feeling is mutual."

"I'm merely asking that you give her a chance. And I want it known that I've also made the same request of her."

Xiomara cast a sidelong glance over at Joran, who was little help as he had chipmunked what remained of the popcorn and was now crunching noisily.

"Fine," she conceded.

"Thank you," Gabriel sighed. "I have to get through this meeting with Blake, and then I have conference calls for the rest of the day." He took a long look at Joran and shook his head. "You can hang out in my office for a bit, but I'm afraid I'm out of popcorn."

"He can stay here if he wants," Xiomara countered, surprising herself. Gabriel opened his mouth to retort just as Blake appeared in the doorway, looking in surprise first at Gabriel and then at Joran.

"Ah, Gabriel!" he said in his customary, good-humored greeting. "I was wondering where you'd gone."

"I was just informing Miss Grant that we'll need coffee in about an hour," Gabriel lied without hesitation. "I thought she might like to make sure that everything is all set up."

"Oh, it will be," Blake said. "Ruby's on top of it, as I mentioned before. She'll bring in everything we need." A familiar clap on the shoulder almost buckled Gabriel's knees. "But, we should get started. I wanted to go over some key elements that were somehow omitted from the latest version of the contracts... again."

"Great," Gabriel said, sounding as though it was anything but.

"Well, well!" Blake boomed, having taken a second look at the occupant of the sofa. "Joran Talbert! Isn't this my lucky day?" Blake walked over to Joran as the latter got to his feet, having discarded the bag and bottle. They were almost equal in height—two titans shaking hands. "My wife and I are such fans of Tourists of Dreams!" Blake enthused. "The name's Blake, Edmund Blake. We were so glad to hear about the tour dates here in the city. Now we can see you closer to home rather than having to travel."

"I really appreciate that, sir," Joran said with a gentle smile. Xiomara's own smile faltered as she caught sight of the vitriolic look in Gabriel's eyes shifting between Joran and Blake.

"And lucky you, Xiomara!" Blake beamed when he turned to her. "I had no idea that you knew this amazing young man! You must get to hear him play all the time!"

"Are you kidding?" Joran said with a laugh, happy to play along. "This one tries to take over each time we have a rehearsal!"

"Brilliant!" Blake laughed. "That's simply marvelous. I can imagine the fun the two of you must have."

Gabriel, meanwhile, looked ready to spontaneously combust.

"Have you already secured tickets for one of the upcoming shows, Mr. Blake?" Joran asked, focused on the older man.

"Please—call me Edmund! And, I certainly have. There'll be no living with the wife otherwise. We'll be seeing quite a few of your performances since I know your fondness for making each one unique."

"And, please call me Joran. I'd like to see about getting some premier seats for you both, if I may, for as many of the shows as you'd like."

"That would be a tremendous pleasure and an honor!"

"No, Edmund—the honor would be mine," Joran insisted. "Would it be all right if I arranged the details with Xiomara? She and I can take care of everything while you have your meeting with Gabriel."

"Say no more!" Blake clapped his massive hands together. "I'll leave you to it." He strolled toward the door with a bounce in his step. "We can go back to my office, Gabriel."

"Xiomara, I think we'll be needing that coffee for the meeting," Gabriel said, his jaw tight and his eyes like chips of blue steel. "Now rather than later."

"Nonsense!" Blake informed the room. "Ruby will take care of that, and we can leave Joran here to visit with Xiomara."

Unable to broach further protest, Gabriel trailed out after Blake. When Xiomara looked over at Joran, she saw him still watching the doorway, looking deep in thought.

"You wanted me to do something about the upgrades for Mr. and Mrs. Blake?" she asked after a few minutes.

The golden curls shook, and Joran reached into his pocket to extract his phone. Several keystrokes later, he looked up with a smile.

"I texted my business manager," he explained to Xiomara. "I gave her Blake's name. She'll see that the seats are upgraded and toss in some extras. Since he and his wife are such fans, I think I owe them a tour backstage, too."

"Just like that?" Xiomara asked with wide eyes. "I thought you were going to need..."

"Did you see Gabriel's face?" Joran interrupted before grinning.

Xiomara shook her head and could not resist chuckling. "You did that on purpose," she surmised.

"Serves him right," Joran shrugged. "I had to yank him down a notch or two. He was in here ordering you around and talking to you like he's your boss or something."

"Hmm," Xiomara answered, reaching into a nearby desk drawer and extracting a medium-sized cellophane bag containing what looked to be three handfuls of bright white cotton candy. "About that..."

"About what?" Joran asked with interest, though he was also eyeing the bag.

Chapter Ten

The quartet sat as before: Diana and Joran across from Gabriel and Xiomara at a table set in white, crystal, and silver. The lone colors on the table were deep red wine in etched crystal glasses with silver stems and bright green salads on silver-rimmed white plates.

After inspecting her salad for raw meat, dragon brains, or the toenails of a chicken, Xiomara felt comfortable enough to eat.

"This merger is taking a ridiculous amount of time to complete," Gabriel said, frowning into his salad after placing his cell phone on the table with a sigh.

"Is he still being difficult, dear?" Diana purred, pouring another inch of wine into Gabriel's glass, her own salad untouched.

Joran pushed his glass near Gabriel's, waiting for Diana to fill it as he removed the phone.

"He insists on adding these little nuances that aren't really important," Gabriel complained. "I keep telling him we should hammer out the important items in the contract. The rest will work itself out later."

"But he doesn't consider the welfare of his employees to be a trivial thing," Xiomara said. "He needs to know that provisions will be made for them within this merger."

"What kind of person does he think I am?" Gabriel said with a chuckle, dimpling. "The type to clean house before the ink is even dry?"

"Certainly not!" Diana chimed in. "*I* would surely never accuse you of doing such a thing." Her pale gray gaze settled on Xiomara, who responded with a sardonic smile as she bit into a grilled asparagus tip. Diana then turned back to Gabriel. "Of course, you know that there are always things you could do to help tip the situation into your favor."

Joran laughed. "And here we go," he said, having already finished his salad.

"Well, there are!" Diana said, nonplussed. "Look at you, Joran. You're throwing yourself into this tour to help you forget the shambles that your life has become, and it never had to be that way."

"Shambles?" Joran repeated, brows raised.

"Had you simply done as Gabriel so generously suggested, Katherine might be dining with us here tonight, and you wouldn't be so... bleak. It's a shame, it really is, that you couldn't pull it together." Her gaze settled on Xiomara. "Katherine is such a lovely young woman."

"That's funny," Joran said, "considering that you never said as much when she was around."

Xiomara balanced her fork along the side of the salad plate before clearing her throat.

"We might be getting a bit off topic," she said.

"So, you can come after me as far as my dealings with Blake, but Diana can't say anything to Joran?" Gabriel asked, tilting his head a bit as he turned to look at Xiomara.

"Now, wait a minute!" Xiomara said, staring at Gabriel. "I didn't come after you. I was speaking of things on a business level. She's attacking on a personal one."

"Oh, and Joran's life is personal to you?" Gabriel asked.

Xiomara leaned back against the tufted cushion. "What exactly is going on right now?"

"It's all right, Xiomara," Joran said with his usual affable grin. "It's nothing I haven't heard at least a dozen times before. The music may change, but the lyrics never do."

"Such wit," Diana snorted as a busser emerged from the kitchen and approached the table.

As he whispered into Diana's ear, Xiomara took a sip from her glass of water, refusing to acknowledge that Gabriel was still staring at her. When Diana got up from the table to accompany the busser back to the kitchen, Xiomara could not help shaking her head.

"I feel we'll be needing another bottle of wine," Gabriel said with a sigh, getting up from the table and heading for the bar.

Xiomara was still shaking her head when she glimpsed Joran focusing on something he seemed to fiddle with beneath the table. She sighed, took up her fork, and picked at the salad.

"Stop worrying about it," Joran said, not looking up. "I told you I'm used to it."

"You shouldn't be," Xiomara said, spearing roasted Brussels sprouts and arugula before sighing again and putting the fork down without taking a bite.

"Stop worrying about it," Joran said again, this time looking up and smiling. Xiomara could not resist chuckling.

"Maybe I should head home," she said. "I don't feel as though this conversation is going anywhere."

"And miss the best part?" Gabriel said, returning to the table with a bottle of white wine. He nodded toward Xiomara. "You ordered the salmon, right? This will go better with it than the red you're drinking."

"Shows how much you're paying attention," Joran said, reaching over to grab Xiomara's glass with one hand while concealing the other beneath the table. "She hasn't touched it." He brought the glass to his lips, peered at Xiomara over the rim, and winked as he took a sip.

"Entrées!" Diana trilled in her nasal tone as she returned, followed by a shuffling busser hefting a large tray filled with food. It surprised Xiomara that her stomach growled at the sight and smell of the salmon Florentine and lemon risotto she had ordered.

"You know, Xiomara," Diana said as the other three tucked into their dinner, "I think you've got it all wrong."

"Do you?" Xiomara replied, more interested in the buttery salmon and the creamy decadence of the garlic-infused sauce clinging to the lemon-zested spinach than anything Diana had to say.

"Of course," came the reply as Diana toyed with the stem of her wine glass. "Gabriel means no harm to Edmund Blake or his employees, and it is rather inconsiderate to keep dragging this merger along. Blake is finished. He should accept that."

"And how would you know?" Xiomara countered. "Have you ever met Edmund Blake? Do you know anything about him?"

The flash of temper in Diana's gray eyes was not lost on Xiomara, and she accepted the challenge with a look of her own. Diana then cleared her throat and turned to Gabriel.

"We should have a little function for the Blakes, dear," she said. "I'm happy to coordinate a little something for them here at Bonne."

Xiomara arched a brow as Gabriel slowly chewed and then swallowed the bit of chateaubriand he had been enjoying.

"A dinner?" he asked.

"Dinner, cocktails, whatever you'd like," Diana soothed. "If things are as dire as you say, it could go a long way toward not only smoothing any ruffled feathers but might also give you an opportunity to learn more about the man outside of work... and about what it might take to gain an advantage in this merger."

"And here it is," Xiomara remarked, shaking her head. "I should have known that extending an olive branch would be much too simple for you."

"This merger is happening regardless," Gabriel said. "What's wrong with having an advantage in the meantime?"

"You already have the advantage, Gabriel," Xiomara said. "Yours will be the controlling company. All this posturing is unnecessary."

Gabriel studied Xiomara for a moment before turning to an eager Diana.

"Next Friday," he told her. "Six courses, superb wines, an interesting cocktail beforehand, and I want you to prepare the meal yourself. Four guests: The Blakes, Xiomara, and me."

Diana's shoulders slumped. "I thought... that you and I might..."

"You would have Diana close her restaurant on a Friday night?" Joran asked, having finished his rosemary and garlic-crusted lamb chops with crushed new potatoes. "Couldn't you have lunch or something during a time when the place isn't usually open?"

"Blake needs to know who he's up against!" Gabriel insisted. "He needs to see what I'm capable of."

"Capable of shutting down a business on a whim and depriving people of their pay," Joran said. "I thought that was the example you were trying to get away from."

"Blake needs to learn," Gabriel stressed, "and I'm going to teach him, Joran." He smiled, dimpling. "Since you won't be here, I'll have to fill you in on my success some other time."

"I guess I'll need to be filled in as well," Diana huffed, "since you have relegated me to kitchen help."

Gabriel turned his amiable smile on her. "Nonsense," he countered in a comforting tone. "You're vital to the success of this, Diana. I wouldn't be able to do it without you."

Xiomara smirked into the glass of water she sipped in response to the unconcealed look of triumph a preening Diana gave her.

"And, what about how vital you are to me, Gabriel?" Diana asked when she turned back to him. "We started filming today. They had to bring in a busload of people pretending to be patrons, to make Bonne look like a success!" She frowned. "I shouldn't need them to do that—I should be successful already! The competition is underway, and we haven't completed our plans, Gabriel."

"What plans?" Joran interjected. "You want to win, so plan to do that."

"It's not solely about winning," Diana countered, looking at him. "I want to be known. I want this season to be like none before it, and all those after it should be nothing in comparison." She turned to Gabriel again. "You need my help, and I need yours. We need a ceremony, Gabriel. We need to combine our efforts."

"We can talk about this later," Gabriel interrupted, casting a sidelong glance at Xiomara.

"It's always later!" Diana snapped, her fiery temper directed toward Gabriel for once. "Who cares if she's here? Who cares what she knows? If you insist on continuing to force her presence upon us, she'll have to take part at some point!"

"Diana, stop..." Joran warned.

"Oh, we've already discussed your failings, Joran Talbert," she shrieked. "You were openly offered help, and you refused it. Your marriage could have been saved, and your career could be skyrocketing. I have learned from your mistakes. I'm snatching up my chance *now*!"

"It's a *cooking* competition!" Joran said. "Maybe you should consider, I don't know, *cooking* something? And I don't mean in a cauldron, either!" He sighed and shook his head, lowering his voice. "Don't you want to win on your own merits? You don't need rituals, Diana. Look at what you made for us tonight. It's the best I've ever had from you. Do this, and only this. It might surprise you."

"What surprises me is that you think I'd give up so easily," Diana said. "I will work from my cauldron, my altar, and whatever else I need to secure what's mine. You may not want to upset what you feel should be the natural order of things. I, however, thrive on doing so."

"That's enough, Diana," Gabriel said, still watching Xiomara. "I said I'd help you, and I will."

"So, let's talk," Diana insisted.

"It doesn't have to be right this minute!" Gabriel said.

"You're just afraid that we're scaring our friend here," Diana said, the hopeful grin stretching her thin features into something ghastly.

"Hardly," Xiomara said with an edge to her voice. "There isn't a thing you can say that would scare me, and I'm not a novice."

The silence at the table was palpable.

"What?" Gabriel asked in surprise, sitting up as Joran blinked at Xiomara before leaning back in his chair.

"You're joking," Diana challenged.

"I am not," Xiomara replied.

"You have to be," Diana insisted. "You probably have no idea of what we're talking about."

"I'm no fool," Xiomara said, "and, you've dropped enough hints. Cauldron? Altar? Natural order? Magick." She raised her eyebrows. "Petition magick, in your case—since you're pleading for something rather than acting upon it."

"I am not petitioning anything!" Diana snarled, red-faced. "I am actively focusing everything I know, and everything I am toward achieving what I want. I am directing my power." She then turned to Gabriel. "But, I can't do this by myself! Help me, Gabriel."

"Wait a minute," Gabriel said before looking at Xiomara. "What do you mean that you're not a novice? Do you practice?"

"I know better," Xiomara replied with a shrug.

"What the hell does that mean?" Diana asked.

"It means that you need to face reality!" Xiomara told her.

"What reality?" Diana asked.

"The reality of the force of power that comes back at you once you've directed your own," Xiomara answered. "The reality that clashes with your delusions of fame and fortune. Diana, Joran is right. You don't need to rely on anything but your own talent to get ahead. You can do this on your own. Do not bring magick into it. You're never prepared for what comes back at you once you put it out there, and it never stops once you start!"

"Nonsense!" Diana snapped, turning for a moment to Gabriel for support. "You just don't want me to succeed! You don't want anyone to succeed! You want to walk around like the golden child, having both Gabriel and Blake sniffing after you! That merger was moving along fine until you came along and attached yourself to Blake like some toxic barnacle! You're the reason it's not going the way it's supposed to!"

"Diana!" Gabriel shouted.

"Nonsense!" Diana said, matching his tone. "It is nonsense—tell her! You can't keep sticking up for her now that she's insulted your legacy!"

"I'm not trying to insult anyone," Xiomara countered. "But, what do you think will happen, Diana? It starts off small—it always does. A sprinkling of herbs here, a line of salt there, the occasional incantation… but, then you'll have to continue to feed it. It'll always want more from you, and you'll keep giving in to get what you want until all you have left to put on that altar is the heart carved from the one that loved you most."

"You're crazy," Diana hissed, "and you're trying to make us out to be equally so!"

"I'm just warning you," Xiomara said. "That's all."

"We don't need your warnings," Diana told her, "or anything else! I can control this! I don't need you to tell me anything!"

"You wanted me to hear this!" Xiomara said. "Gabriel tried to stop you, but you insisted I should hear, didn't you? You wanted me to be alarmed! You hoped that I'd be uncomfortable! Now that you're not getting what you want, and you realize that I have intricate knowledge of what you claim to be dabbling in, you don't need to hear from me, and you can control this? You're fooling yourself!"

"You are rude, offensive, and spiteful!" Diana returned. "I've had you here as a guest in my establishment, and you've been nothing but contrary. I don't for one moment think that a word of what you've said is true, and you did it to belittle me and to draw me away from my true station in this world!"

"As you like," Xiomara sighed, glancing at her watch after Gabriel looked at her without further comment. "Time is short. It's late and I should be going."

Diana grunted. "Turning into a pumpkin before midnight?"

"You don't have to go yet," Gabriel said.

"So says the Fairy Godfather," Diana chortled before being silenced by an icy look from Gabriel. She then busied herself with the contents of her wineglass as Gabriel turned a softer gaze toward Xiomara.

"I can walk you out," Joran interjected before Gabriel could say anything more. "It's time for me to get going, anyway."

"Good!" Diana chimed. "That will give me some time to chat with you privately, Gabriel, about some things I have in mind. Never mind all that other rubbish."

"Plenty of time left for all that, Diana," Gabriel said, his eyes following Joran and Xiomara as they got up from the table, preparing to leave. He then got to his feet. "Can I get a car for you?"

Xiomara smiled. "Walking distance, remember?"

"Still don't know how the hell you manage that," Diana muttered into her glass of wine.

"I'll see you at the office in the morning," Xiomara offered before turning to Diana. "Despite the way things have ended, I appreciate you having me. You really should consider what I've said. Dinner was delicious."

"Wow!" Diana crowed. "With reviews like that, I will surely get a James Beard award! I'll go burn my grimoire right now!"

As Gabriel turned to glare at Diana again, Joran tugged at the sleeve of Xiomara's blouse, jerking his head toward the exit. Before they departed, however, Joran looked at Gabriel.

"By the way, you dropped this," he said, as he tossed something at Gabriel. Gabriel caught it, looking with a puzzled expression at his own cell phone. Once outside, Joran helped Xiomara slip into her light jacket, shoving his hands into his pockets as he watched her smooth a lock of hair away from her face. She noticed him watching her and smiled.

"I'm only about a mile away," she reminded him.

"I remember," Joran replied. "Walking distance—kudos. But, it is getting late, and since you don't want to take a cab and the ex-wife has my truck… looks like you're stuck with me until you get home okay."

"It's really fine," Xiomara smirked.

"Sure, it is!" Joran said cheerfully. "But, you already coerced me into letting you stroll away from here last time. You got that freebie—now it's my turn."

Xiomara shook her head, chuckling. "You win," she said.

"Fiiiinally," Joran said with an exaggerated roll of his eyes before winking at Xiomara and extending the crook of his elbow. "Milady."

"Sir," Xiomara returned with mock coquettishness, placing her hand upon the offered arm as they walked.

Chapter Eleven

Half an hour later, the twenty-minute walk to Xiomara's apartment was still not finished. Joran and Xiomara sat upon a park bench, chatting and passing a half-consumed bag of bright blue cotton candy between them.

"Diana is all right," he conceded. "She really is a talented chef under all the frills. If she would trust her skill and the quality of her ingredients, she'd be fine. But, that raw meat she gave us at the last dinner—yuck!"

"That was her contribution to the elevation of our culture," Xiomara said with a straight face.

"And for that I could have happily contributed the masticated remnants of the courses she served before that," Joran replied. "The rest of dinner that night might have been okay but she insists on adding all these..."

"...flourishes," Xiomara offered.

"Exactly!" Joran agreed, helping himself to a large pull from the cotton candy. He pointed a blue, tufted fingertip at Xiomara. "Don't let her get to you," he suggested. "She's all bluster—about everything, not just food. Like before, with all that crap about an altar. She's not as dedicated as she lets on. She got into it to get closer to Gabriel, but there isn't enough magick in the world to make *that* happen. So now she dabbles when she wants something and has it in her head that she'll actually get what she's after. Meanwhile, she tries to put on a show—like she's some kind of Grand Wizard or something."

"Surely not," Xiomara said. Joran chuckled, eating the tuft before handing the bag back to her. "What about you, Joran? Are you a dabbler as well?"

Joran examined his cyanotic fingertips and sighed. "Not even close," he admitted. "I was curious at first, I'll admit that much, and I know what enthusiasts like Gabriel and Diana claim you can get from it, but..." He hesitated. "There are just... certain things..." His eyes met Xiomara's, and he reddened, suddenly becoming very interested in the designs on the bag of cotton candy she was holding. "Certain things should happen as they're meant. It upsets the natural balance otherwise, and I don't get off on doing it like Diana does."

"I didn't realize," Xiomara said. "You showed no discomfort during the conversation."

"It's not that the topic doesn't bother me," Joran said. "But, I don't feel a need to defend something I'm not part of. The two of them are on guard, especially Diana, and that's why she was so offended. Gabriel and I have discussed it. He knows where I stand."

"Has this always been a subject of disagreement for you and Gabriel?" she asked.

"Gabriel and I have known each other since middle school," he began after a time. "We were in Band together—which is how we met. To look at him now, you'd never..." He paused, and Xiomara was patient as she waited for him to start again. He gently took the bag of sweet treats from her and studied it for a moment before starting again.

"He got picked on a lot," Joran continued. "I'd get it sometimes, too, before I had my growth spurt... but, it was terrible for him: scrawny kid, no money, mom on a first-name basis with every dive bar inside four counties... and he played the flute." Joran shook his head, and a shock of golden curls fell forward, covering his eyes before a head toss settled them back into place.

"It was pretty brutal for a few years. Then one summer, I didn't see him around. He didn't show up for band camp, and even though he hated for me to go by his house, I went over to see if I could find out where he was because I was worried. All I could get from his mom was that her sister had swooped into town and snatched him up. She wouldn't tell me anything more than that, so I figured I'd never lay eyes on Gabriel again."

"But you obviously did," Xiomara interjected.

Joran's brow furrowed. "There are two schools of thought on that," he explained. "Gabriel came back at the beginning of the school year, but he wasn't the same. The time with his aunt really made a difference. He was confident, you know? He dressed differently; he'd grown a few inches and filled out some. He quit Band, so we no longer shared any class time, but I sometimes saw him in passing in the hallways. I honestly don't think I've seen him so much as glance at sheet music since.

"Even more... he petitioned the courts to be made independent of his mother—and won, too! I guess they had some kind of falling out, and she packed up and left town shortly after that."

"Did he say why?" Xiomara asked.

Joran shook his head again. "He wouldn't talk about it. He got a job working after school and on weekends. He rented a house of his own right outside of town and got a car..." He absently plucked at some of the cotton candy and shoved it into his mouth as if fighting the taste of bitterness. Xiomara waited, and eventually Joran's green eyes again met hers. "I wasn't jealous."

"The thought hadn't crossed my mind," she assured him.

"You'd be the first," he said, handing her the bag of dwindling blue. She took it and continued to focus on him. "We saw each other even less to where we didn't even pass one another in the halls anymore. My life was revolving more around music, and he started hanging out with the Entrepreneur's Club and the Junior Business League. I felt weird going to his house. Those same jerks who wouldn't have given him a second thought unless it was to do something messed up to him, were always scheming on how to get him to let them use his place for parties." The golden head shook again.

"But, you stayed friends somehow," Xiomara prompted.

"He came to my house one night during Christmas break," Joran went on. "Like I said, I hadn't really seen much of him and didn't want to bother him. But, there he was... outside my door with that stupid grin as if we hadn't been virtual strangers for the last four months."

"What happened after that?" Xiomara asked, dipping her fingers into the bag of cotton candy.

"Nothing," Joran said. "Everything. I don't know. We had to get to know each other all over again and reestablish our relationship since we no longer had music in common. He taught me to drive, and I taught him to play chess. He offered to let me stay with him at his house, but it would have killed my mom if I did that. She had a hard enough time with me going on brief trips to play at concerts."

"Nothing and everything?" Xiomara repeated, and silence hung between them for a time.

"Xiomara, listen," Joran began, "I didn't really mean to sit here and talk about Gabriel or any of that other nonsense except to tell you that..."

"What the hell are you two doing out here?" came a voice from behind them. Joran skittered to his feet and turned around. Xiomara was calm as she got to her feet and turned to face Gabriel, who was looking back at them with an expression devoid of amusement.

"Cotton candy?" Xiomara offered, extending the nearly depleted bag.

"What?" Gabriel said, his gaze shifting from Xiomara to Joran and back again. "You guys left the restaurant like forty-five minutes ago." He looked back at Joran. "When you didn't come back right away, Diana and I figured you'd gone home."

"Everything okay, sir?" called a voice from behind them.

They all turned toward the black Cadillac Escalade that was idling at the curb. The rear passenger-side door was still open, and the driver, a small man appearing to be in his late fifties, peered at them through an open window, his widened eyes darting from one to the other as he gripped the steering wheel. Gabriel pulled his cell phone from his pocket and made a few taps.

"I've ended the ride," he sneered at the driver. "You can go." He turned back to Xiomara and Joran as the driver of the SUV rushed to close the door, climbed back into his vehicle, and departed with a light screech of his tires. "Want to tell me what's going on?" Gabriel asked.

"Xiomara said she didn't live far," Joran offered. "I thought I'd walk her home."

"So you live on a park bench now?" Gabriel pressed, still looking at Joran, though the question was directed toward Xiomara. "Have I interrupted something?"

"What's the problem, Gabriel?" Xiomara asked in her usual soft tone.

"What are you even doing out here?" Joran asked with a dry chuckle. "You live about half an hour away... by train... in the *opposite* direction."

His chuckle faded, cloaking the trio in silence. The evening stilled. Joran exhaled when Gabriel's gaze rested once more upon Xiomara.

"I'll walk you the rest of the way home," he offered.

Joran snorted and claimed the remains of the cotton candy from Xiomara's grasp.

"Since you were headed that way anyhow?" Joran said, walking away from the duo and heading back in the restaurant's direction without a backward glance.

"Joran, you were about to tell me something?" Xiomara called after him.

"It'll keep!" he replied without stopping.

A few minutes after watching Joran depart, Gabriel turned to look at Xiomara. She looked back at him; her face a blank mask while he appeared to be seething.

"You should go after him," she remarked after a moment.

"What for?"

"Because I think the two of you need to talk," she answered. "Things got more than a little tense at dinner."

"Is that what you two were out here talking about?" Gabriel pressed.

"You can still catch up to him," came the answer.

"I can talk with him later. To use your peculiar phrasing from earlier, 'time is short,' so I'd better see you home. Shall we?"

Gabriel stepped to the side, extending the crook of his arm to Xiomara in a polite gesture, though his face was still cloudy.

"I guess we shall," Xiomara replied, opting not to accept the arm and instead slipping her hands into her pockets as she walked.

Xiomara was not oblivious to the occasional glances in her direction from Gabriel as they walked along the well-lit street toward the building that housed her loft apartment. She walked at a moderate pace, her leather satchel bumping against her hip as the evening breeze toyed with her loose locks.

"And, suddenly, you're not so talkative," Gabriel said. When Xiomara's sigh carried through the evening air, Gabriel turned to look at her. "What?"

"Was I so talkative in the park?" she queried.

"You know what I mean," Gabriel said as he stopped walking.

"Obviously, I don't," Xiomara returned as she also stopped.

"What is it with you and Joran?"

"Out of everything that was said tonight, you want to talk about Joran?"

"Diana means nothing to me," Gabriel said. "This isn't about her."

"And, it's not about Joran!" Xiomara said.

"We need to talk, Xiomara."

"Actually, we don't. We have nothing to discuss outside of Matheson Media and EJB Advertising."

"Xiomara!" Gabriel said, reddening.

"I'll see you at the office in the morning," she said. "I can get home from here—alone. I trust you'll thank Diana for a lovely evening."

"Xiomara!" Gabriel said again. She had, however, already turned on her heel and walked away.

"Xiomara Grant," she answered after the first ring.

"Joran Talbert," came the response.

Xiomara stopped walking. She had been on her way to her bedroom when the call came through.

"Joran?" she said.

"Yeah," he confirmed. "Hope I'm not disturbing you."

"No, not at all," she replied, detouring into the kitchen and turning on the light. "How'd you get my number?"

"From Gabriel," he said, "in a way."

Xiomara laughed, walking over to the counter to look at the bowl of fruit.

"In a way, huh?" she asked, selecting a green apple. "Is that what you were doing with his phone during dinner?"

"It was indeed!" Joran said.

"You could have asked me," Xiomara commented before biting into the apple. "No need for such intrigue."

"After the conversations we had tonight—both at the restaurant and then at the park?" he asked. "Gabriel's likely afraid he'll never see you again. Diana's probably sacrificing a goat to the Foam Gods hoping she doesn't."

"And you?" Xiomara asked before taking another bite of the fruit.

"I stole your number from Gabriel's phone so that I could call and, hopefully, convince you we're not all bat shit crazy."

"Crazy isn't the word I'd use," she murmured, leaning with her back to the counter as she studied the fruit in her hand.

"Well, it's one I use often, and it admittedly fits."

"Why are you really calling, Joran?"

"Am I being transparent?" he asked after a brief pause.

"A bit," Xiomara admitted, savoring another bite.

"I wanted to apologize," he said. "That's what I was going to say before Gabriel showed up. I am genuinely sorry, Xiomara."

"For what?"

"All of it! All the craziness that you didn't sign up for when you went to work for Blake: Gabriel's mood swings, Diana's manic desperation, rituals and power trips... and I keep thinking each time we get together that one or both of them will say something and you'll walk away for good. So, yeah... I took Gabriel's phone, looked up your number, and memorized it so that I could call you and try to explain."

"You don't owe me an explanation," Xiomara told him. "There's nothing to explain."

"How can there not be anything to explain?" Joran asked, his voice tense. "Diana is close to getting what she wants, and with Gabriel's help. They're finalizing plans."

"It didn't escape me," she said.

"And?"

"And, what?"

"What else did you think about it? What's been going through your mind since you left us tonight?"

"What do you mean?" Xiomara asked. "Obviously, I'm on the phone with you and not out somewhere with Diana helping to wrangle another goat."

"I'm being serious."

Xiomara straightened, cleared her throat, and placed the half-eaten apple on the counter.

"Yes, I suppose you are," she acknowledged. "Look, Joran, I can't help what some people choose to believe."

"Not what I'm asking," Joran insisted.

"I am not taking part in whatever Gabriel and Diana are cooking up—no pun intended," Xiomara said. "It doesn't interest me. Is that better?"

"You said you were familiar," he reminded her.

"I also said that I don't practice because I know better," she countered.

His deep sigh rumbled through the phone, and Xiomara retrieved her apple. She finished it and tossed the core into the trash.

"I'm not like them," Joran said at last.

"So, we've established," Xiomara returned. "And, you're right. I don't think Diana is as eager as she tries to make it seem."

"Even though she brings it up every chance she gets?"

"Exactly," Xiomara said, turning off the light as she exited the kitchen to pad down the hallway toward her bedroom. "She has Gabriel's phone number. She could always call him. Yet, she makes a point of begging and trying to bring him to her side, with us as the audience."

"To bother you, no doubt, and to stake her claim."

"Partly," Xiomara agreed. "The other part is to show Gabriel what she's willing to do for him by openly proclaiming her allegiance." She entered her bedroom and sat on the bed. "I'm honestly hoping that this dinner she wants to have for Gabriel and the Blakes will be a positive distraction. I'm hoping to bring out more of a human side—to everyone. Maybe Diana can glimpse what's possible through genuine, hard work."

"You'll have to let me know how that goes," Joran mused.

"I won't have to because you'll be there."

"They did not invite me, Xiomara," he said. "I was, in fact, purposely left out. Surely, you noticed."

"Edmund and Lavinia Blake are big fans of Tourists of Dreams," Xiomara said. "As the leader of that group, it would be a wonderful treat if you played for them before the dinner. If I know Mr. Blake as well as I feel I do, he'll insist that you remain afterward to eat with us."

"You are a marvel," Joran said after a pause.

"Gabriel's wrong for excluding you. I see no reason you shouldn't be present, and I'll tell him so. Making sure that Mr. Blake expects to see you will seal it."

"That's devious," Joran commented.

"That's fair," Xiomara said with a smile.

"What a triangle," Joran surmised. "Diana wants Gabriel, and Gabriel wants you."

"That isn't a triangle," Xiomara said after a pause. "That's only two parts."

"You're the third part, Xiomara," Joran said softly. "What do you want?"

"To go to bed," she answered with a smirk, pressing the END button after hearing Joran's hearty laugh.

Chapter Twelve

Xiomara was standing at one of the massive bookshelves inside Edmund Blake's temporary office at Matheson Media when she heard a soft click behind her. Finding the binder she'd been looking for, she pulled it from the shelf before turning to Gabriel, who stood with his back pressed against the closed door.

"Good morning," she said pleasantly.

"What do you think you're doing?" he said.

"Pardon?" she asked.

"What are you doing in here?"

"Mr. Blake has an afternoon meeting with some of his key investors," Xiomara explained as she approached the desk and flipped through the manual. "I'm refining the presentation he's giving them."

Gabriel advanced into the room as Xiomara sat and tucked a stray curl behind her left ear.

"Why are you in here doing that when Blake is in my office right now for a meeting?"

Xiomara looked up, brow furrowed. "I don't understand," she admitted.

"I already know about the meeting this afternoon with the investors," Gabriel said. "I imagine explanations are due since the merger is unnecessarily delayed. I'm not talking about that."

"Then what are you talking about?" Xiomara asked as she used the keyboard to enter information into a waiting document.

"Why is Ruby at the meeting instead of you?" he demanded.

"Because I asked her to attend in my place so I could focus on this," Xiomara responded, her eyes glued to the monitor.

"You didn't need her to do that!"

"And you're qualified to know that—how?"

"You're sore from last night," Gabriel accused. "You're trying to avoid me."

"As if it is possible to do that," Xiomara sighed.

"So, you are still sore," he said.

"No, Gabriel," she said, looking up at his flushed face. "I am busy. I needed to prepare for this afternoon, and Ruby was free. It was a logical exchange."

"Always logic with you."

"You should try it sometime," Xiomara murmured as the office door opened and a red-faced Ruby peered in.

"Did you need something?" Gabriel snapped.

Ruby's blush deepened. "Mr. Blake sent me to make sure everything's all right."

"He sent you searching for me all over this place to ask if things are all right?" he drawled sarcastically.

"No," Ruby said, glancing at Xiomara. "He sent me here. Just here." She turned around and departed, leaving the door open.

Gabriel turned to Xiomara, eyes wide, and then opened his mouth to speak.

"Have a good meeting, Gabriel," Xiomara offered. "I'll also be working through lunch, so I hope the rest of your day goes well."

Gabriel stared at her for a moment as the color drained from his face. He left the office without another word, leaving the door open behind him.

Chapter Thirteen

Xiomara arrived at La Bonne Vie as the mist turned into an insistent downpour. Standing beneath the dark green awning, she reached into her purse to retrieve her cell phone and turn off its ringer as Gabriel jogged up and joined her.

"I thought that was you!" he said with a smile. "I hoped we'd walk over together, but when I got to your office, I saw that you'd left early."

"I did," Xiomara said as he pulled the heavy door open and held it. As she passed him, putting her phone away, she could hear a low buzzing coming from the pocket of his jacket.

"It's probably Diana again," he said as they went inside. "She started calling not long after I left the office. But since I was on the way anyway, I thought whatever it was could wait."

"Hopefully, nothing's gone wrong," Xiomara said.

"I'm sure everything's fine," Gabriel replied. "I'll take your coat."

"Thank you," she said, loosening the belt of her black trench coat as Gabriel helped slip it from her shoulders. She paused, noting his glance.

"That isn't what you wore to the office today," he said of the dusky pink silk crepe sheath dress.

"This is why I left early," she responded with a light shrug. "I thought a blouse and slacks seemed a bit too informal for the occasion, so I went home to change."

"It's very nice," Gabriel stammered, his breathing shallow. "You... look..."

"Ah, look who we have here!" came the booming voice of Edmund Blake. Gabriel reddened and retreated to the coat rack to hang their coats.

Xiomara turned to look up into the smiling face of Blake, who stood with one arm wrapped around the waist of a petite blonde with radiant violet eyes that beamed back at Xiomara. Her lustrous, silver-streaked hair was styled in a neat French roll, and the designer lilac boucle crepe dress and matching jacket complemented her rosy complexion.

"Xiomara, I'm very pleased to introduce you to the beat of my heart: Lavinia Pascale Blake."

"Such gallantry," Mrs. Blake said in a Southern accent before giggling. She wrinkled her patrician nose as she aimed a playful swat at her husband. She then reached out to clutch one of Xiomara's hands between both of hers. "I am glad to finally meet you, Xiomara. Edmund speaks so highly of you, and often."

"Thank you, ma'am," Xiomara said, overwhelmed by the warmth emanating from the older woman. "I must say that it's an honor to be in the presence of the woman who brings so much light into Mr. Blake's eyes at the mere mention of her name."

"Oh, Eddie, I do like her," Mrs. Blake announced as she squeezed Xiomara's hand. "Are you sure we can't keep her?"

"Not if Gabriel has anything to say about it!" Blake said, looking past the ladies to where Gabriel stood near the collection of coats.

"Well, hello again, Gabriel!" Mrs. Blake called, laughing as she released Xiomara's hand.

"It's nice to see you again, Mrs. Blake," Gabriel said as he approached.

"It's been a while, too," she chided, still smiling. "I haven't caught sight of you since this whole merger business first started!"

"Now, Lavinia," Blake said, bending to kiss the crest of his wife's plump cheek. "Tonight is for breaking bread and beginning anew. The merger will fare as it's meant to."

Mrs. Blake's sparkling gaze found Xiomara again. "My dear," she breathed, "I can see why his face lights up so."

Xiomara's brow furrowed as she looked from the Blakes to a crimson-hued Gabriel.

"Ma'am?" Xiomara asked, as a burst of commotion from the kitchen interrupted them.

Joran was dabbing at the lapel of his starched white dress shirt with a cloth napkin, trailed by a nervous-looking busser holding another cloth in one hand and a bottle of clear liquid in the other.

"Joran, sweetheart," Mrs. Blake called, "I was just talking about you. Were you able to get that stain out?"

"Almost, Mrs. Blake," Joran responded as he looked up, noticed Xiomara, froze, and reddened.

Xiomara had never seen Joran in anything other than T-shirts and jeans, which she felt suited him well. Tonight, however, the unruly curls were in a ponytail, and he wore neat, dark green slacks. Warmth touched her face as she drew a breath, catching an amused glance from Mrs. Blake.

The room grew silent enough for Xiomara to hear Gabriel's slow exhalation.

"That looks simply wonderful!" Mrs. Blake said as she walked over to Joran and peered up at his shirt. "You can't tell at all that red wine was ever spilled."

"All thanks to you, Mrs. Blake," Joran said with a smile. "I never would have thought to use seltzer water."

"I thought we'd already established that you are to call me Lavinia," she told him, taking the dry napkin from the busser and dabbing at the dampness on Joran's shirt with it.

"Joran," Gabriel said at last, "I didn't know you'd be here tonight."

"It was a wonderful little surprise!" Mrs. Blake beamed. "The idea was for him to come here tonight to play for us a bit before and then after dinner."

"And what is he to do with himself during?" Gabriel asked, averting his gaze to rest on Xiomara.

"He'll be dining, of course," Diana said as she emerged from the kitchen and snatched the seltzer from the busser. "Cocktails," she hissed at the departing form before treating everyone else to a toothy grin. "Mrs. Blake practically insisted that we include Joran. Took a bit of rearranging, but I'm happy to accommodate our lovely guests."

She sidled over to Gabriel and fixed him with a look. Xiomara guessed Diana must have been calling to warn him of Joran's presence, and by ignoring her, Gabriel missed out.

"Drinks are going to be served shortly," Diana said, addressing the group. "It's a signature cocktail to be added to the menu here at Bonne."

At that moment, the busser returned holding a large silver tray upon which sat six twelve-ounce martini glasses filled with a froth-topped ombré liquid layered in shades ranging from pale peach to deep orange. He distributed the drinks among those present, and Diana, her own glass held aloft, aimed her gleaming tusks in a sulking Gabriel's direction as she grinned.

"To the continued success of Gabriel Quentin Matheson!" she crowed. "Let this acquisition be but one of many cobblestones along his road to greatness!"

"Well, I declare..." Lavinia Blake murmured into her drink before sipping it.

Xiomara looked over at Joran, who returned the glance with wide eyes. Their gazes shifted to Gabriel, who glared back with a somehow already-empty glass clutched in his hand. Diana, still beaming, at last tore her eyes away from Gabriel to take in the rest of the guests.

"Dinner will be served soon," she said. "Please continue to enjoy yourselves in the meantime."

"I should get back to my cello," Joran said to Xiomara with a gentle smile, the otherwise-untouched drink still in his large hand. "I meant to be playing as everyone arrived, but I was so nervous that I spilled wine all over the place."

Xiomara peered at his shirt. "I can hardly tell," she commented, returning the smile.

"Thanks to Mrs. Blake and her genius save," he laughed.

"Lavinia!" Mrs. Blake chimed in from not far away, causing both Joran and Xiomara to laugh.

"What could you have possibly been nervous about, Joran?" Gabriel asked, moving to stand closer to Xiomara. "Even at a career low, you've played for larger crowds than this."

Joran looked at Gabriel for a moment before shaking his head.

"Tonight's different," came the reply as Joran walked away.

"You didn't tell me he'd be here," Gabriel said to Xiomara in a lowered tone, even as the melodic hum of the cello resonated around them.

"Don't you think it was a pleasant surprise for the Blakes?" Xiomara asked. "They're both such big fans." She looked over at them and at the way they embraced one another while watching Joran play.

"Once again, you've done well looking after Blake," Gabriel muttered.

"And, once again, it's Mr. Blake that I work for."

"Not for long," Gabriel said, placing his glass atop one of the nearby tables before walking away.

Chapter Fourteen

"I certainly hope that the completion of the merger won't mean I never get to see you again, Xiomara," Mrs. Blake said, her eyes alight.

The dinner was cordial enough; the addition of Joran reducing Gabriel to a short-tempered, monosyllabic mess, though he still tried to be charming. Mrs. Blake, with years of practice as a successful hostess and socialite, kept the evening from imploding.

"You're too kind," Xiomara responded with a smile. "I'm awfully glad to have met you. As I said earlier, Mr. Blake lights up at the mention of your name, and I can see why." Xiomara's hazel gaze shifted to Gabriel as he leaned against the bar, sipping at a short glass half-filled with amber liquid. "The way you overcame the peculiarities of this gathering is an example we could all learn from."

Mrs. Blake giggled. "Says the sun around whom all planets revolve."

"Ma'am?" Xiomara said for the third time that evening, blinking at Mrs. Blake in confusion.

"I feel for him, you know—young Gabriel over there drowning his sorrows. He's fighting a losing battle."

"I know that there are still a few things to work out," Xiomara said. "But, I wouldn't say the merger is lost."

"Who said anything about the merger?" Mrs. Blake said, her eyes shining with mirth as she squeezed Xiomara's hand before approaching her husband and Joran. "And, what mischief are you two over here concocting?"

Xiomara walked over to the bar, standing beside Gabriel.

"Something to drink?" he asked, nursing his glass, bright blue eyes focused on the Blakes.

"No, thank you," Xiomara said.

"She's something else, isn't she—Mrs. Blake?"

The duo watched as Mr. and Mrs. Blake held hands. Xiomara could not resist a smile.

"She is," she responded. "They both are."

"He loves her very much," Gabriel commented. "You can tell she means the world to him." Xiomara turned to look at him, brows raised.

"Are you all right?" she asked. "Do you feel any better at all about how things will end up?"

Gabriel turned to meet her gaze, and at last he smiled.

"I actually feel better about the merger than I have in weeks," he said, placing his glass atop the bar. "Listen, I have some work to do back at the office. I can get an Uber to take you home if you'd like."

"Thank you," Xiomara said, "but I'll be here a while longer to make sure Mr. Blake and his wife are taken care of."

"Of course," Gabriel said, studying her for a moment before dimpling again. "I'll leave them in your capable hands and wish you an enjoyable weekend, Xiomara."

"To you as well, Gabriel," she told him, watching him walk away from the bar and to the coat rack to grab his jacket. He extracted his phone from the pocket, perhaps to summon a ride for himself.

"Everything okay?" Joran asked as he approached, leaning his cello case against the bar.

"One never really knows with Gabriel," Xiomara said. "Seems like something's thrown him for a loop tonight, though, and not just the fact that you were here."

"The look on his face when he saw me," Joran said with a grin.

"I don't get it," Xiomara said. "You guys were close and seemed to be close for several years. Now, it seems as if you barely tolerate one another and enjoy getting a rise out of each other."

They watched as Diana emerged from the kitchen and walked over to join the Blakes in quiet conversation.

"He's getting worse," Joran answered, picking up Gabriel's discarded drink, sniffing at it, and setting it back down. "Every acquisition, every advancement, every award... takes him farther from the guy I knew. My guess is that I won't know him at all anymore in a few months."

"And that's okay with you?" Xiomara asked.

Joran shrugged. "What else can I do? I've told you how things changed for us in high school. I guess this has been years in the making, but I keep hoping for more than the occasional glimpse of the kid I knew then. Seems less and less likely."

Xiomara glanced at Diana again and then sighed.

"I suppose I shouldn't be rude," she said, smoothing her dress. "Coming?"

"Nope, I'll be rude. Thanks, though!" Joran said with a grin. Xiomara shook her head, moving toward the trio to wait until Diana finished speaking and the Blakes moved to the bar to join Joran. Diana looked Xiomara over, brow arched, and said nothing. Refusing to take the bait, Xiomara smiled.

"Thank you for hosting us tonight, Diana," she said. "The meal was amazing, and I believe your suggestion to have this gathering may have provided the breakthrough needed as far as how things will proceed from this point."

Diana rolled her eyes. "Do you?" she asked.

"It's because of you that Gabriel and Mr. Blake could take advantage of a wonderful opportunity to step away from the politics of business and find common ground—as men with shared interests."

"What they have in common is you," Diana said in a low voice. "Neither of them can seem to do anything without you having a hand in it."

"Diana," Xiomara said, matching her tone, "I do not want Gabriel. Since my actions have obviously not been enough for you to catch on, listen to what I am telling you."

"And so you punish him by flaunting Joran in his face?" Diana responded in a shrill whisper.

"I did not flaunt him! His presence was a gift for Mr. and Mrs. Blake!"

"Something you could have orchestrated at any other time," Diana commented. "They're going to see him at a show next week, aren't they?"

"Make up your mind, Diana," Xiomara sighed. "You're bothered because you think Joran's presence upset Gabriel but would have been equally riled if Joran weren't here. You can't have it both ways."

"Neither can you!" Diana sneered.

"I'm not trying to. I do not want Gabriel."

There was a pause as the women stared at one another.

"Then you're a fool!" Diana spat before turning away and heading back into the kitchen.

"Unbelievable," Xiomara muttered as Joran approached with her coat draped over one arm.

"She's a lost cause," he offered, holding out the coat and helping her into it.

"I like to believe that there's no such thing," Xiomara answered as she worked the buttons.

"The Blakes are offering to let us ride with them if you're ready to go."

Xiomara took a cursory glance outside through the windows and then shook her head.

"It's stopped raining," she said. "I think I'd rather walk and clear my head."

"I'll walk with you," he said.

"Joran, you have your cello. You can't walk me home."

"Xiomara, I've been schlepping a cello around since I was ten years old. I'm sure I can manage."

She laughed. "You win again. We can see them off and then go on our way."

"After you," Joran said with a bow, grinning.

"We actually made it all the way here without Gabriel sneaking up on us," Joran commented when they reached the entrance to the building Xiomara lived in.

"Well, he said he had work to do back at the office," Xiomara commented.

"Will wonders never cease?"

Xiomara walked over to the door, opening it. "You coming up?" she called over her shoulder.

"You inviting me?" Joran returned. Xiomara turned and smirked at him.

"Seems like a walk with you isn't complete without cotton candy," she explained.

"We passed three stores!" Joran exclaimed.

"I have some upstairs," Xiomara explained. "Kiwi-strawberry and mango-coconut."

"Looks like I'm coming up," Joran said, rubbing his hands together as he followed her inside.

"Where in the world did you find mango-flavored cotton candy?" Joran demanded later when Xiomara walked him out.

They stood facing one another in the lobby of her apartment building. The thick strap of Joran's cello case stretched diagonally from his right shoulder to his left hip, and he wore the cello backpack-style. On the average man, it would have seemed comical. On Joran, it somehow didn't.

Xiomara ran a hand through her hair. "I am a woman of many mysteries," she deadpanned.

"Oh, yeah?" Joran asked. "What else are you hiding?"

Xiomara's smile was sweet as she said nothing.

"My life is gonna suck in about an hour once all that sugar wears off," Joran commented.

"I've supplied reinforcements," she said, pointing at the small paper bag Joran was holding. "Just consider the use of moderation."

"Ah, I can't eat this," he insisted, though he cradled the bag. "I'd be breaking tradition. You said yourself that a walk with me goes hand-in-hand with the gluttonous consumption of cotton candy."

"I don't think I said it quite like that," Xiomara disagreed with a gurgle of laughter.

"I'll have to save it," Joran said. "Until next time."

"Next time?" she asked, brows raised.

"The next time we go on a walk," he replied with a grin before turning to leave.

"Now, wait a minute!" Xiomara protested, still smiling.

"Have a wonderful weekend!" Joran called over his shoulder, pushing against the heavy glass doors and slipping out into the night.

Chapter Fifteen

"Good morning, Mr. Blake!" Xiomara said cheerfully as she entered his office, hefting the day's mail.

She found him sitting at his desk, appearing to be deep in thought as he stared at the computer monitor. It was not until she got closer that she realized the monitor was off. She frowned and placed the stack of mail on the corner of the desk.

"Mr. Blake?" she said, brow furrowed.

He blinked and turned to her with unfocused brown eyes before flashing the familiar smile that she had grown to appreciate. The recovery, however, was not fast enough, and Xiomara was concerned.

"Um, sir," she began, "is everything all right?" She attempted a smile. "Have I interrupted your daydreaming? Tonight's one of the first performances of Tourists of Dreams. You and Mrs. Blake have been looking forward to it for weeks."

"I don't think we'll be going," Blake said, the smile faltering a bit as he reached for the mail and shuffled through it.

"Sir?" Xiomara said, puzzled.

"I shouldn't even be here today," he said into the stack. "She started feeling under the weather a couple of days ago." He looked up at Xiomara. "This morning, she wasn't even well enough to get out of bed."

Xiomara was stunned. "What's wrong?"

"We take walks every night after dinner, no matter the weather. Nothing big, just a couple of turns around the grounds. At first, we thought maybe she caught a bit of a chill, but now I don't know what this is." He tossed the mail back onto the desk. Some of it slipped from the stack, slid across the smooth wood, and landed on the floor. "It was her idea for me to come in today, with explicit instructions not to worry. No chance of that."

"Then go home, Mr. Blake," Xiomara said. "There isn't much on your calendar today at all, aside from a lunch meeting with Gabriel."

"I can't deal with that one," Blake muttered. "Lavinia and I want to go to Paris next month. We still can if Matheson would stop dragging his feet."

"I hoped things would get better after the dinner last week, sir."

"The dinner was very nice," Blake admitted. "That Diana is a wonderful chef." He looked at Xiomara again. "I know why you set that up. You hoped that I'd see another side to the young man."

"The idea wasn't mine," Xiomara admitted. "But I hoped it might help things a bit."

"I hoped the same." Blake adjusted his generous bulk as he settled back into the mahogany leather chair. "Has it helped you?" he ventured. "Do you now see another side to him?"

Xiomara shook her head. "Not in the way you're implying, sir," she said. "I haven't forgotten your warning, and I can't ignore things I've seen. But, I hoped that the dinner might reset things a bit and give you both a fresh perspective."

"Yet here we are. We're going around in circles because he keeps excising employee provisions from the contract, or he uses his lawyers to rewrite the terms into flowery gibberish that means nothing!" He got up from the desk. "I shouldn't even entertain this farce anymore! I wish I could take myself and my company elsewhere. Merging with Matheson Media could be a boon for both sides, but he can't be trusted!"

"Mr. Blake," Xiomara began, "you warned me about his business acumen. If I may ask, why did you decide to go through all of this if you felt that way?"

Blake ran a hand over his bald head and exhaled. "It looked perfect on paper," he explained. "Here he is, a shooting star in our industry. Here I am, an established name with a lucrative client base. What was there to lose? It wasn't until after my investors began drooling at the prospect and money started funneling in that I saw things differently."

"Gabriel is not a stupid man," she said. "He wants to wear you down so that you'll give in."

"I can't abandon my employees," Blake insisted. "I won't. I must continue to fight for them. There are investors willing to support the EJB side—but, on the condition that this merger takes place. If I pull out now, it will do my company more harm than good. Too many people have sunk their teeth into this."

"I'll help you, Mr. Blake. All of us on the team would love to. We can band together to make sure that Gabriel does what's right." She smiled. "I'll have a meeting with the others. Why don't you go home, sir? Spend some time with Mrs. Blake. Despite what she said, she'll be glad to have you there. We'll handle things here."

Blake considered her for a moment, and then frowned.

"Xiomara, I need to ask you something," he said.

"Of course," she responded. "Please do."

"Why do you stay?"

Xiomara blinked in surprise; brows raised. "Sir?" she asked.

"No offense, but you are not Junior Secretary material," Blake answered. "I knew it from the moment your application and portfolio came across my desk, but I wanted you for my team. Your abilities far exceed the position you are in, and your wealth of knowledge belies your years.

"You're handling dual workloads for both EJB and Matheson Media and you send daily reports back to my corporate office to make sure that everyone's kept in the loop. I have yet to see you bothered by any of it or come anywhere near missing a deadline.

"You have endured Gabriel's attention and intrusions in a climate where he should have already been brought to bear for harassment. Lavinia, who never has an unkind word for anyone, could not help commenting on Gabriel's behavior at that dinner—particularly where you were concerned."

"Mr. Blake..."

"Why do you stay, Xiomara?" he asked again. "You could do so much better."

Xiomara smiled again and shrugged. "I have a job to do," she answered. "I intend to see things through."

"And what about Gabriel?"

"Gabriel likes to think that he has the upper hand," Xiomara said. "He'll realize soon enough that he does not, and hopefully the shock of it will force him to rethink his actions."

"Would take an act of God for that to happen," Blake chortled.

Xiomara giggled. "I appreciate your concern—yours and Mrs. Blake's. I intend to see this through. We'll worry about what comes after later."

Blake nodded. After several moments, the smile returned to his face.

"We should talk, you and I, when this merger is completed," he told her. "There are bigger things in store for you than hanging around here."

"I believe you're right, sir. For now, though, please give Mrs. Blake my best. I'll let Joran know about tonight, but I'm hoping she'll rebound and feel well enough to attend after all."

She watched, still smiling, as Mr. Blake retrieved his coat and left the office. Xiomara then reached for the phone atop the desk, picked up the receiver, and dialed.

"Donna, how are you this morning?" she said into the phone. "It's Xiomara Grant. I'm well, thank you. I would like a custom order, please. I want your biggest spread of the best of the season—roses, lilies, what have you—and I'd like for you to send it out to Mrs. Lavinia Blake at home." She paused and listened. "No, don't charge it to the account for EJB, I want to take care of it personally. Please include a card that reads, 'With love from all of us,' and I will come around before lunch to settle the bill. You're the best, Donna. See you soon."

Xiomara replaced the receiver before bending to retrieve the mail that had fallen to the floor, slipping it back into a neat stack. She glanced around Blake's office to make sure that nothing was out of place before exiting to head to her own, closing the door behind her. Her black silk-georgette shirt dress swished about her suede-covered calves as she sat at her desk, wiggled the mouse to wake the computer, and then typed.

Chapter Sixteen

"That's fantastic, Caroline," Xiomara said later that morning. She looked over the shoulder of a petite older woman with a neat coif of dark brown curls while they both studied the screen of the laptop Caroline held. "That's exactly what we'll need for the report. Make sure that you and Judy compile your findings so that we can add them to the presentation."

She then moved to her desk, at which sat a willowy redhead with black cat's-eye glasses perched on the bridge of her Roman nose. She divided her attention between Xiomara's desktop computer and an open laptop. Her method of typing data into the first machine and then the other was seamless.

"How's it going over here, Loraine?" Xiomara queried.

"Cake," Loraine replied, not taking her eyes away from either screen. "Just need those figures from Ruby. Once I plug those in, I'm done and can hand off to Caroline and Judy."

"You sent her for them an hour ago," Judy commented in an undertone from her place on the sofa, where she also wielded a laptop. "What kind of archives do they have in this place? We'd be able to find everything much faster at EJB headquarters."

"It's not whether I could find it, but why I'm even looking," Ruby said from the doorway, her brow furrowed. "If you're going to bash me, you could have the decency to do so behind a closed door."

"No one's bashing you, Ruby," Xiomara assured, admonishing Judy with a look before turning back with a smile. "I asked because we need that information for EJB's investors."

Ruby wrinkled her nose. "Why would you need Matheson's fiscal reports from the last two years for the investors behind EJB Advertising?"

"To give them what they haven't been shown so far: hard evidence as to the pros and cons of this merger," Xiomara said. "What we have given them are puff pieces and smokescreens to support every reason this merger needs to happen."

"So?" Ruby said.

"I think they need to see reasons to the contrary—why EJB can survive on its own and even surpass Matheson Media."

The room went quiet as four sets of eyes rested upon Ruby, who stiffened as her mouth fell open.

"You would undermine Mr. Matheson?" she whispered; her eyes wide. "You mean to undo this merger?"

"No, Ruby," Xiomara said with a shake of her head. "I mean to show Mr. Blake concrete reasons he doesn't have to settle and, at the same time, show Gabriel every reason to be fair in the process based on what he could lose. Presenting this information to the investors is a key step in ensuring that they'll support and promote the outcome that will serve both companies best."

"That's what Mr. Matheson is already doing!"

"Ruby," Xiomara said quietly, "I think you know he isn't. He's stalling. EJB has a lot to gain from these combined efforts. But so does Matheson Media. Yes, Gabriel could walk away, but what he will lose in doing so is something he honestly can't afford as a young company on the rise—and that's the tremendous investment of time.

"He needs Mr. Blake's clientele and reputation, and Mr. Blake needs Gabriel's vision of the future. Why should one come out of this any less than the other when they're equally formidable? You'll be here, Ruby, to see it through. No one's trying to leave you out or belittle your contribution."

Ruby reached into the pocket of her gray pinstripe slacks and extracted a flash drive, which she then held out to Xiomara.

"I gave you the last three years of reports," she said. "We had an uptick of business in the second year, so I thought a representation of how that carried over into the third year along with a showing of the results might be helpful. We met every deadline we set."

"Thank you, Ruby," Xiomara said, taking the drive and holding it to her left, where it was snatched up by Loraine and inserted into the laptop.

"I guess that's all, then?" Ruby said.

"Not even close," Xiomara told her. "You should stay. Now is as good a time as any to learn from the EJB side, since I've brought these ladies in for the day. Collaborate with them, Ruby. Show them what I already know of you."

"Mr. Matheson..." Ruby began.

"...is in his office closed away doing God knows what," Xiomara finished. "The only pressing item on his calendar for today was the meeting with Mr. Blake, and that's been canceled."

"Pull up some sofa, Ruby," Judy said as an offering of peace. "There's always room for one more."

Xiomara watched as Ruby's brow furrowed again, her green eyes flitting from one woman to the next before settling upon Judy and the space beside her. She then walked over and took a seat.

"I have a couple of errands to run," Xiomara said, walking over to the coat rack to retrieve her leather outerwear. "At the top of my list is catering in a late lunch. We'll have it in the main conference room."

"I could take care of that," Ruby said, looking up from the illuminated screen of the spare laptop she had been given.

"You are exactly where I need you," Xiomara replied, "and I won't be long. I also need to stop in and see Donna over at Garden's Gate."

"And when Mr. Matheson comes looking for you?" Ruby asked.

"You're so sure he will?"

"He always does," Ruby stated. This time, all eyes were on Xiomara, who smirked in response.

"None of you need answer to Gabriel on my behalf," she told them. "If need be, I'll deal with him when I get back."

Chapter Seventeen

Xiomara waited at the back door of La Bonne Vie, after ringing the doorbell at the service entrance. She smoothed a lock of hair behind one ear and adjusted the strap of the purse that dangled from her left shoulder, marveling that even the alley behind the restaurant was kept in pristine condition.

When the door opened, Xiomara wasn't surprised to be greeted by the proprietress herself who, despite having several hours before the restaurant was due to open, was already clad in her chef's whites.

"Is Gabriel with you?" Diana asked, looking past Xiomara and further out into the alley.

"He is not," Xiomara answered.

"What do you want?"

"To discuss business."

"What sort of business could I possibly have with you?" Diana sneered.

"You are a chef with a restaurant. I want food. Simple enough."

"Simple enough that you can go somewhere else. We're not even open yet, and I'm already behind. I had the crew of the show in here filming at six this morning."

"It's Monday, Diana," Xiomara said. "How many covers do you get on a Monday night—with your prices? Six? Four?"

"That's no concern of yours!" Diana said, reddening. "Did Gabriel send you here?"

"I came on my own... to ask you to cater lunch for five over at Matheson Media."

Diana straightened at that. "For Gabriel?" she asked, her tone eager.

"Not everything has to do with Gabriel," Xiomara said. "This is a lunch for a group of very hardworking ladies. They could use the nourishment... and you could use the cash-flow."

"What!?" Diana snapped, offended.

"You could make as much off this lunch as you will the entire night peddling rose water foam to the handful of toadies that show up."

"Do you really think that insults will somehow entice me to help you?"

"Asking nicely didn't seem to have an effect," Xiomara shrugged. "But, if you're really able to turn down $2,500..."

"What did you say?" Diana said, on alert. Xiomara smiled.

"I said you could make as much off this lunch as you would on a typical Monday night."

"Serving a dozen courses to the dregs over at Matheson?"

"Five," Xiomara corrected. "We'll need to get through the rest of the day, so five courses at the cost of what you normally charge for more than twice that. Start with an appetizer, end with an array of sweet things—all of them light. None of them drowned in that bullshit foam.

"No alcohol, obviously, which will leave even more of the profits for you to absorb. I'll want everything set up in the main conference room no later than 2:30, with one of your bussers available to set up, serve, and dismantle. That's four hours from now, which is more than enough time. You'll be done with time left for dinner prep. Will you do it?"

"With time left to prep for my four covers?" Diana asked in a mocking tone, to which Xiomara responded with a shrug.

"As you like," she said with a roll of her eyes before covering an indelicate yawn. "I could always book a private room at Morton's for lunch, which I know they'd appreciate. EJB has a longstanding relationship with them, after all."

Diana bristled. "I suppose EJB is footing the bill for this lunch?"

"No," Xiomara said, "I am." Diana's eyes widened. "Consider it a show of good faith and a token of good will. I could go anywhere and spend much less than what I'm offering you, and without the serving of attitude."

"Then why come here?"

"It's an olive branch, Diana, and the last one I'm offering. I would not be here if I didn't think you were talented, and the ladies you'd be catering for have tenure and could do a lot to spread a positive word. You should have more than the crumbs that Gabriel offers you, and I know that closing last Friday night had to hurt. I can't compensate you for that, but a good rapport with EJB will benefit you in the long run." Diana's lips pressed into a thin line, and she didn't respond. "So, may I come in and discuss the menu, or should I give Morton's a call?"

The ladies stared at one another for several seconds before Diana stepped to one side and allowed Xiomara to walk through the door.

As Xiomara emerged from the vibrant and colorful storefront of Garden's Gate Florist, her cell phone rang. Fishing it from her pocket, she was surprised that the display revealed Joran's name rather than any of the numbers associated with Matheson Media.

"Xiomara Grant," she answered, continuing to walk.

"So formal," Joran said with a chuckle.

Xiomara could not help smiling. "You're a surprise," she said. "I thought you'd be working on sound checks."

"We are, but I'm having a break. I tried you at your office and got your voicemail."

"I'm heading back there, actually. There have been some developments."

"Are you okay?"

"It's not me," Xiomara assured him. "It's Mrs. Blake. She isn't well, so she and Mr. Blake are not likely to make it tonight."

"That's too bad," Joran said. "They were both really looking forward to it. So was I. They're amazing people."

"They are," Xiomara agreed, stepping away from the sidewalk to stand near one building and out of the path of the sparse late-morning foot traffic. "I was planning to call you when I got back to the office to let you know."

"Is it bad?"

"It's too soon to say, but it's probably just a bug and they're being cautious. He was concerned enough about it that I suggested he go home to spend time with her. I'm sure they'll make it to the other performances."

"I'll bet he loved that," Joran surmised.

"Huh?"

"Gabriel. Without Blake around, he gets to have you all to himself."

"He gets no such thing," Xiomara said, walking again, the heels of her black suede boots clacking against the concrete. "I had some ladies come in from EJB so that we can work on some things in Mr. Blake's absence, and Gabriel has been holed up in his office. In the meantime, I've been to see Diana."

"What in the world would you do that for?" Joran asked, shock evident in his tone.

"I have something that Diana needs badly," she said.

"A roofied-out Gabriel covered in crème caramel foam?" Joran offered.

"Money."

"What?"

"That restaurant is a money pit as it is, and Gabriel made her close on the busiest night of the week," Xiomara explained. "Since she won't listen to me, I let my wallet do the talking."

"What'd you do, bribe her to burn the place down for the insurance?"

"I simply asked her to cater a lunch. The opportunity to showcase the skills that we know she has could drum up business for La Bonne Vie. EJB caters business functions all the time—not to mention any personal gatherings the Blakes might have."

"Why? Why are you being so nice to her after the way she's behaved toward you? She hasn't earned one bit of your help!"

"Diana isn't the issue," Xiomara said. "She's just caught up in Gabriel's self-serving manipulation."

"By choice! She's been thriving under his lukewarm attentions for a while now. You're wasting your time."

"I don't believe that anyone is a waste of time. Diana and I are not friends and probably never will be, but she needs to know that she has options. Gabriel doesn't do anywhere near as much for her as he could."

"Now, wait a minute," Joran said, lowering his voice. "You're not talking about what she asked him to do for that show, are you?"

"Of course not, Joran!" Xiomara said. "We've gone over this, and you and I both agreed that she doesn't have to resort to that. I am talking about the fact that he's in marketing yet hasn't bothered to create any buzz for her. What do you take me for?"

"I'm sorry!" he blurted. "It's not that I doubt you, or at least I try not to. But, you're with him all day and I know he's waiting to wear you down."

"Stop!" Xiomara said, pausing on the sidewalk again. "Just stop. Why does everything always have to come back to me and Gabriel? You're no different from Diana!"

"I'm sorry!" Joran said again. "I really don't mean to keep doing this."

"Then don't. Look, I'm heading back to the office, and you need to get back to rehearsal."

"Wait, Xiomara... hang on. Not like this, okay? I don't want this conversation to end with us fighting."

"I'm not fighting," Xiomara said, "I'm merely withdrawing from the eventual."

"I don't want you to do that, either!"

"Go back to rehearsal," she said again. "I'll send word if the Blakes will make it after all, okay?"

"No, seriously... wait..."

Xiomara pulled the phone away from her ear, pressed the END button, and slipped it into the pocket of her coat, continuing to walk while ignoring the incessant buzzing as the phone came to life again.

Chapter Eighteen

Xiomara sat at the computer in her spare bedroom. Her gaze focused on the PowerPoint presentation that she and Ruby compiled based on the investor report put together by Caroline, Loraine, and Judy. She had already reviewed the presentation half a dozen times throughout the day but wanted to be certain that it was airtight and streamlined to perfection.

She wore her hair in a thick twisted braid thrown forward over the left shoulder of gold, relaxed-fit silk pajamas. Xiomara picked up a glass of apple juice and sipped it as she continued to read. The sudden and loud knocking coming from the living room startled her, and she nearly dropped the glass.

Juice in hand, she padded through the apartment, sighing along the way as she opened the front door. She blinked, taking in the sight of Joran in a black Parisian tuxedo, wielding an enormous multi-colored array of roses, their buds spun from cotton candy. He wore a ponytail again, a look she appreciated almost as much as when he was windswept.

"I should have moved into an apartment building with a secured entrance," she said.

"You don't answer your phone," he returned.

"It's in my bedroom charging. I was in my office working. Do you have any idea how late it is?"

"I am acutely aware of the time, thank you," Joran said, Xiomara's golden attire reflected in his appreciative green gaze. "The performance ended at precisely 9:47 p.m., after which I shook hands, toasted with an empty glass, and autographed a few babies that were likely conceived during one of my songs.

"By 10:32 p.m., I was at the confectionery near the Plaza when I started calling you, and where I happily paid an exorbitant amount for the toothless matron in charge to produce this dazzling arrangement." He extended the bouquet, his eyes not leaving hers. "And, then I got a taxi and came straight

87

here." His gaze softened, and he exhaled. "Xiomara. Please don't be angry with me."

Xiomara accepted the composition of spun sugar with her free hand, breaking the gaze to admire the craftsmanship.

"These are beautiful, thank you," she said.

"Xiomara," he said again.

She looked up at him. "I'm not angry, Joran," she told him.

"But?" he prompted, to which she shook her head.

"There is no but," she said. "I know how our conversation ended earlier today, and it upset me. I've since let it go. I wasn't intentionally ignoring your calls tonight."

"This afternoon," he suggested. "During the early evening..."

"You needed to focus on your show then," she explained, moving away from the doorway so that he could come inside. "You couldn't be on the phone debating with me for half the night, and that's exactly what you would have done."

"I sure would have!" he agreed with enthusiasm, following her and shutting the door behind him.

He continued to follow her through the living room and into the kitchen, where she deposited the glass of juice atop the counter and shifted the bouquet to cradle it in the crook of one arm.

"I don't suppose that you stopped to have something to eat amid your apology tour?" Xiomara said.

"Who could eat?" Joran answered, leaning against the wall.

Xiomara sighed and placed the sweets atop the counter as well, shaking her head. "Well, you're certainly not about to fill up on cotton candy."

"That wasn't my intention. I don't know what I intended, to be honest. I didn't know if I'd even get to see you at all tonight, so I made no plans. I was so focused on my quest that it wasn't until I was three-quarters of the way here that I realized I left the keys to my apartment in the jeans that I wore to the Plaza tonight. All I could think to grab before I left was my wallet."

He held his arms out at his sides, once again drawing Xiomara's attention to his impeccable attire. She gaped.

"Everything else is back in the dressing room?" she asked.

"I was in a hurry," he responded.

88

"I'm not mad, Joran."

"I didn't want to risk it."

Xiomara nodded. "Are you hungry now?" she asked after a brief pause.

His side-to-side headshake was slow and deliberate.

"Honestly, I am so tired from being wound up for the last twelve hours that food isn't even a consideration," he said. "I just wanted to see you—that's all."

"Wait here a moment."

Xiomara could feel him watching her as she exited the kitchen and walked down the hallway, past her bedroom. She reached a sliding door near the end of the hall and opened it, extracting a set of linens, a cream-colored duvet, and a large pillow. Xiomara brought the items to Joran, showing with a nod of her head that he should follow her back to the living room.

"It's not a sleeper, but it's very comfortable," she said of the sectional. "As you can see, it's also pretty big. You should be able to stretch out with no problem." Xiomara placed the stack atop one of the sofa cushions before turning to Joran and continuing in a conversational tone. "The spare bathroom is at the end of the hall on the left. I have a pack of new toothbrushes in the top bathroom drawer nearest the door, and all the towels hanging in the bathroom are clean. You can toss whichever towels you use into the bathroom hamper. Help yourself to anything in the kitchen. There's some leftover Mongolian beef in the fridge that is phenomenal."

"I certainly wouldn't get service like this at the Hilton down the street," Joran said, smirking.

"I guess it's a good thing you don't have to worry about that," Xiomara said, smiling. "Wake up call at six, so I'd better let you settle in."

"Thank you, Xiomara," Joran said after she had turned to leave.

She glanced at him over her shoulder, shaking her head.

"Good night, Joran," she replied before heading to her room.

Chapter Nineteen

Xiomara sat at the desk in her office, sifting through the enormous stack of mail sent over from EJB Advertising for Mr. Blake. Though she tossed some into the nearby trash can, she was methodical in sorting the rest into three separate piles. She had almost finished doing so when the cellphone atop the desk rang. She glanced over at the display, arched a brow, and then answered.

"Interesting to see the name La Bonne Vie on my Caller ID," she said.

"Not any more interesting than it was for me to make this call," Diana said, her shrill voice sounding even more so over the phone. "I got your number from the invoice for that lunch."

"I gathered as much. To what do I owe this unexpected event?"

"I received a fax this morning from Loraine Stanfield," Diana said after a pause.

"The accounting executive at EJB?"

"She didn't tell you?"

"No. I've spoken to Loraine several times since you catered for us a couple of weeks ago, but she never mentioned contacting you." Xiomara waited while Diana paused again.

"Apparently, her daughter has gotten engaged," Diana said at last. "She wants to hold a dinner for her at Bonne."

Xiomara set aside the remaining stack of mail and settled back in her chair. "Well, that's good, isn't it?"

"She's asked to hold the dinner on a Monday night. You so readily pointed out that I'd only have four covers on that night of the week anyway... and she's requested seating for thirty."

Xiomara whistled. "Will you do it?"

"Have you lost your mind?" Diana retorted. "Thirty covers will fill the entire restaurant."

"You'll have to close for the evening to give Loraine's party your full attention," Xiomara commented with a soft smile.

"Which is exactly what I intend. You really didn't put her up to this?"

"Diana, all I did was ask you to cater lunch. You did the rest on your own, as I said you could." There was yet another pause, and Xiomara instinctively knew that Diana was struggling for something more to say. "Will you be serving five courses again?"

"No," Diana said. "She's requested the full experience—all thirteen courses." Xiomara made a series of swift mental calculations and then chuckled. "Don't you dare," Diana warned.

"I wasn't going to say a word," Xiomara assured her, "other than congratulations." Diana choked on something that sounded like a thank you, and Xiomara thought it best to let it pass without drawing more attention to what seemed to be an uncomfortable moment.

"Did you mean what you said?" Diana asked.

"About what?" Xiomara said, puzzled.

"About not wanting Gabriel."

Xiomara sighed. "Just when I thought you and I might have reached an understanding..."

"Gabriel's going to help me win that competition, and I want nothing to get in the way. Now tell me—did you mean it!?"

"I meant it and cannot emphasize it enough."

"Good," Diana said before disconnecting.

Xiomara was still shaking her head as she returned to sorting through the mail. The first pile comprised things she could take care of on her own. She would send the second pile via messenger to Edmund Blake at his home, where he had remained for the last week, once it became clear that Mrs. Blake's recovery might not be as swift as everyone had hoped. Xiomara would reroute and distribute the third pile among other departments for review.

Mr. Blake spoke with Xiomara every morning via phone, discussing how things should proceed at the office in his continued absence. She had yet to review the financial report and presentation with him in person, but she sent copies over with the messenger so that he could go over them at his leisure. The efforts made to entice and excite the investors of EJB moved him, and he promised to reschedule the meeting with them as soon as Mrs. Blake recovered.

Xiomara wished she could do more and made a few offers to visit the Blakes personally. Mr. Blake, however, often assured her it was a matter of time before things would be back to normal and he could return to the office without worrying.

What was not normal was the fact that Gabriel had become a rare sight at his own company. The rumor mill was rife with speculation that he was hard at work plotting his next acquisition, since the Blake merger was all but officially signed. Xiomara was not so sure about the latter half of that rumor, but the former wouldn't have surprised her at all and was a testament to Gabriel's greed. Ruby, unfettered and left to reign, had blossomed. It thrilled Xiomara since Gabriel appeared to be giving Xiomara some space, too.

"Xiomara Grant," she answered after the office phone trilled beside her.

"My lucky morning," Joran responded.

Xiomara's eyes widened, and she sat up in her chair. "Good morning," she said. "How are you?"

"I'm okay. Going over tonight's set list and thinking of changing up a few things. How're you?"

"Oh, chugging along," she said. "I'm tackling a few things here, and then I was thinking of heading out to EJB for the day."

"Don't you usually have people come out to see you?"

"If it pertains to dealing with Matheson Media, yes," Xiomara explained. "But, this visit would be more specific. Mr. Blake has been out for so long that I thought going out to the company might help them feel that someone is still looking out for their best interests. They're not just part of a merger."

"That's very thoughtful of you," Joran said. "Shouldn't that be something for Gabriel to do, though?"

"I'm not even sure that Gabriel is here today," she admitted. "He has been behaving like a *persona non grata* for days. Ruby is having the time of her life."

"As she should," Joran said, laughing. "Since you're heading out to EJB Corporate, does that mean what I think it does?"

Xiomara laughed. "Yes, I'm actually going to drive. It would take two hours to get there by train."

"And here I thought you might try to hoof it!"

"Hilarious. This is a beautiful city. There's no harm in the occasional stroll."

"Occasional," Joran mocked, though his tone was warm. "I've worn down the soles of two pairs of sneakers since I met you."

"Fibber," she said, sitting back in her chair.

"I have to head back," he said. "Should I call you later?"

Xiomara paused. "Okay," she responded after a moment.

"Such enthusiasm!" he said before adopting a falsetto. "Why of course, Joran! I would love for you to call me! I SO look forward to our chats!" Xiomara laughed again but refrained from responding. "I'll talk to you later," he said in his normal voice.

"Bye," she said before hanging up. Just then, Ruby appeared in the doorway. Her coloring and demeanor had improved by leaps over the last few weeks, and it thrilled Xiomara.

"Any updates?" Ruby asked, to which Xiomara responded by shaking her head in the negative.

"Sadly, no," she said. "I'm glad to say that Mrs. Blake has gotten no worse. However, she doesn't seem to improve, either. How about for you?"

Ruby took a cursory look down the hallway toward Gabriel's office before turning back to Xiomara with a shrug.

"The door was already closed by the time I came in this morning," Ruby said. "I've heard him talking here and there while walking by, but he hasn't asked for anything. He's even been ordering his own meals."

"I'm heading out to EJB, so I'll be gone for the rest of the day. Do you need anything before I leave?"

"No, everything's fine here," Ruby said. "I imagine they're feeling panicked out there, though."

"Nothing so drastic," Xiomara said. "But, I want to make sure they get more than a daily briefing from me. They're owed more than that. I would have gone out sooner, but I think we all hoped that Mr. Blake would be back by now."

"What time are you going?"

"Within twenty minutes. I needed to finish with the mail that came by messenger this morning. Some of it needs to be returned for review."

"I have your cell number," Ruby said, "and be sure to take your laptop just in case."

"Check and check!"

"Say hi to Judy, Loraine, and Caroline if you see them?"

"I'll make it a priority," Xiomara said, smiling.

Ruby smiled back before disappearing into the hallway.

Chapter Twenty

Xiomara stood in the center of the large space that once served as the auxiliary office of Edmund Blake. Loraine, Judy, and two junior secretaries from EJB Advertising bustled around the room, packing various items into boxes. Standing nearby, beside a uniformed courier, was Xiomara, watching as he took notes and checked items from a list attached to a clipboard.

"We're making excellent time," Xiomara commented.

"We could make even better time if you'd let me get my guys in here," she was told.

"I've already explained that. These ladies have been on Mr. Blake's team for years. They want to be the ones to do this. Your guys can do the heavy lifting later."

"I've done work for Mr. Blake before," the man said. "Brilliant man. Great reputation. I was deeply sorry to hear what happened. It's a shame..."

The room went still, drawing Xiomara's attention as she looked around in confusion. The others were staring behind her, and Xiomara turned to follow their collective gaze. She locked eyes with Gabriel as he stood in the doorway with a bashful grin. She drew a breath as her jaw tightened. Xiomara had seen little of Gabriel in the last month, and while his presence was not unexpected, the timing of his reappearance was not ideal.

Turning back to face the others, while doing her best to ignore the puzzled expression on the courier's face, Xiomara offered a warm smile.

"Ladies," she began pleasantly, "this is as good a time as any to have a break, don't you think? In about an hour, we can go for the final push and get these things squared away so that Mike and his team can clear out the boxes." As the ladies first glanced at each other and then at Xiomara, the latter turned to Mike with that same smile. "Will your guys be ready in about two hours?"

"They were ready this morning," he said, chuckling. "But, we're here whenever you need us."

"Then I'll see you back in an hour," she offered, "and we can go over the last bit of inventory before we send for them."

Xiomara waited as the others filed out, the women taking great care to give Gabriel a wide berth, before walking over to where Mike had discarded the clipboard containing the paperwork. She picked it up and glanced through it, not bothering to look up after hearing the door close.

"Is this what we're resorting to?" Gabriel asked.

"Hmm?" Xiomara asked, looking over the second page.

"The silent treatment," he commented.

She took her time looking up at him. "Is that what you think?"

"What else could it be?" he asked, arms out at his sides, blue eyes wide. "I've hardly seen you, let alone spoken to you, for weeks. You didn't respond to the message I left the other day inviting you to dinner. What am I supposed to think?"

"You're not supposed to think," Xiomara said, tossing the clipboard atop the nearby empty desk with a clatter. "You're supposed to know that I am busy. You're supposed to know that, as one of Mr. Blake's assistants, I have a lot to do to help him right now. He has lost his wife and is losing his company within days of each other, and I still have work to do." She folded her arms and studied him. "So, why don't you tell me what you think you could have done to earn the silent treatment? Unless you'd care to enlighten me as to your reasons for being so sequestered during the last few weeks?"

Gabriel reddened before looking away. Xiomara watched as his face remained flushed, and his hands retracted into refined fists. He then turned away and placed a hand on the doorknob.

"Will I see you at the funeral on Sunday?" Xiomara queried.

Gabriel froze for a moment before yanking the door open and stalking out.

Chapter Twenty-One

Xiomara awoke drenched in sweat, gagging and gasping for air as she clutched at her throat. Scrambling from the bed, she almost did not make it to the toilet before the remains of her dinner splattered into the bowl.

Tears mingled with the sweat on her cheeks as she flushed, still struggling to catch her breath. She sat upon the floor beside the toilet, hugging her knees to her chest as she sobbed—open-mouthed yet soundless as the tears continued to flow.

After several minutes, Xiomara scrambled to her feet, sniffling as she returned to her bedroom. She snatched up her cell phone so abruptly that the charging adapter snapped loose from its connection. She scrolled through her contacts, selected Joran's name, and dialed. As the line rang, she disconnected.

"Stop," she whispered to herself. "What are you doing? You cannot call him. You can't..."

Xiomara took a deep breath, tossing the phone onto the bed before leaving the bedroom again. This time, she went to the spare room and over to the large desk. She yanked the cover of the rectangular wooden box free, tossing it to the floor and seizing the sketchpad. Xiomara ripped each page until she reached the one upon which she had drawn the man with the hazel eyes.

She stared at his picture for a moment and narrowed her eyes before it, too, was ripped from the booklet and, unlike the other pages, torn into even smaller bits that she allowed to fall onto the floor.

Xiomara was standing in the bathroom, towel-drying her hair after having showered to reclaim her wits and temper. The mess in the spare room was cleaned, and she returned the pictures that were ripped from the sketchpad to the wooden box. Even the shredded portrait went back into the box because, for reasons she still did not understand, she was not ready to part with them.

As she studied her reflection, determined to return to bed to embrace the five hours of sleep that would have to suffice, she heard knocking coming from the front door. Her body tensed as she waited, thinking someone had gotten off on the wrong floor and would soon realize the mistake. She was prepared to ignore the intrusion.

The knocks came again, louder this time, and Xiomara crept down the hallway toward the living room, debating whether to glimpse through the peephole in the door to see who it was. She was mere steps from doing so when a voice called out.

"I know you're standing there. Let me in!"

"What are you doing here!?" Xiomara asked after flinging the door open. Joran, who was holding two large paper bags by the handles, looked relieved to see her as he smiled.

"You called me," he stated.

Xiomara reddened and stepped to the side so that he could enter. She leaned back against the closed door and tucked a lock of hair behind her ear. Joran entered the living room and placed both bags on the floor near the sofa.

"Joran, look," Xiomara began, stopping when he held up a hand.

"Don't bother," he said, still smiling. "You're going to pretend that you didn't mean to call. I am going to ignore that. We're going to pig out on the food I brought, and you'll tell me what's wrong."

Xiomara could not help chuckling.

"Oh, really?" she asked and then paused as her senses picked up the aroma wafting from the contents of one of the paper bags. Her stomach growled, and her blush deepened.

"Guess I have your attention now," Joran laughed, rubbing his hands together. "Shall we?"

Chapter Twenty-Two

Xiomara nibbled through a large 'breakfast bowl' of buttery grits topped with cheesy scrambled eggs, crumbled sausage, sautéed spinach, and blistered cherry tomatoes. Joran, meanwhile, had already plowed through two such bowls, a blueberry muffin, and was working on a slice of moist banana walnut bread as Xiomara looked on in awe. They had gone through the contents of one bag, however, and she could not help wondering what the other bag contained.

"I wouldn't have ever guessed that you have such an appetite," Xiomara confessed. Joran laughed, sipping at a glass of orange juice.

"Because the only other things you've seen me eat are cotton candy and Diana's scraps," he said. He brought the glass to his mouth, peering at her over the rim. "We should fix that."

Xiomara averted her gaze, suddenly fascinated by the embroidered cuffs of her pajama shirt.

"Fix Diana's scraps?" she asked in an offhand manner.

"Nice try," he said, lowering the glass. "Why'd you call me?"

Xiomara sighed, looked up at him, and then shrugged.

"I had a nightmare," she said at last. "I got freaked out. I wasn't trying to bother you, Joran."

"You don't bother me, Xiomara," he countered. "Want to talk about it?"

"About bothering you?" she smirked.

He smiled and settled back, leaning against the leather ottoman behind him.

"You have a doctorate in deflection," he remarked. "Lucky for you, I am a patient man."

"Lucky?"

"Want to talk about it?" he asked again after laughing.

Xiomara shrugged again. "What's to talk about?" she asked. "It was a nightmare. It was awful. I honestly don't even remember the details of it now. I never do, but in the moments right after waking up..."

"...you were terrified," Joran said.

"More than terrified, if that's possible."

"Do you think it's because of Mrs. Blake?" he asked. Xiomara looked at him and did not answer. "You're arranging the funeral of a woman who otherwise seemed healthy a month ago before suddenly dying. That can't be easy."

"No," Xiomara said, studying the other cuff. "It isn't easy at all."

Joran shifted from where he sat, scooting to the place beside Xiomara in front of the sofa. She felt conflicted by his nearness; enjoying the comforting presence he provided and the clean smell of him, while wondering if letting him in was a good idea. She mulled it over, noting his unwavering gaze as she nodded, cleared her throat, and took a deep breath.

"My mother died when I was fourteen years old," she said. "It was the first time that anyone close to me had ever died, and... I guess I thought I'd put it far enough behind me, but apparently not, even though it happened so long ago."

"The death of a parent isn't something that just gets put behind you, Xiomara," Joran said in a soothing tone. "What was that, ten years or so ago that it happened? That's still recent."

"It's been enough time!" Xiomara stressed. "But I started planning this memorial, and suddenly I remembered things about my mother that I thought I'd forgotten—little things at first.

"She was a classic Southern lady: always perfumed and coiffed, with impeccable taste and manners... and though she seemed delicate and demure she had a wicked sense of humor and an I.Q. that was off the charts.

"Daddy's face... he would light up when he saw her, or even if anyone said her name. They were a force, the two of them... and meeting Mrs. Blake at dinner that night and getting to see her reflected in her husband's eyes made me think of my parents." Xiomara frowned, and her voice became harsh. "Doctors diagnosed my mother with bone cancer. It was a tremendous shock to us. My beautiful mother, who got up at dawn every morning to jog and went on walks with Daddy every evening... the woman who cooked three nutritious, five-star quality meals a day made from items picked fresh from our gardens and greenhouses... was suddenly extremely sick and it made absolutely no sense at all."

"Xiomara..." Joran said.

"We initially thought that she was responding well to the treatment prescribed," she continued, ignoring him. "But then it was like a bomb went off inside her, and the cancer was everywhere. Daddy tried everything, consulted everyone, flew in specialists, and paid for experimental treatments. We even went to Switzerland for six months because we knew a clinic there known for groundbreaking progress on her specific type of bone cancer, and we were hopeful.

"But, Mama got tired and wanted to come back home. She told Daddy that if it was her time, she wanted to meet it on her own terms and be in her own bed surrounded by the colors and smells of the flowers from her garden, rather than filled with so much medication that she might risk sleeping away the last of the time she had with us.

"They're two different people—Mama and Mrs. Blake—I know they are. But, the nonsensical means of their loss and the loss to us is too much the same, and I hate it."

"I'm so sorry, Xiomara," Joran said, turning to reach out for her.

"I hate ALL of this!" she burst, snatching up her glass of juice and taking a long drink, causing Joran to pause.

Xiomara also hated the itchy burn behind her eyes as she got up from the floor, walked into the kitchen, and placed her glass on the countertop. She thrust her hands beneath the faucet at the sink, activating the automatic sensor controlling the flow of water. It was freezing, which gave Xiomara the jolt she needed as she struggled to reclaim herself.

She knew Joran had followed. When she turned around, he was holding out a paper towel taken from the dispenser on the wall. Xiomara accepted it, drying her hands as he watched.

"Better?" he asked in that same gentle tone.

"No, Joran!" she answered, tossing the balled-up and damp bit of paper into the trash can. "I cannot reconcile how bad things keep happening to good people! I refuse to get used to it, even after all this time."

"Then, don't!" Joran said. "Don't get used to it. But, don't be so hard on yourself, either. What happened to your mom... what happened to Mrs. Blake... none of it makes sense. Not much in this world makes sense, but there is nothing we can do about it. We can't help what happens to good OR bad people. We don't get a say."

Xiomara studied him and did not respond.

"I'm sure that Edmund would understand your inability to organize his wife's funeral if you let him know the reason," Joran said.

"I'm able," Xiomara countered, running a hand through her hair.

"Don't do this to deal with what happened to your mother, Xiomara."

"That's not why I'm doing it," she said. "I'll be fine—really. I just... lost myself for a moment. But, I can finish my work. I haven't lost sight of what it is I'm meant to do."

"Calling me was not a mistake," he said again. "I'm willing to help however you need it."

"You have the tour," she reminded him. "Lights, sound checks, set arrangements..."

"I know how to multitask."

"You'd help me plan a funeral?" Xiomara asked, wrinkling her nose.

"I'd help you plan a funeral, I'd help you NOT plan a funeral, I'd help you eat the breakfast bowl you haven't even opened yet."

Xiomara giggled, and the lightness of the sound seemed to cut through the tension that hung between them. "Is that what's in the other bag?" she asked.

"No, that bag's filled with packages of cotton candy," he said with a straight face.

"Joran!" she said in surprise.

"What?" he answered with a shrug. "You call me after midnight and then don't respond when I try to find out what's going on... I needed to be prepared for anything. There's a bottle of Fireball in the bag, too."

"Breakfast bowls, pastries, cotton candy, and cinnamon whisky," Xiomara said, counting on her fingers.

"And orange juice," Joran offered helpfully, reaching out to extend her thumb.

"You, sir, are definitely prepared," Xiomara said, lowering her hand.

"On to the cotton candy, then?" he asked.

"No," she stressed. "I have to be up for work in a few hours. I'd say it's time for bed." Joran looked at Xiomara as a slow smile spread across his face. "Oh, my God!" she shrieked, leaving the kitchen to return to the scattering of empty bowls and packaging on the floor between the sofa and ottoman.

"I can clean that up!" he said from behind her. "You go ahead and crash."

"Joran..." she began, turning around to face him.

"No strings!" he stressed, hands up. "The door has a lock on it that'll engage when it's closed, right?"

"Yes."

"Then I'll clean up and let myself out afterward," he assured her.

"I'm sure we can do it much faster if we both worked on it," Xiomara said.

Joran considered her. "Do you allow no one to help you or do things for you?" he asked.

"It's just dishes. We're not trying to coordinate a peace treaty between warring nations," she told him.

"Exactly. It's just dishes. Go to bed, Xiomara Grant."

Xiomara sighed and shrugged.

"Leave the cotton candy," she said as she began walking toward her bedroom. "You can take that Fireball with you, though."

"What could you possibly have against Fireball?"

"Good night!" she returned. "Thanks for the food... and the conversation."

"Anytime—and I mean that."

Xiomara entered her bedroom with a smile. She felt fatigued from the storm of emotions that she had gone through for the last couple of hours, yet pleased that she had allowed them to process at a natural pace.

She went over to the bed to retrieve her cellphone, which had been tossed aside during her earlier panic. A quick check of the display revealed nine missed calls and fourteen text messages—all from Joran. She decided she would sift through the lot in the morning.

Returning the phone to its charger, she went over to her dresser to grab something to help pull back and secure her hair. Looking up at the mirror atop the dresser, she studied her reflection. Despite the lateness of the hour, her hazel eyes were bright and there was color in her cheeks. She watched as a wrinkle crept into her brow, and the smile faded as her eyes rounded.

"What are you doing?" she whispered to her reflection. "What the hell are you doing?"

Xiomara turned toward the still-open door. She could hear Joran moving about, humming to himself. She left the bedroom, having decided that she would again ask him to leave, but then lost her resolve as she traveled down the hallway.

She paused, wringing her hands together as she leaned against the wall. She frowned again and dropped her arms to her sides, her body stiff as her hands formed into fists before she padded along the hallway toward the living room.

"Hey!" Joran said with a laugh, having stepped out into the hallway from the kitchen. Startled, Xiomara took a step back, the rest of her tenacity melting away at the sight of his serene smile. "I thought you were heading to bed."

"Yes, yes... I am."

"What's wrong?"

She stared at him for a moment and then shook her head. "Nothing. I forgot something."

"Yeah?" Joran asked, wiping his wet hands on his shirt.

"The door," Xiomara decided at last. "I didn't show you how to make sure that it locks behind you. There's a button on the panel beneath the latch. Push that until it clicks, and the door will lock when you leave."

"Easy enough," Joran said. "Can I get you anything before you head back to bed? Tea? Maybe more juice?"

Despite her very recent reservations, Xiomara could not help chuckling.

"Thank you," she said. "I appreciate it, but I'm fine. Good night, Joran."

"Sleep well, Xiomara," he returned before continuing along the hallway toward the living room.

Chapter Twenty-Three

Xiomara entered the church, pausing for a moment to glance at the guest book sitting to the right of the doors leading to the sanctuary. Though the morning started with the promise of sunny skies, the horizon had shifted beneath menacing dark clouds that made it appear to be much later in the day than it was. Even the heavens seemed to grieve the unfair loss of Lavinia Blake and intended to make the displeasure known.

Slipping into the very last pew on the left, Xiomara removed the black wool peacoat, draping it across her lap. She placed her purse nearby and smoothed the bodice of a black embroidered lace sheath dress. She had pulled her long hair back, and the diamond-accented Akoya pearl earrings and matching necklace glowed under gentle lighting.

She removed dark glasses, unable to resist a gentle smile upon seeing Joran settled to the right of the altar, playing the cello alongside fellow musicians on the piano and violin as the other guests settled into the pews.

Joran was immaculate in a black suit, black shirt, and silver tie that almost matched the casket that held Lavinia Blake at the altar. His hair was in a neat ponytail, save for one spiral, defiant in its resistance to confinement. Though his expression was initially somber, he looked up as he was playing, and his green eyes sought and somehow found Xiomara in the back pew. Though he did not smile back, Xiomara could still see that his posture had eased, and she was glad of it.

During the funeral, Xiomara slid the dark glasses back onto her face. She was having trouble reconciling how an event could be both uplifting and heart-wrenching. However, leaving mid-service was not something she would allow herself to do.

She saw Mr. Blake in the front row, flanked on either side by people unknown to her. She saw Judy, Loraine, and Caroline among the rows of others from EJB Advertising. She even glimpsed Ruby, dressed in a tailored black pantsuit and wearing a delicate fascinator. There were so many in attendance, but everyone that Xiomara invited or expected seemed to be there—except for one person.

When the ceremony ended with a closing prayer and blessing, most of the attendees dispersed—some lingering to wait their turn to speak with Mr. Blake, and others paying their respects to Mrs. Blake by approaching the casket and bowing their heads before departing.

Xiomara watched as Ruby left the pew she was sitting in and walked along the center aisle toward the exit. As she got to the last row, she looked over, saw Xiomara, and gave a nod of recognition and a slight smile. Xiomara returned the nod and lifted a hand in greeting, watching as Ruby continued through the doors.

She turned back in time to see that Joran was making his way down the aisle toward her, stopping along the way to speak with those who were, despite the occasion, star-struck. Xiomara got to her feet and removed the dark glasses, smiling up at him as he approached.

"Hey," he said, his brow furrowed as he looked her over. "How are you? Are you okay?"

Xiomara blinked in surprise. "Me? Mr. Blake is saying goodbye to his wife today, and you're asking how I'm doing?"

"You know what I mean," Joran said. "You don't have to keep that wall up, you know."

Xiomara sobered at that. "I'm not," she said. "I mean, I'm okay... this is just... a lot."

"Have you heard from Gabriel?" Joran asked after nodding. "I expected him to be here."

"I think many people did," Xiomara answered. "But, he didn't answer any of my texts, and my one call was sent directly to voicemail."

"What is he thinking?" Joran demanded. "Let's forget that we're talking about how it looks to skip the funeral of a colleague's wife. There's also an actual human component to this, and a clear lack of any compassion on Gabriel's part."

"I'm sure he has a reason," Xiomara said.

"I'm sure he has an excuse," Joran countered before sighing. His face relaxed a bit as his green eyes settled upon Xiomara. "You're not coming to the burial, right?"

"I don't think so, Joran," Xiomara sighed. "I... I wanted to be here to pay my respects, but I don't know that I can do much more than that. It was hard enough. I... couldn't stop thinking."

Joran nodded. "I know," he said. "I remember, and I understand."

Xiomara tilted her head. "You're so understanding of me and not of Gabriel?" she queried.

"Considering the difference in the circumstances, of course. Besides, I'd say you've done enough in planning all of this."

"Almost all of it," she smiled.

"True enough," he said, smirking. "But, I was honored when Mr. Blake called to ask if we'd play here today." Xiomara nodded. "He also told me he sensed you were reluctant to ask, so he wanted to spare you that and did it himself."

"Joran, it's not that I didn't want to ask..."

"...but, you thought I had enough going on already," Joran finished. "I know, Xiomara. You don't have to explain, and I appreciate it."

"He probably thought I'd have some sway over your decision," she admitted with a chuckle.

"You do," Joran said, fixing her with a look, "and you should know that by now."

Xiomara clutched her small black bag, unsure of how to respond. She was saved when they were joined by one of the other musicians, the young man who played the piano.

"Sorry to interrupt," he said with a gentle smile before nudging Joran. "Michael's pulling the van around. It's really started to pour out there. Want me to take your baby?"

"Yeah, thanks Devin," Joran told him. "Xiomara, this is Devin. Devin, Xiomara."

Devin's smile widened; straight, white teeth encased in a trimmed black goatee.

"It's nice to finally meet you, Xiomara," he said. "Very nice, indeed."

"Nice to meet you, too, Devin," Xiomara said, glancing at Joran, who appeared to be studying one of the stained-glass windows behind her.

"We'll be outside," Devin remarked to Joran before departing. When at last Joran looked back at Xiomara, it was with an amused expression.

"I'm sure I'll hear about that later," he said.

"And not just from him," Xiomara returned.

"Did you drive?"

Xiomara shook her head. "Train," she answered.

"We can take you home," Joran offered with a frown.

"No need," she said with another shake of her head. "The station isn't far, and I'm rather fond of rain."

"What's happening outside right now isn't rain," Joran told her. "There might be actual cats and dogs falling from the sky."

"You'd better get going," Xiomara said, laughing. "Traffic is bound to be a nightmare, and you don't want to be late. Besides, I live in the opposite direction of where you're going."

Joran considered it. "If you're sure?" he asked.

"I am," she said.

"Take a taxi or something, though," he urged. "Don't walk in this. I'm sure that Mr. Blake would agree."

"He would," she admitted, "and I will."

"Want me to call you later?"

"Okay."

Joran grinned before heading through the doors leading out of the sanctuary and toward the front entrance of the church. Xiomara turned back toward the altar, noting that only she and those working at the service remained. She watched as most of the attendants hastened to remove the arrangements of flowers, carrying them from the room to be transported to the service yet to come, as a duo closed and secured the head panel of the silver casket housing the body of Lavinia Blake.

Xiomara shook her head as a shuddering sigh escaped her lips. She had met Mrs. Blake once, but was sure to be haunted by her musical laugh and open warmth for the rest of her days. It was unfair. Her brow furrowed, and she blinked as moisture collected in her eyes and blurred the room. Reaching into her purse, she was dismayed to find that she had not even thought to pack any Kleenex.

"Damn!" she whispered, dabbing at her eyes with her fingertips, when a blue-embroidered white handkerchief came into view from her left. She looked up in surprise into the kind eyes of Edmund Blake.

"I was hoping you'd still be here, Xiomara," he began gently. "I wanted to talk with you."

"Mr. Blake," she said, feeling foolish, though she accepted the handkerchief. "I didn't know you were still here." She found herself unable to look at him and used the gesture of wiping her eyes as the perfect excuse not to do so.

"I've just seen Joran," he said, "and he mentioned you were still inside, so I wanted to come back and talk with you."

Xiomara shook her head. "You didn't have to," she said.

"I did," he insisted. "Sit with me for a moment."

They sat next to one another in the pew. Xiomara busied herself by folding the handkerchief, though she could feel Blake's eyes studying her.

"Gabriel is outside," he said in a clipped tone, to which Xiomara responded by looking up in surprise. "He didn't attend the services, but as I was speaking with some attendees, they brought it to my attention that he was here... standing beneath a tree across the street."

Xiomara gaped at him and then shook her head as her mind struggled to process the information.

"Mr. Blake, Joran asked if I'd heard from Gabriel," she explained. "Neither of us had. I certainly didn't know he'd be lingering outside."

"Gabriel is not your responsibility," Blake asserted. "That's something I need for you to understand—particularly since we signed the merger and I won't be around anymore." Blake reached into his suit jacket, extracting a sealed envelope and holding it out to her. "I wasn't sure that you'd be here, but I'm glad that you are. It was my preference to give this to you personally rather than have it delivered by courier."

"Sir?" Xiomara said in confusion as she took the envelope from him.

"You and I have talked before about Gabriel, and I've already voiced concerns I don't feel bear repeating."

"Yes?"

"There's a letter in the envelope as well, but you can disregard it, since I'm talking with you now," Blake continued. "I mentioned before that you and I would talk once I settled everything, though neither of us counted on things going quite this way. I still mean, however, to honor my original intent.

"My wife spoke of you on a day where she seemed back to her normal, brilliant self, and I was sure that she'd pull through just fine. I've told you about how she had concerns about Gabriel and his behavior toward you, and she was adamant that something be done on your behalf.

"That envelope contains a cashier's check for the equivalent of five times your salary, Xiomara. It's for you to do with as you'd like. You have been invaluable to me, to my company, and if I paid what you are worth, I'd be bankrupt. I hope that you'll not only accept this check and remember us fondly, but that you'll take it, use it, and leave Matheson Media."

Xiomara let the envelope fall from her grasp and into her lap as if burned by its touch. Blake snatched it up and pressed it back into her hand.

"Mr. Blake," she began.

"I don't think for one minute that Gabriel came here to pay respects to Lavinia or to me," he revealed, his words brisk, "and he's too cocky to even consider that doing so would improve his standing among our peers— particularly since his reputation has taken something of a beating as of late. He's here for one reason, Xiomara, and that reason is you."

"Mr. Blake," she said again.

"You think I don't know that he's going to dismantle everything I've worked thirty years for?" he said. "And, when he's done, the last ones left standing will be Gabriel, his chosen few... and you, Xiomara. He already has his sights on the next target, and it will all begin again. If Lavinia hadn't become so ill, I would have continued to fight or delay this merger with everything I have. The presentation that you put together with the others could have sealed it. But... she's gone, and I'm tired."

"Mr. Blake!" Xiomara insisted. "I've already told you I see Gabriel for who he is. There's nothing going on."

"No, Xiomara," he said, placing one large hand over both of hers. "I don't think that anything is going on at all, not on your part. That is not what I am saying. I don't want you to feel that staying at Matheson Media is the only option available to you. I also know that it might take some time for you to find something else, and you should want for nothing in the meantime.

"When you walk out of here and see Gabriel, and I am certain that you will, know that you have a way out and that you don't have to settle for anything he offers you. You can now afford—truly afford—to walk away and not look back, and you don't owe him anything.

"He's out there ruining his coif, you know." Blake's eyes twinkled with mischief. "I understand why you didn't take Joran up on his offer of a ride, but the look on Gabriel's face if you had would have warmed these weary old bones." Xiomara gaped again. "Of course, you could always ride with me, but... Joran mentioned you weren't planning on attending the burial."

"I'm sorry, Mr. Blake," Xiomara said, staring down at the corner of the envelope that peeked from beneath the large hand that still held hers. "I'm just not very good at... what comes next."

"No need," Blake said, removing his hand and patting Xiomara's shoulder with a tenderness he never exercised with Gabriel. "You arranged all of this when I couldn't, and I can never thank you enough." His eyes ventured toward the altar where the casket was being prepared for transport. He smiled, pressing a palm against his heart before turning back to Xiomara. "You gave my Lavinia a beautiful home-going." He tapped the envelope. "You'll consider this?"

Xiomara nodded and then looked up at him. "You don't have to worry, Mr. Blake," she said with an indelicate sniffle. "I won't transition to Matheson Media." She picked up the envelope and held it out to him. "In fact, I'm returning this to you. Even before your offer, I knew that staying is not a viable option."

"All the more reason for you to keep it," Blake said, shaking his head. She watched as his body seemed to relax, and he sighed. "I can't express how glad I am to know this, and now I feel settled enough to go." He got to his feet, but then looked down at her as she sat in the pew. "Never hesitate to reach me for any reason. Take time for yourself, Xiomara. Look after yourself. Let Joran help you. He's a wonderful young man."

"He is," Xiomara whispered.

"I think that, had he known that Gabriel was here, he never would have left your side."

"I think you're right," she answered. "Please don't mention it to him, Mr. Blake. He'd worry for nothing."

"All right then, Xiomara," Blake conceded. "And, you'll handle everything with Gabriel now?"

At this, Xiomara could not resist a smile. "Doing so is at the top of my list, Mr. Blake."

He returned the smile, and Xiomara watched as Edmund Blake approached the double doors, pulled his shoulders back, and went outside.

Once Blake departed, Xiomara took a deep breath and reached into her purse for a small black and silver compact. She examined her reflection in the mirror, reaching up to smooth back the neat chignon, even though nothing was out of place. Returning the compact to her purse, she folded the envelope Blake had given her and placed that inside as well, along with the handkerchief. Bundling within the warmth of her coat, Xiomara slipped the strap of the purse onto one shoulder, leaving the pew and the church.

He was still there when she got outside: small, soaked, and sullen. As Xiomara crossed the street and approached Gabriel, she noticed his eyes were red. Whether because of crying or from copious amounts of hair product washed into them, she was unsure.

The tree under which Gabriel stood did nothing to shield him from the torrent. His dark blue jacket looked to be soaked through, as were the light gray shirt and black pants he wore with it. His expensive-looking leather shoes had also sunk a bit into the wet earth.

"Bit dramatic, don't you think?" Xiomara asked. "You could have come in."

"No," Gabriel said, the word leaving his mouth in a single puff. "I couldn't."

"You didn't think it was appropriate to pay your respects to the wife of the man whose company you've just absorbed?"

"I couldn't come in, Xiomara," Gabriel said again.

"So, what are you here for, then? I didn't think voyeurism was your style. Everyone else came inside, even Blake's longtime competitors, and yet you're standing out here like a creeper."

Gabriel paused and looked down. A large raindrop nestled within the thick lashes of his right eye entranced Xiomara before it dropped and disappeared like those before it into the lapel of his jacket. She then sighed, her own exhalation chasing after Gabriel's before dissipating, and turned to leave.

"Did you drive?" he asked from behind her.

"Train," Xiomara replied without facing him.

"Come with me then."

She turned around at that. "Where?" she asked with narrowed eyes.

"I live a few blocks from here," he said.

"And?"

"I want to talk to you!" Gabriel said, arms extended at his sides as he shrugged.

"What do you think I was trying to do just now?" Xiomara returned.

"Not out here," he said. "My apartment is warm and dry."

"So's the office. We can talk there—tomorrow." She turned away again, moving a couple of steps along the sidewalk.

"Xiomara, please!" Gabriel's lithe, wet figure was suddenly blocking her path. Xiomara realized she had underestimated how far his footwear had descended into the mud for his extraction to have been so swift. "Don't."

"Don't what?" she said through clenched teeth. "Don't freeze out here in the rain talking in circles with you? Shouldn't you be offering me an Uber right about now? That's your usual M.O."

Gabriel glared at her before the fight seemed to go out of him and his shoulders slumped. He shook his head, ran a water-wrinkled hand through his shock of hair, and shrugged again.

"I don't know what you want from me," he whispered.

Xiomara stepped closer to him. "I'm not the one stalking a funeral. You were out here waiting for me, so how about you tell me what you want?"

Gabriel nodded. "My apartment?" he asked again.

She studied him. "Just a few blocks?" she asked. Gabriel nodded again. "Fine. Lead the way."

Chapter Twenty-Four

Several minutes later, Xiomara felt as though he had transported her in time as Gabriel led her into an older apartment building. He had been correct in that he lived a short distance away, but the difference between the neighborhood housing the church and the one in which Gabriel lived was startling. The area seemed untouched by the rezoning that had altered the rest of the city. She was drawn to its quaint charm, with its cobblestoned side streets and amber-tinged streetlights that warmed the block despite the rain.

"I've never been to this side of town," she commented as they moved through the lobby, past the large group of wall-mounted mailboxes, across a gleaming floor covered in alternating squares of gray and black, and along a short hallway with a single door on each side. Turning to the door on the right, Gabriel inserted his key into the lock and stepped inside.

"We should hang your coat up," he said as she entered, surveying the room with a cautious gaze.

He yanked off his own soaking outerwear and hooked it onto a nearby coat rack. He then turned to her, taking her purse before helping to remove her coat and placing the latter on the prong across from his on the coat rack. Returning the purse to Xiomara, Gabriel ran both hands through his hair and then glanced around the room.

"Please make yourself comfortable," he offered. "I won't be long."

Gabriel turned the corner to the left of the apartment's entrance as Xiomara closed the door behind her and lingered nearby. Even the inside of the apartment appeared untouched by the trappings of the modern world, down to an antiquated and somewhat large grandfather clock against a far wall on the right. It looked to be well over seven feet tall, and she could not help wondering how Gabriel wound it when needed.

The rest of the room was minimalistic, decorated in burgundy and brass, from the burgundy brocade drapes at each window to the brass sconces dotting some walls. The plush leather sofa and brass-edged, glass-topped coffee table resembled those present at Matheson Media, and Xiomara surmised that the company's interior designer had done some work in Gabriel's apartment as well.

He returned and was watching without comment as she drank in the space. She turned to look at him, noting that he had changed into dry clothes and had toweled his hair into multi-directional ebon shards.

"The bathroom's this way," he offered. "I've left you some dry towels. If your clothes are too wet, there are hangers inside the bathroom closet and something clean to change into on top of the vanity."

"Thank you," Xiomara said. Gabriel nodded and crossed the room before pausing and turning back to her.

"Something to drink to warm you up?"

"Tea, if you have it," she answered.

"I do," he nodded again. "Black, green, or white?"

Xiomara could not help chuckling. "Black, thank you."

"With a bit of brandy?" Gabriel asked. "I have some of that, too."

"No brandy, thank you."

There were three doors along the hallway when Xiomara rounded the corner: one on either side, and another at the far end. She had little trouble figuring out which was the bathroom, since it was behind the sole door that had been left open.

The bathroom was nearly the size of a standard bedroom, and she wondered if it was the most modern room in the entire apartment because of the way it had been appointed. The tiles along the walls were a shade of bone, accented by a backsplash of ivory and tan checkered tiles above the dual-sink vanity. Xiomara could feel the warmth of the floor through the soft soles of her shoes, and she guessed that a heating mechanism lay beneath the sand-shaded tiles.

She eyed both the large soaking tub and the separate glass-encased shower with unconcealed longing but turned to the mirror above the vanity to study her reflection. Rainwater dripped from the bun in her hair, and she reached up to first loosen and then remove the pins holding it together.

With a sigh, Xiomara tossed the collected hairpins into her purse, reaching to her left for one towel among the short stack that Gabriel had provided. It was then that she inspected the stack and realized that the top of the stack held a pair of long-sleeved silk pajamas in a shade resembling port wine.

Xiomara could not resist touching the rich fabric, though only long enough to rub her palms along the lapel of the shirt before moving the set to one side in favor of one of the fluffy cream-colored towels. Drying her hair as best she could, she used her fingertips to manipulate it into a style that extended past her shoulders in a tangle of waves. She folded the towel, draping it along the countertop before returning to the living room.

Gabriel hopped to his feet when she entered, his recovery time not fast enough for the disappointment on his face to be missed.

"Thank you," Xiomara said in response to the look. "Turns out that the dress survived the deluge, and I didn't need to change."

Gabriel did not have the chance to respond as a shrill whistle came from the kitchen.

"That's the kettle," he explained in a rushed mumble, leaving Xiomara alone to ponder his behavior. She moved further into the room and took a seat on the sofa, placing the purse beside her before interlacing her fingers atop her lap.

"Need any help?" she offered.

"No, I'll be out in a moment," Gabriel responded. "But, it looks like I'm out of sugar. Is honey okay?"

"Honey is fine, thank you."

He returned after another minute, holding two large and steaming red mugs with the gold Matheson Media logo splashed across them. He placed one mug on the coffee table in front of Xiomara before placing his own and taking a seat.

"It's scalding," he explained. "You should let it cool a bit."

"Thank you," she said, turning toward him. "Maybe in the meantime you can explain what's going on." He reddened. "That is why I'm here, isn't it? Because if not, I can go home."

"Your tea..." Gabriel began.

"...is too hot," Xiomara finished with a smile. "Now, spill some tea of your own."

Gabriel sighed and then shook his head.

117

"I came to the funeral to see you," he admitted. "That's the one reason I was there, so I waited for you to come out."

"You didn't think for a second about how that might look to everyone?" Xiomara challenged, wide-eyed.

"Come on, Xiomara," Gabriel said, getting up again and padding around the room in bare feet. "In the end, no one will care whether I showed up. Everyone is just interested in what's coming. All eyes are on what Matheson Media will do next. This merger was huge!"

"This merger was unfair," she countered. "You could have delayed the process to allow Mr. Blake to focus on his wife's care. You should have."

"Why?" Gabriel shrugged. "There was no stopping it, so what would slowing it down have accomplished? Things were dragging on too long as it was. This was a money deal—I had too much tied up in it to let it fester." Xiomara snorted. "Oh, you don't believe me? I'm not rich, Xiomara, not yet. But, I'm smart and I know how to place my bets well."

"What do you mean?" Xiomara asked.

"This building," Gabriel said. "I own it, though none of the tenants or even the staff are aware. I run it through a property management company so, for all they know, I am another idiot paying the rent. I also own the building that houses La Bonne Vie."

"Diana's restaurant?"

Gabriel nodded again. "I leveraged them both along with every cent I have in savings to make sure that this merger was a success... and it was."

"Is that why Diana is always talking to you about how things are going and what she needs in order to improve?"

"She owes me," Gabriel said with a shrug, returning to the sofa. "She wouldn't have that place if not for me. Her husband could have helped her at any point, but he wanted her to stick to catering and being a personal chef."

"Nothing wrong with either of those," Xiomara said, picking up her mug.

"Diana wants to be bigger than that," Gabriel said, staring down at the coffee table, but leaving his mug where it was.

"Then why didn't you help her more?" Xiomara demanded. "Did the thought ever occur to you that, as someone working in advertising, you might have the unique ability to lift a finger for La Bonne Vie? Even if you didn't have a personal and financial stake in it—what about helping a friend?"

"Diana's destined for a specific purpose," Gabriel remarked, getting up again, "and, I'll make sure she meets it."

"Ah, I see now..."

Gabriel turned to look at her. "You see what?"

"You don't intend to help her, not in any way that's visible to others," Xiomara commented. "This goes right back to the conversation we had when last we were all together." She picked up the mug again and blew into it. "I'm not stupid, and I know it has something to do with why you refused to set foot in that church. Just admit it."

Gabriel paused, his bright blue eyes darting about for a moment before focusing on Xiomara.

"There's nothing to admit," he began. "She wants me to help her with that cooking show, and I've agreed."

"Yes, I know that much," Xiomara said, "and I know the methods she expects you to use in that regard. But, you seemed to leap from dabblers to devotees in a brief time, unless I'm missing something." Gabriel paused again for a moment, and then shrugged.

"You're not missing anything, Xiomara," he commented.

"That's all you have to say?" she scoffed. "That I'm not missing anything?"

"I didn't know what you would think if you knew everything!" he said. "I was hoping to... ease into things, but Diana... isn't so patient. Her ambition forced my hand, and now everything's arranged for next weekend."

"So soon?" Xiomara mused. "And here I thought you were so methodical that nothing could touch you."

"Must you always do that?" Gabriel said, running both hands through his hair before wringing them together. Xiomara couldn't help focusing on the slenderness of his fingers. "I'm trying to explain—as you asked!"

"You're talking in circles," she corrected, putting the mug down again, "somehow saying a lot and nothing at all. Diana has gone from being unsure that you'd help her win that competition, to certain that you will—why?"

"Come with me," he said after a pause, turning to leave the room. Upon realizing that he was not being followed, he turned back to appraise his guest. "What?"

"Come with you where?" Xiomara asked.

"To the room that I've allowed no one to see—not even Diana," he answered. "But, it will answer your questions in a way that... I apparently can't quite manage directly, it seems."

She got to her feet and followed him, a few paces behind, as they went along the hallway of Gabriel's tidy apartment, passing the bathroom that she had exited minutes before. Stopping at the door on the right, Gabriel opened it and pushed it wide, stepping to the side so that Xiomara could enter while he lingered in the hall. She took a tentative step forward, paused in the doorway, and then went inside.

He had filled the wall along the right side of the room from corner to corner with bookshelves extending from the floor to about six feet up. The shelves appeared to be a recent purchase because of their condition and design, but several of the books looked quite old, with leather spines crackled from repeated openings and the titles rubbed into obscurity. There were other books, though, concealed beneath a protective covering of dark suede tied with a strap.

Xiomara moved through the space, missing nothing and not saying anything. The titles of most of the books seemed ambiguous enough, but the accompanying diagrams, drawings, and depictions on two of the other walls made the remaining pieces of the Gabriel-Diana puzzle fall into place.

She stopped below a painted depiction of a nude woman kneeling before a large-breasted, goat-headed figure with a brief loincloth covering its lower extremities and concealing a tented erection. The woman was reaching for a silver platter held by the goat figure, and there was a black and silver snake coiled around the woman's left wrist. Atop the platter lay a bloodied human heart, and behind the duo was an ebon-swathed altar, upon which was draped the body of a male with a cavernous wound at the center of his chest.

Xiomara's eyes shifted to the glass cabinet near one side of the window that housed talismans, trinkets, and a pair of hook-handled silver stiletto daggers. She then glanced back toward the painting, focusing on the altar beside the body. The bloodied dagger depicted there was of the same hook-handled design.

There was no other furniture in the room; nothing to mask the floor, which was painted in a highly glossed blackness, and nothing to mask the large, inverted red pentagram settled in the center of the shine.

She turned to glance at Gabriel, who was leaning against the doorway and watching her.

"This is why," he said.

Chapter Twenty-Five

"It's true that I met Diana at a gathering awhile back," Gabriel said. "I just didn't mention the kind of gathering. But it was nothing too involved, nothing like..." His bright blue gaze held the painting that Xiomara had been studying. He then looked back at her. "It was a dinner for a very select group, honoring my achievements in business and advertising.

"She had to sign a Non-Disclosure Agreement promising to keep the details to herself, but... it didn't stop her from wanting to befriend me or wanting a taste of the sort of life my faith provides."

"Your faith?" Xiomara repeated, walking across the pentagram to move through the room to have a closer look at the long rows of books. "Blood magick?"

"Please don't do that," Gabriel sighed. "Don't be dismissive."

"I'm not trying to be," she said. "But, at no time during any of the conversations at dinner did you seem this serious. Not, 'come into my parlor' serious." She flicked a finger toward the painting. "Definitely not, 'Hey, check out my illustration of Baphomet,' serious."

He blinked at that, his brow furrowing. As he appeared ready to ask a question, Xiomara turned away from him to study the items inside the glass-enclosed cabinet.

"This has been part of my life for almost fifteen years," he said, continuing. "I've worked at it, I'm devoted to it, and it's served me well. I am very serious. But, I... wanted to discuss it with you in my own way."

"Fair enough, I suppose," Xiomara said with a slight nod, turning to him once more.

Gabriel indicated the bookshelves with a nod of his head. "As far as collections go, this one is admittedly rather light," he continued, keeping his voice steady though he was frowning. "I'm still building it, you see. Some of the older, better books are awfully expensive... and others are few so they're still being kept by learned families."

"Learned?" Xiomara asked, looking over the books again.

Now fully aware, she couldn't help shuddering at some of the titles and, upon closer inspection, had a horrifying feeling that some of the older books weren't covered in leather at all—but something else. She did not want to think of the horrors hidden by the suede covering the other books.

"My family is fairly new to this," he admitted. "Our heritage goes as far back as my great grandfather on my mother's side."

"Magick has no color," Xiomara mused. "There is no white or black; it's all in the heart of the user."

"What?"

She turned to him again. "I may have heard that once... somewhere a long time ago, it seems." She crossed to the window and looked at the cabinet, which rested on facsimiles of clawed feet. "The books, the collections of trinkets, this locked cabinet, and that... on the floor... make me wonder what color your heart is."

"Xiomara," Gabriel said, his arms out at his sides and his eyes wide, "I have no idea what you're talking about."

Xiomara sighed, closed her eyes for a moment, and then shook her head as she walked back to the wall that contained the bookshelves.

"I suppose that you're afraid of me," Gabriel commented. "Now that you know the truth."

Xiomara turned away from the collection of tomes to look at him. He had advanced farther into the room and was now a few feet away from her.

"Should I be?" she asked.

"Again," he said. "You definitely have a fondness for answering questions with questions—particularly at the most inconvenient moments."

Xiomara nodded, conceding the point. "Try again," she offered.

"What?"

"Ask me again, Gabriel," she said.

"Are you afraid of me?" he asked in a whisper.

"No," she answered.

"How could you not be?" he said. "After what I've just told you... and shown you? With everything you see here in this room?" Xiomara studied him for a moment, and then slowly raised her right hand. "What are you doing?" he asked, puzzled.

"Seeking permission to ask a question," she responded, her eyes twinkling.

"This is funny to you? Really?"

Xiomara sighed and lowered her hand. "Of course not. And, if you needed a way to describe how I'm feeling right now, afraid is not it."

"Then what is?"

"Concerned," Xiomara stated.

"About what?"

"Not what."

"Xiomara..."

"I'm concerned for you, Gabriel," she said. "What color is your heart?"

"What?" he asked, brow wrinkled.

"What could you possibly hope to gain from this?"

"Are you kidding?" he scoffed. "I've already gained so much! You know my accomplishments, the awards... you know what I'm capable of."

"I know you aren't happy," Xiomara remarked.

Gabriel's eyes steeled. "You know nothing like that!" he snapped. "How could you? You've never even asked me anything about my life!"

"I'm with you five days a week," Xiomara countered. "I know."

"I think I like you better when you ask questions," he shot back, "rather than making assumptions about something you can't possibly know anything about."

"Are you happy?" Xiomara returned.

Gabriel walked over to the window and stared out. Xiomara wondered how much he could see through the sheets of rain and the low-hanging fog.

"I'm twenty-nine years old, and people are begging to work with me," he finally responded, his breath adding more fog to the view. "Men I used to intern alongside are outbidding one another to be part of one of my projects." He turned toward her. "You have no idea how that makes me feel, and it gives me what I've always wanted and wouldn't be able to get otherwise."

"Who says you couldn't get it, Gabriel?" Xiomara said. "You are amazingly talented, with a brilliant mind for advertising and graphic design.

You own that. Those skills belong to you, and they are what will help you get ahead!"

"That's not enough for me! I don't want to just get ahead. I want to be known! I plan to put a mark on this world that will never be forgotten."

"By using this?" she asked, sweeping the room with one gesture, recalling the night at dinner when Diana made a similar declaration about her own goals.

"Yes, this! Advertising and graphic design aren't the only skills that belong to me, and definitely aren't all that I'll use to help me get to the place I deserve." He sighed. "Look at you, Xiomara. You are also amazingly talented. Blake's presentations improved by leaps once you came aboard. I saw your work. I saw what you did for him.

"You... picked out these little nuances—things that others would overlook—and you enhanced them with splashes of brilliance. Because I am so aware of you, I'm able to recognize everything you touch. If Blake had you by his side before I set my sights on his company, it probably would have been impossible to take over.

"And, Ruby showed me the presentation that you put together. Had Blake's investors gotten their hands on that, they might have chosen to fully back him instead of encouraging the merger with me. That's how good you are."

"Gabriel..."

"And you're beautiful," he continued, as his eyes softened. "You're so lovely, Xiomara. But, I'm sure you know that. I'll bet that you always have been and have always been at the center of attention. Things have probably come easily to you your entire life. But, me..." He scoffed. "I was short and bony. The biggest thing about me was my hair. My mother thought it was a good idea for me to master the flute because I had what she called 'delicate hands' so I'd excel at it... and it made me a joke.

"I got my ass kicked by bigger kids on an almost daily basis from the time I was ten years old. If it wasn't because I was so small, it was because I had raggedy clothes. If it wasn't the clothes, it was because I was in Band. If not Band, then it was because my mother was a drunk. If not all that... it was because I got a crush on a pretty girl, and she thought it was funny to get her brother or cousin to come beat me up for even thinking about trying to approach her."

He nodded toward the bookshelves. "Some of those are heirlooms. Can you believe that? My mother's family is filled with powerful and successful people. All of them, one way or another, amounted to something. Well, all except my mother. She wanted nothing to do with it. My mother rebelled against her faith... drank to wash the sweet taste of it away... and raised me without ever telling me what I should have been. She ran from it and from them... had me living in some dump while my life was being ruined continually.

"She'd wipe the blood off me, tell me how everything was going to be okay, and it was a rough patch that wouldn't last much longer... Do you know how much better things could have been for me then had I known? My life... my entire existence... would have been so much different. Nobody would have messed with me, but she kept me ignorant!

"Everything changed the summer that my aunt, Sasha, came to visit." He looked at Xiomara again. "I know Joran told you about my mom's older sister."

"He shared that an aunt came to claim you one summer," Xiomara remarked.

"That she did," Gabriel said with a sardonic smile. "So much changed for me at that point, and I gladly said goodbye to the life my mother tried to pigeonhole me into. I freed myself of her, of her inhibitions, her ridiculous rules... and she tucked tail and ran out of town, even after I told her she could still stay with me and live the life she was born for. She ran. She might still be running if she hasn't drunk herself to death by now."

He spread his arms. "But I didn't run," he continued. "I've embraced it, and it's empowered me. I've taken over one of the biggest agencies in town—and I'm nowhere near done. I have meetings lined up next week with executives from other companies, because they have all seen how I handled Blake, and they're hoping to stave off the inevitable. But, it doesn't matter... because they're all eventually going to either become part of the Matheson name or end up crushed beneath it."

He moved closer to Xiomara, and for the first time since they met, she saw uncertainty in his bright blue gaze. He reached for a lock of her hair, which was still damp, and snaked his long fingers through it.

"Come with me," he pleaded in a whisper.

"Excuse me?" Xiomara said.

"Not everything has to be so clinical," Gabriel told her. Xiomara stared at him without responding. "Don't get me wrong. I already have a few unsigned deals with the handful of people at the company that are worth a damn—and I fully intend to poach them before I shut the whole thing down—but, I need you, too."

"Mr. Blake already told me about your request," she revealed. "I know that I wouldn't remain under his company but would instead become a part of yours."

He blinked at her, his hand dropping to his side. "He told you that?"

"Yes," Xiomara answered.

"When?"

"That doesn't matter."

"What else did he say?" he demanded.

"That doesn't matter, either," Xiomara said. "But, I think I'm beginning to see things clearly now."

"What does that mean?" Gabriel asked, taking a step back.

"You tried to placate him," she said. "Edmund Blake cares about his employees, and I witnessed the fact that you removed various items he requested from each meeting's itinerary—as well as from the contracts—knowing that the welfare of those in his employ was an important item that he wanted addressed."

"And?"

"And, you were trying to wear him down and throw obstacles in his way, but it didn't work at first—did it? So, you had to up the stakes."

"Xiomara..." Gabriel said, shaking his head.

"When we had dinner with the Blakes that night, all you could think about was how much of an asset Mrs. Blake was to her husband. You were fixated on it, and Diana was practically sick with grief at how your perfect evening wasn't going to plan."

"Wait..." Gabriel said.

"What did she do, Gabriel?" Xiomara plowed on. "Was she so willing to show you that she was only too happy to do dirty work for you that you agreed once and for all to do whatever she asked if she found a way to rattle Mr. Blake's resolve?" Xiomara blinked away angry tears.

"Then Mrs. Blake became so ill, and no one could figure out why. It made no sense that a woman so vibrant at her age suddenly lacked the ability to even get out of bed in the morning.

"Mr. Blake was sick himself watching her fade... and he caved just like you wanted him to and allowed himself to be defeated so that he could be by her side.

"And still... it wasn't enough for you."

"That wasn't my fault!" he shouted.

"So, you're telling me that I'm wrong?" Xiomara shouted back.

"No... but, it wasn't supposed to end up that way!" he insisted. "I had no control over what Diana did! She only told me what she'd done after Mrs. Blake had already become ill."

"Did you bother telling her to stop it?"

"How?"

"Exactly! Exactly, Gabriel! You do not know what you're doing and Diana, who probably learned from you, doesn't either. Neither of you understands that you are working from some idyllic fantasy that your aunt, Sasha, created for you, and it's all wrong!

"I told you... I told you about the force of the power that comes back once you put it out there. Diana meant to help you by making Mrs. Blake sick enough to keep her husband occupied, didn't she? And while you hid in your office for three weeks because you didn't have the guts to face me, Diana did so well that she killed Mrs. Blake and her husband practically gift-wrapped a company that took him years to build and handed it to you out of grief so that you can turn around and dismantle it!"

"If you think that's what I am," Gabriel began, "and I'm such a monster that I would purposefully kill to gain control of a company that would have been mine anyway..."

"You know I never said it was intentional," Xiomara replied. "Both you and Diana took a leap of misguided faith and took the life of someone innocent in the process. That's why Diana is so sure she'll get your help now. You owe her."

"Xiomara, what do you want from me?" Gabriel asked. "What more do you want?"

"Think about what you're doing, Gabriel!" Xiomara cautioned. "Look at what's happened and learn from it. Think about all of it: the way you handle business, the way you foster relationships, and the way you are living your life. Think about consequences, the long-lasting consequences, of all of it. This has to bother you on some level!"

"I don't need to think about any of that!" he shot back. "I'm creating my natural order, and I don't find fault in it, though you do!"

"I find fault in how easy this seems to be for you! Lavinia Blake is dead. She was an unwilling pawn in a game she was not even playing! You exchanged her life for a company you don't even care enough about to keep!"

"And if I kept it? Would that make things better for you?"

"I'm not your conscience, Gabriel. That would do nothing for me."

"Then what would?" he challenged, once again stepping closer. "You're so good at asking questions—how about you answer one!"

"What do you mean?" she said, blinking in surprise.

"I have just opened myself up to you," he reminded her. "I have brought you into the core of my world; into something that I've never shared on this level with anyone outside of my circle and told you I need you. I need you, Xiomara! You insist on addressing everything else, but that."

They stared at one another for a time, and the room was silent aside from the tap-tap-tapping of the rain against the window. Xiomara's temples throbbed as the full weight of the discovery hit her all at once. Gabriel's eyes had never seemed so bright, and she could see the tautness in his posture.

Gabriel's eyes narrowed, and his hands curled into trembling fists. Just as she prepared to respond, he pulled her into his wiry yet strong grasp with one arm around her waist and his other hand curled into her dark hair as he sealed his mouth against hers.

Chapter Twenty-Six

"Gabriel..."

"Wait..."

"Please, let me go."

"Wait, just wait a minute. Let me explain. Let me talk to you..."

"We've been talking, and you don't have to explain anything. Let me go."

Xiomara extracted herself from Gabriel's loosened grasp, leaving the room to walk along the hallway, into the living room, and back to her discarded mug of tea. She sighed, picked it up and, though it was no longer hot, sipped at it as Gabriel slowly made his way from where she had left him. Though she would not look up, she knew he was watching her.

"Granted, kissing you in a room with a pentagram painted on the floor probably isn't the most romantic setting," Gabriel said with an attempt at levity, though there was a tremor in his voice. Xiomara stared down into the cup and said nothing. "Don't do that, not now. I have dealt with your silent treatments before, but this isn't the time. I need you to talk to me. Tell me what you're thinking."

"I'm thinking that you don't need me," Xiomara said, looking up at him, and Gabriel paused.

"What did you say?" he asked. He walked over to her, sat on the coffee table, and then took the mug from her hand before looking into her eyes. "What, Xiomara?"

"I said that you don't need me," she repeated, watching as Gabriel crumpled a bit as he put the tea onto the table with a soft thud.

"That's your response?" he asked, wide-eyed. "That's all you have to say... to... to not only all that I've said, but to what just happened is that I don't need you?"

"Yes," Xiomara said after a pause.

"The one time I counted on you to ask a question, and you didn't," he said. When she did not answer, he plowed on, staring into her eyes. "You were supposed to ask me why."

Xiomara arched an eyebrow. "Why you need me?"

"Yes!"

"How could you answer that if I asked?" Xiomara commented. "I don't think you know why, because I don't think it's a need at all. None of this has anything to do with need. Your entire life has nothing to do with need, and that kiss was not at all about a need. Wants drive you. I think you want me—on a rudimentary and most likely carnal level."

"Oh, really?" Gabriel said with a frown. "So, I guess now it's my turn to ask a question."

"Why you want me?" Xiomara said with a dry chuckle. "You've been stumbling over that since the day we met in the lobby. You even hinted as much after the first day we worked together. I'm the riddle that you can't solve. I don't fawn all over you, and I pay you minimal attention unless it's business-related.

"You brought me here today and showed me your secret little room and tried to make me think you were unlocking some part of your soul. When that revelation didn't achieve the desired results, you tossed compliments at me and talked about my beauty—as if that would flatter me into submission—before you threw a kiss at me. I'm your challenge, Gabriel. I'm the acquisition that's out of your reach."

"You're not out of my reach," he insisted. "You're here, sitting right in front of me and flowing through me. I can see you with my eyes closed. I know your scent, Xiomara. Just now I've tasted you. You don't have to keep fighting me. We are alike, don't you see that? We walked this path together—it's yours and mine!"

"This is not my path, Gabriel!" Xiomara said. "I cannot and will not join you on it."

"You can't tell me you felt nothing throughout all this!" Gabriel countered. "The deal, Blake, closing in on an opportunity of a lifetime—you've already walked this path, even when you tried to undermine me with that presentation. That move alone showed that you have what it takes to be beside me!"

"No!" she countered, getting up and walking past Gabriel toward the hallway. "I was never on any path with you, not like this! Our goals were always different, which is why we clash. You have this deeply myopic view of what it is you need to do to get ahead, and I don't share that view!"

"What's wrong with the way I see things?" Gabriel demanded. "Is it really so bad to be on the winning side?"

"You are not on the winning side," Xiomara said with a sigh, turning to face him. "You're being allowed to feel that way now, but it's a façade. It will crumble around you, Gabriel. It will bury you."

"I will reach the top," Gabriel said. "This is the beginning, and you still have a chance to be there with me. You can't want to be a lackey all your life."

"If you're so sure that it's what I want... what I need... and if you are so sure that what you believe is so... life-altering and rife with rewards... why don't you use your faith, your gifts, or your... knowledge to lure me in?"

Gabriel shrugged. "Because it would be so much more amazing if you joined me voluntarily," he said. "I want you to want it. I want you to want me."

"Free will," Xiomara said.

"Yes."

Xiomara returned to the sofa, lowering herself onto it, and did not speak for a moment. Gabriel was still watching her, though, and remained silent.

"About your... gathering with Diana next weekend..." she said, breaking the silence after several moments.

"What about it?" Gabriel asked with a puzzled expression.

"Are you sure you want to go through with it? You don't have to, you know."

"We're back to this now?" Gabriel accused. "You're going to ignore what I've shared with you—again."

"You won't change my mind about being with you, Gabriel."

"And, you won't change my mind about my destiny. So, yes—I'm sure that I want to go through with it. I owe Diana. I owe myself as well. Lots of things will be different after next weekend."

"You're having it here?" Xiomara asked as she looked around.

Gabriel moved to sit once again on the edge of the coffee table. "Not exactly," he said. "Like I told you, Diana's never seen my sanctuary. I planned to have it somewhere else nearby. Why?"

Xiomara rested her elbows on her thighs, steepling her fingers beneath her nose as she looked at Gabriel. Gabriel leaned forward, and their eyes locked. Finally, Xiomara tilted her head, sighed, and lowered her hands.

"Don't go, Gabriel," she whispered. "Don't do this."

Gabriel studied her for a moment and then flashed a dimple. "Have something better to offer me for the weekend?"

"I'm being serious!" Xiomara said.

"So am I!" he returned.

Xiomara smoothed away a stray lock of hair and brushed his suggestion from her mind, moving forward with the initial topic at hand. "Are you sure that the place you have in mind is suitable?" she asked him.

She watched as he crumpled again, stung by yet another rejection. He ran both hands through his hair before he shrugged.

"It always has been," Gabriel revealed. "Why?"

"I was thinking of another venue," Xiomara offered.

"You were thinking..." His brow furrowed. "You just spent all this time trying to talk me out of this, you blatantly rejected me—now you're offering accommodations?"

"Are you certain that there's no chance that you'll change your mind?" Xiomara asked again.

"Are you certain that there's no chance that you will change yours?" he countered.

"I'd say I'm pretty clear on this," she said.

"And, like I said, so am I. I won't be like Joran." He scoffed. "I've tried to get him to listen for years, and he never would. Diana was right, you know. Something so simple could have kept Katherine by Joran's side, but he insisted on doing things his way." He shook his tousled head. "No. I want this. I'm going to get everything that's rightfully mine." He studied her. "If you won't be there, why do you care?"

"I never said that I wouldn't attend," Xiomara said, grabbing her purse, getting to her feet, and walking toward the front door. She could feel Gabriel's eyes boring into her as she reached for her coat, choosing to drape it over one arm rather than put it on. "But, I'm sure my location is better. I'll get back to you with an address."

"Why are you doing this?" Gabriel asked. "After all we've discussed—why?" Xiomara paused while opening the door to look back at him.

"Because you've made your decision," she answered, "which means I've made mine."

"Xiomara, I don't understand you," he admitted. "I don't understand what's going on."

She chuckled. "I know," she answered. "But, what you should understand is this, Gabriel. There's still time for you to make a different choice. There's always time." She moved through the door and closed it behind her with a soft click.

Chapter Twenty-Seven

"Xiomara?" Gabriel answered, surprise clear in his tone.

"Yes," she responded. "I said I'd be getting back to you, yet you don't seem to have expected it."

"With the way things ended earlier, what I expected was to find a resignation letter waiting for me at the office tomorrow," he admitted.

"Oh, ye of little faith," Xiomara answered. "First thing's first—I sent a text right before calling with the address I said I'd give you."

"Wait, Xiomara," Gabriel said before pausing. Xiomara assumed he was glancing at her message. "What is this place? Why are you doing this if you want no part in the ceremony?"

"It's a cabin outside of town," Xiomara said. "You told me yourself that you don't have a lot of money, so I don't imagine that the place you have in mind is as private as what I'm making available to you."

"How in the hell do you have access to a cabin?"

"I'm sending word in the morning to make sure that it's cleaned and aired out," she told him. "What time did you want to meet? It's a suitable distance away so you'll need to accommodate for travel time."

"Now, hold on a minute!" Gabriel insisted. "Things with you have been moving at a snail's pace for months. Now, you're speeding through and still without bothering to answer my questions!"

"Oh, I don't know, Gabriel," Xiomara said with an exaggerated sigh. "I've owned the cabin for years. And let's not forget that I can afford to live within walking distance of work, yet can pull my car out of the garage for those pesky, longer trips. Maybe it's you that needs a taste of the sort of life MY faith provides."

The silence lasted for several seconds before being broken by Gabriel's laughter. "I'll let you have that round, Xiomara," he said. "On Friday night, though, I'll expect you to see things differently."

"Before then, however, there's the matter of that resignation letter," Xiomara said.

Gabriel groaned. "Come on—I was mostly kidding about that!"

"My work for Mr. Blake and EJB Advertising is done."

"But Matheson Media..."

"...will endure," Xiomara finished. "For now it's late. We both have a long week ahead of us."

"There's still time to turn this around," Gabriel said.

"I continue to hope," she answered before disconnecting. Xiomara had not yet put the phone down when it rang again. She read the display and took a deep breath before answering.

"I didn't wake you, did I?" Joran asked.

"No," Xiomara said. "You didn't wake me."

"How are you feeling?"

Xiomara shook her head, running a hand through her hair. "Conflicted," she admitted.

"I'm sorry," he said. "I know that this has been pretty rough-going for you. I wish I wasn't so busy this week."

"You booked these shows long before you even knew who I was," Xiomara told him.

"If I had the chance to do it over again..."

"Second chances... that seems to be the theme."

"What?" Joran laughed.

"I've gone silly," Xiomara said, frowning. "I'm spouting nonsense."

"I've got shows every night this week until Friday—and on that day I have two, including a matinee," he sighed with dramatic flair. "Guess I won't have time to make it to Gabriel's little party."

"As if you had any plans to," she said. "I mean, you don't—do you?"

"No," he said. "It wasn't my thing before, and it certainly isn't now. I can't believe I ever entertained it. It just seems so... I don't know. Hearing you talk about the strength of what gets sent out and being unable to control the way it comes back struck a nerve with me. Before, Diana and Gabriel made me feel like maybe I was missing out. Now, I feel like I've been saved from something."

"I'm glad to hear that, Joran," Xiomara said. "You really shouldn't be there, anyway. Now, if I could be as successful with swaying the other two."

"Fat chance of that!" he exclaimed. "Diana would gladly trade her Benz for a broom if she thought it would get her any closer to Gabriel."

As he continued to laugh, Xiomara could not help focusing on the sound, timbre, and warmth that reflected Joran's genuine nature. It became easy to picture his face and the almost shy smile that came so easily and paralleled his calming influence.

"So, listen," he was saying, "is there any chance of you making it to any of my shows this week? I can leave word at the box office."

Xiomara pulled the phone away from her ear, pressing her free hand to her chest as her eyes filled. She took a deep, shuddering breath, held it for a moment, and then slowly exhaled as the tears fell.

"Oh, I don't know, Joran," she said into the phone, her voice not betraying her feelings. "There's still so much left for me to do with EJB." She wiped at her cheeks with the back of her hand.

"Well, my last three shows are next week," Joran said. "Think about it, okay? I'd really like for you to see me perform the full set."

"I will," Xiomara promised. "I definitely will think about it."

"Have you given any more thought to what you'll do next?" he queried. "With credentials from both Matheson Media and EJB, you could probably write your own ticket and choose from among the best companies in the city."

"I think I'll need a break for a bit," Xiomara admitted. "A lot of unexpected things happened with this assignment. I don't know that I'll be ready to jump right into something else."

"Well, I meant what I said to you last week. You really should come out with me, see me eat something more than fluffy confections or one of Diana's bovine massacres. Once the shows are done, my schedule is wide open for a bit."

"I'll keep that in mind," Xiomara said.

"I'm tucking that raincheck away to be redeemed soon," Joran promised. "For now, though, I'll let you get to bed. But, listen—I don't care how early or late it is, or how busy you think I am—if you need anything, or even just want to chat for a minute, don't hesitate. I'll take my phone onstage if I have to."

"That'll go over well with Michael and Devin," Xiomara laughed, though her eyes were still moist.

"Somehow, I don't think that either of them would be surprised."

"Good night, Joran," Xiomara said, "and, thank you."

"Good night, Xiomara Grant," he returned. "I'll see you soon."

Chapter Twenty-Eight

"So, it's true."

Xiomara turned around, holding the framed photograph she had just lifted from the wall, to find a red-faced Ruby standing in the doorway. Ruby entered, closing the door behind her.

"Mr. Matheson has been closed up in his office all day," Ruby continued, her brow furrowed. "Even so, it's all over the office that you're leaving."

"Of course, I'm leaving, Ruby," Xiomara said, walking over to her desk, upon which lay, among other things, a large plastic tote. She placed the photograph beside it. "They completed the merger, Mr. Blake is planning an extended trip to Paris, and you are free to work and prepare for the projects of your own that you've wanted for so long."

"But it's not fair!" Ruby said, stomping her foot in protest. "If you leave now, it'll ruin everything!"

"Ruby, what are you talking about?" Xiomara asked in genuine confusion.

"I need you here to back me up!" she said. "I want Judy, Loraine, and Caroline to be hired by Matheson Media! They are valuable, brilliant women who would be an asset to us, but Mr. Matheson doesn't seem at all interested in securing their futures with the company. You have to help me!"

Xiomara could do nothing but sigh. Over the last few days, as she completed her business with EJB Advertising, Gabriel had been busy. He adhered to the pared-down version of his agreement with Edmund Blake that made it into the contracts by extending offers of employment to twenty percent of the company's workforce—half of which would be for a probationary period of six months. Those who accepted would transition into the office at Matheson Media within a month. The rest, including Judy, Loraine, and Caroline, received no offer at all but the most basic severance package and a blanket employment reference.

The investors, those with a tangible financial stake in EJB Advertising, had so far been unable to refute the way things were being handled. Gabriel had the foresight to arrange a swap between those coming in from EJB's corporate office outside of town with certain employees at Matheson Media who, while important, did not need to maintain a constant physical presence. These "auxiliary employees," as Gabriel termed them, were expected to relinquish their offices to those coming in.

Xiomara, hearing the news through word of mouth as it trickled from one of the many meetings that had taken place, could not help but be surprised. Though the methods weren't very encouraging, they were still a long way from Gabriel's initial plans to liquidate EJB Advertising altogether.

"I handed in my resignation on Monday," Xiomara said. "I won't even be staying the full two weeks. Besides, contract negotiations have already ended."

"There were no negotiations!" Ruby countered. "You and I both know that he had a list of people he wanted especially. But I want to add to it, and the only way it'll work is if you back me up!"

Xiomara sighed again and then nodded. "There might be something that can be done," she revealed. "But it won't be immediate."

"What does that mean!?" Ruby demanded.

"It means that I need you to trust me," Xiomara said. "Be patient, Ruby. I know that it's asking a lot with everything that's going on, but I will make this right—okay? Please."

"Okay," Ruby said at last, seeming to deflate. Her green eyes roamed over the office. "Wow. Almost done, huh?"

"Almost," Xiomara said amiably. "I drove in today so that I can take these things home later. I can work minimally for the next couple of days—not that I have much work left to do."

"Mr. Blake is really going to Paris?"

Xiomara nodded. "He and his wife intended to go to celebrate and unwind after the merger was completed, but..."

"Yeah," Ruby sighed. "But where will you go, Xiomara?"

Xiomara paused in her effort of taking a few more photographs from the wall. She looked at Ruby and then shrugged.

"I don't know yet," she admitted. "Once I'm done here, I'll take some time off and then... maybe spin a bottle and go in the direction it leads."

"When you get settled, let me know," Ruby said. "I'd like to know how you're doing."

Xiomara smiled at her. "Stop worrying," she said. "You're going to be fine, Ruby. Of that I have no doubt."

"Thank you, Xiomara—for everything," Ruby told her before opening the door and leaving the office.

Xiomara intended to pick up where she left off with her packing when her cell phone rang. Following the sound, she found it beneath other items on the desk. Spying the words "La Bonne Vie" on the display caused her to take a deep breath before answering.

"Diana," she said, "what can I do for you?"

"You can start by sharing your secret," Diana greeted. "Swanky address, a wardrobe to kill for, and now a cabin on acreage? Are you a trust fund baby or something?"

"Is there something else that I can do for you, Diana?"

"Have you talked with Gabriel today?"

"Long enough to tell him this morning that the key to the cabin will be in his hands by tomorrow afternoon. The team I sent out should be finished cleaning it by then."

"You're giving him access a day before the ceremony?" Diana asked. "Isn't that cutting it a bit close?"

"He made no mention of needing more time than that," Xiomara said. "From what I understand, things will not get underway until shortly before midnight on Friday, which gives Gabriel plenty of time to leave here, go to his place, and get whatever he needs to bring out to the cabin."

"Finally given up on talking him out of it, have you?" Diana asked.

"I have not given up on him," Xiomara conceded, "but, the choice has to be his. You also have a choice, Diana."

"I knew it," Diana said coldly after a pause. "You don't really want me there, do you? What have you done—set up a little love nest for the two of you?"

"Diana..."

"We all know that Joran doesn't have the balls to show up, so you'll have your little lanky boy-toy well out of the way, won't you?"

"Diana," Xiomara sighed, "there might still be hope for Gabriel, but I seriously doubt that there's any left for you at this point."

"Don't you dare think to keep me away on Friday night!" Diana warned. "I already have the address."

"I suppose you'll drive over after closing at Bonne?"

"No!" Diana said in a proud tone. "Gabriel is sending a car to take me to the cabin!"

Xiomara paused. "You're riding in with Gabriel?" she asked.

"Well, no," Diana said. "He's sending the car and I'm to ride alone. But, he obviously needs me to help him because you said he told you that things were starting before midnight, and I was told that the car would be here to pick me up at closing and I should get out to the site before ten-thirty."

"Hmm," Xiomara said, thinking.

"And don't you dare think about coming early!" Diana spat. "He obviously staggered the times like this purposefully, and I don't want to ruin whatever surprise it is that he has in store for me."

"Diana, how many times do I have to say..."

"Don't bother!" Diana snapped. "Prove it by not being there until you were told!" Xiomara rolled her eyes heavenward before closing them, and then shook her head without offering a response. "I'm sure you know not to tell Gabriel that we've talked."

"Of course, I know that," Xiomara said, opening her eyes.

"I'll let you get back to work," Diana said, as if granting a gift. "You only have a couple more days, you know, before you're done with Matheson Media—and Gabriel—for good."

"I think this is the first thing you've got right, Diana," Xiomara said.

"You're going to witness something amazing on Friday, Xiomara," Diana crooned. "Maybe then you'll realize what else I'm right about."

Xiomara pulled the phone away from her ear, knowing that Diana had already disconnected. She set the phone atop the desk and looked around the room at what remained. She would likely be done packing within the hour and could then tie up other loose ends.

She glanced at the phone again as it lay on the desk. She knew that Joran, with shows scheduled on subsequent nights for the entire week, was not likely to call her. Xiomara could not help wishing he would, though, or that she had the courage to call him. She was also aware, however, that he was better off not knowing about the plans made with either Gabriel or Diana.

"Just a couple more days," she whispered, keeping in mind what Diana had said. "I'll be done with all of this."

Chapter Twenty-Nine

"Joran, what are you doing here?" Xiomara asked in a whisper, even though hers was the sole loft on the top floor and there was no chance of being overheard.

"I need to talk to you," Joran said, a leather jacket thrown over a white T-shirt and red-striped pajama bottoms. "Can I come in?"

"It's almost two in the morning," Xiomara said, keeping her body wedged in the doorway. "You have a matinee performance today!"

"I'm aware," he answered. "Like I said—I need to talk to you."

Xiomara stepped out into the hallway, closing the door behind her. "What's so important that it can't wait?" she asked.

"I need to know if it's true," he said.

"If what's true?"

"Diana called me, telling me all about the glorious night I'm going to miss and how I'm such a fool to let the opportunity pass by..."

Xiomara groaned, mentally cursing Diana for her selfishness. She probably panicked, so afraid of Xiomara's alleged designs on Gabriel, that she used what she felt was her single insurance policy: Joran.

"...you know how Diana is," Xiomara interjected. "Ignore her."

"I do know how she is," Joran returned, "and I was planning to ignore her—until she told me that Gabriel moved that little shindig from his usual place to one that you set up." He studied Xiomara, who sighed and looked away. "I guess that answers my question." Still, Xiomara said nothing. "You're helping Gabriel? After everything we talked about and all you said to convince me not to go? You're helping him?"

"Joran, you don't understand," Xiomara began.

"You're damned right I don't! Why?"

"I'll explain everything to you later."

"No, Xiomara, you can explain to me now! I'm here now!"

"But I can't do it now!" Xiomara said. "After tonight, after... after everything is done..."

"No, now!" Joran insisted. "Explain to me how, according to Diana, you apparently set all of this up with Gabriel on Sunday. Sunday, Xiomara! That was the day of Mrs. Blake's funeral, and I talked with you that night. You said nothing to me about this!"

"He showed up at the funeral," she said at last.

"When?" Joran said, confusion etched into his handsome features. "I was there for the duration. We even talked about it before I left for the burial..."

"He didn't come inside," Xiomara clarified. "You had already left, and Gabriel was standing across the street from the church."

"Waiting for you," he surmised, and then scoffed. "I thought you said you weren't able to reach him that day."

"Before the funeral, no. But I didn't know he'd be there."

Xiomara looked away from Joran again, feeling uncomfortable under the scrutiny of his stare. Joran cupped her chin in his hand and tilted her head until their eyes met. After a moment, Xiomara took a step back and pressed against the door, averting her eyes again. Joran exhaled, let her go, and stepped away. Xiomara folded her arms and a curtain of dark hair fell into her face as she made a point not to look in Joran's direction.

"You and Gabriel," he said.

"What?" she blurted, her head shooting up as she stood straight. "No, Joran!"

"No? Really? Because all of this seems strange and very convenient."

"You're wrong about that!" Xiomara insisted.

"Is that the real reason you don't want me to be there?" he asked.

"How could you even..."

"That's what Diana has been after this entire time, you know that!" Joran spat. "What do you think is going to happen at that ceremony, Xiomara? It is not about incantations or bloodletting or drinking from a silver goblet.

"Sex heightens the experience. It... amplifies the ritual. There were things... certain things... they both suggested that I do to my ex-wife while we were making love to get her to stay with me. Other ways to bind her to me... I didn't want it—not that way.

"But Gabriel will do anything to get what he wants. He is never satisfied, and Diana is just as bad. She thinks this is her way to stardom. She wants to win that cooking competition, and she wants to replace her husband with Gabriel. She's counting on tonight."

"That is why she told me, isn't it? She knows that you're planning to be there, and we all know that Gabriel would gladly trade her for you."

"That is not what's going on!" Xiomara maintained.

"Don't you think I want to believe, more than anything, that you're telling me the truth?" Joran said, voice raised. "I know what I see, and your half-explanations aren't working this time!"

Xiomara dropped her arms to her sides and then ran a hand through her hair. The brief shift away from the door was all Joran needed as he brushed past her, went inside, and then paused—his mouth agape.

"What is this?" he asked with wide eyes that swept the room. He turned to her. "Why is it like this? Are you moving in with Gabriel?"

Xiomara rushed back inside, closing the door behind her. Joran backed away as she approached, almost falling backward over one of the many boxes. They almost filled the living room, though a few were still open and in varying stages of fullness. Someone had also rolled the rug up, secured it in plastic wrap, and leaned it against the wall.

"I am not moving in with Gabriel. There is no me and Gabriel!"

"I don't believe you," Joran admitted. "How can I after this? I want to so much, but I know what I see... and what Diana said."

"Forget about Diana!" Xiomara exploded.

"I know Gabriel," Joran went on, "and he has had his eye on you from the start."

"Joran, I need you to stop..."

"You said that I shouldn't go to the ceremony," he continued, "that I didn't deserve to be there. What exactly does that mean, Xiomara? What don't I deserve?"

Xiomara took a deep breath and turned away.

"*You're not... like them...*" she heard echoing in her mind.

"Xiomara!" Joran shouted, causing her to jump.

"You're not like them," she said.

146

"What?" he asked, walking a half-circle around her until they faced one another again. "What did you say?"

"You're not like them, Joran," she said louder. "I... I've seen that. You have to know that. They're not... they're not your friends. They never were! They're just the people you settled for while you tried to find your way. You're not like them. Don't *be* like them."

To her horror, Xiomara felt a warm wetness on her cheeks and realized she was crying. Her jaw clenched as she scrubbed the tears away, scraping one cheek with a fingernail. The resulting sting was sobering, and she fixed Joran with an unyielding gaze as he looked at her with great concern.

"Go home," she stressed. "Forget about what Diana said. Put Gabriel out of your mind. It'll all make sense later."

"You're not here for Gabriel?" Joran asked with hesitation.

"No," she said. "I don't know how many times I have to say it."

"He told me he was going to ask," Joran said. "Not just about you continuing to work with him, I mean. I should have told you that before."

"I know what you mean," Xiomara admitted. "He did ask." Xiomara noticed he looked away from her then. She took the opportunity to study the shock of golden curls, the bit of stubble that enhanced his upper lip, jawline, and chin, and even the stiffness of his body, as if struggling to maintain his composure. "He asked, and I said no. I said it and I mean it."

The relief in his eyes, when they finally met hers again, was palpable, and a bit of color returned to his cheeks as he nodded.

"I'll ignore for now the fact that there are dust covers on your furniture and boxes everywhere," Joran offered. "I can try to keep from focusing on the fact that, despite everything, you seem to be helping Gabriel with this nonsense.

"I know how I feel, and I also know that I'm not imagining the connection that you and I have, even though it seems to contradict whatever else it is that's happening right now. I will do as you ask and go home and wait, but... I don't understand any of this."

"But, do you trust me?" Xiomara asked.

"There are so many ways I could answer that," he said.

Xiomara chuckled, recalling an echo of that same sentiment, and then wiped at her eyes—with more care this time.

"Answer with the truth," was all she said.

"Yes," he replied. "I do trust you. Gabriel's not for you, Xiomara. I hope you know that."

"I know it," she said.

Joran was watching her, and his posture seemed to waver as he took her in from the distressed waves of her burgundy-black hair to the oversized, blue-starred white pajamas and bare feet.

"I'll go," he said at last. "For now." He brushed a fingertip along the welt that had formed on Xiomara's cheek before opening his mouth as if to say something more. He then appeared to reconsider it and turned to leave. Xiomara watched his form become a blur as he departed, and she closed her eyes at the sound of the door closing behind him.

"God help me..." she whispered, feeling the hot sting upon her cheek again.

Chapter Thirty

The chime sounded on Xiomara's phone, announcing an incoming text message. She glanced over her shoulder toward the phone before returning her attention to the clipboard and its papers.

"And I'll need you to initial here and here," a young man said, smiling as he showed where Xiomara should sign. Gracing the spaces with her neat script, Xiomara handed him both the clipboard and pen.

"Thank you," she said.

"No, thank *you*, Ms. Grant," he enthused. "And please let us know where to deliver your belongings once you arrive at your eventual destination."

Xiomara smirked. "I don't think you deliver that far," she muttered under her breath before clearing her throat and gracing the man with a winning smile. He beamed at her, tipped his hat and walked to the door, where he let himself out.

Xiomara turned with a sigh, looking at the abundance of space before her. They had removed all her belongings from the loft, except for her leather satchel, which leaned against the far wall beside the matching duffel bag, plump from its contents.

Barefoot, Xiomara padded over to where her cell phone rested atop the duffel bag. Her hazel eyes scrutinized the display, and she realized that she still had roughly four hours before it was time to depart.

She scrolled through varying screens with expert precision. Once she confirmed what she was looking for, she checked her text messages. There were more than a few, as the chime sounded at least a handful of times from the moment the movers had arrived almost two hours earlier.

Hope that ur not 2 sore, read the text from a number that wasn't familiar to Xiomara. Not that Joran wud show up neway but i needed leverage. Xiomara sighed, realizing that the text couldn't have come from anyone else but Diana. No hard feelings, tho.

"Right," Xiomara said in disdain, scrolling through the other messages. They were mostly from a few of the ladies at EJB wishing her well, and one from Ruby that contained just the crossed fingers emoji. "Best of luck to you, too, Ruby," Xiomara said before putting the phone back atop the duffel bag.

It was after six o'clock. Xiomara imagined Gabriel had already left work and was on his way home to put the last details in place for the evening. She still did not understand why he was manipulating the arrival times, but in the end, it would have little effect.

Diana was sure to be doing meal prep at La Bonne Vie, salivating at the prospect of at long last claiming Gabriel as her own. Xiomara could not help wondering what Diana's husband was like... and why he would want a woman like Diana. Then again, Diana might not always have been as she was now. Something in her might have changed, or awakened, the night she met Gabriel when catering the dinner he attended. Xiomara knew that the allure of Gabriel's lifestyle—or faith, as he called it—had not wavered. For every person who had turned away from it, others still embraced it and praised what it could do.

Xiomara paused and leaned against the wall, closing her eyes. Joran was likely preparing for the evening show while worrying about what might take place at the cabin that evening. She would not call him, though the desire to do so felt like a scorch mark across her heart, and she prayed the night would pass quickly enough to set things right.

With a sigh, Xiomara opened her eyes and moved toward the center of the room, settling upon the floor with her legs folded in front of her. Closing her eyes again, she took a series of deep breaths, each becoming slower than the one before. Before long, she allowed herself to drift away.

This place is incredible! read the first message under Gabriel's name and number. We'll need to talk about using the space more often – until I can get one of my own, that is.

It was almost ten o'clock. Xiomara was giving the loft-style apartment she'd lived in for the last several months a final walkthrough. Finding nothing amiss, she put her phone inside the black satchel before slipping the strap onto one shoulder, grabbed the duffel bag, and departed.

Traffic was light, which was typical considering the time, and Xiomara drove a few miles under the speed limit so as not to risk arriving too soon. True, she would likely still arrive a bit before Gabriel intended, but in the end, it would be of no consequence.

A chime heralded the receipt of another text message. Having already linked her phone to the car's navigation system via Bluetooth, she waited for the message to be read aloud to her.

"From Joe-ran," the automated voice began, causing Xiomara's grip on the steering wheel to tighten, "You're not answering. Please tell me that you haven't changed your mind."

She felt bad for ignoring two calls from Joran earlier in the evening. She imagined he had finished his evening performance and tried contacting her right away. Worrying him was the last thing she wanted to do, and the familiar ache in her chest nagged at her.

"Wait, Joran," she whispered. "Just wait until tomorrow."

Another chime, and the automated voice continued: "I trust you. I do. I don't trust Gabriel."

Xiomara shook her head and then groaned as the chime sounded yet again.

"From Diana," the automated voice announced, "I have been in this car forever! This is some Blair Witch shit. What exactly is the use for a cabin so far away from everything? If Gabriel wasn't also texting to make sure I'm on my way, I'd think this was some sort of prank."

Ten minutes later, also from Diana: "I'm here."

Xiomara continued to drive, realizing that within a couple of hours, everything would be set in place for the night's events. She had been on the freeway for twenty minutes when the chime sounded again.

"From Gabriel," she was informed, "Don't forget to show up at around eleven-thirty. I'm going to check with Diana to make sure that she's still coming. See you soon?"

"Soon enough," Xiomara commented with a frown. She wondered why Gabriel would need to check with Diana when Diana had already said that she had arrived at the cabin.

Something vexed Xiomara, yet she could not quite determine the root of her discomfort. She was unsettled by what was about to take place, and the mixed messages from Gabriel and Diana did nothing at all to help. Ignoring her previous decision to travel at moderate speed to the cabin, Xiomara sped up and continued.

Xiomara jogged toward the cabin, the heels of her black suede boots tapping along the cobblestone path and wooden steps leading to the covered porch. She stepped around the debris scattered across the porch and examined the damage to the front door. It hung from the few bolts that remained intact when it was snatched open from the outside, and there were jagged, three-pronged claw marks gouged into the heavy wood.

Xiomara glanced to her left, her brow furrowing as she noticed a shovel lying just inside the doorway among the debris. She spun on her heels, looking around before considering the shovel once more. Casting a sidelong glance, she shrugged and then entered the structure.

As her hazel eyes surveyed the condition of the space, she noticed that Gabriel or Diana had swathed the large foyer in swirls of black, silver, and red. Approaching the dining room, Xiomara coughed, becoming inundated by a thick, coppery stench and the bitterness of sulfur at the back of her throat. Mindful of the distant sounds of snarling, smacking, and gurgling, she steeled herself and entered the room.

Her eyes fell upon what looked to be a makeshift altar near the dining room table; draped in black and littered with half-melted black candles nestled into silver candelabra. Some candles upon the altar were still burning, and a single candelabrum had tipped over and fallen, burning almost to the scalp a large patch of what was once the lustrous white-blonde locks of Diana, who lay nude and obscenely stretched across the table.

Her gray eyes were wide, and her mouth hung open as if in surprise. Her left hand was pierced palm-side up with the stiletto tip of a hook-handled silver dagger, the point going through the flesh and pinning the hand to the surface of the altar. Xiomara recognized the dagger from what once lay among the other accouterments inside Gabriel's apartment.

Diana's throat had been slit, and rich, red blood pooled around her neck and shoulders. Her legs were splayed, and there were dry and darkening smears of blood on her lower abdomen and between her upper thighs, as well as a distinguishable, crust-edged and congealing white substance streaked across both bare breasts.

"That's what Diana has been after this entire time, you know," she heard Joran echo in her mind. *"Sex heightens the experience."*

"Gabriel," Xiomara whispered, shuddering as tears filled her eyes and spilled down her cheeks. "This is why you wanted her here early. This is the purpose you claimed she was destined for, and you planned it all along. It's why you never helped her. I wanted to be wrong about you, but this…"

There was a flicker of movement behind her, and she turned away from Diana's stiffening body. The shadow had gone past the doorway and down the hall. They were still around then—hunting and feeding, which meant that Gabriel was probably in one of the other rooms hiding somewhere. But not for long. One could never hide from those things for long.

"Please, I know you're in there. I saw you come this way…"

She heard the scream then; no doubt masculine, but no less terrified, coming from the direction of the living room. Another of the things raced by, intent on joining the first for hellacious fun and games. Sickened, Xiomara turned back to the stomach-churning sight atop the dining room table. She tugged at a corner of the black cloth that covered it, intending to conceal the body. There was no sport to be had here for those things; no joy in hunting and killing something that was already dead before they arrived. Xiomara wondered what reward Gabriel sought in the killing of the one person who loved him above all others.

The act of moving the cloth drew Xiomara's attention to something beneath the table. Kneeling in the sticky and wet, she peered inside and gasped in uncomprehending horror at the picked-over and tortured remains of Gabriel Quentin Matheson.

His thick hair was spiked with blood, and the same three-digit jags that scarred the front door marred the left side of his face from forehead to chin. The left eye was missing, and the empty socket was moist, yet oddly free of blood, as if someone had wiped it clean—or something worse.

Xiomara stared in disbelief as the screams behind her came again—more frenetic and hysterical.

"No! No! No! Help! Help me! Oh, my God, no!"

Xiomara jumped up, almost slipping in the muck, as a chilling realization dawned. She raced through the dining room into the hallway, following the direction of the commotion. She heard the all-too-familiar sounds of cackling as the things tormented their prey, and she came upon the two of them as they wrestled with their new toy, who was fighting with everything he had left in him.

Joran's blond curls were stained scarlet with blood—his blood. One thing sat upon Joran's chest and was licking at his forehead and nose, recalling the sight of Gabriel's eye. The other sat nearby; its long, pointed tongue lolling lasciviously as it leered down at Joran's writhing form.

He was panting, flailing, kicking, struggling to free himself from his tormentors. The pointed tongue had now worked its way into Joran's hair, caressing the blood-stained curls.

"Stop!" Xiomara yelled, having gone from frightened to alarmed to outright furious. "You get away from him right now!" She was dismayed to see and hear that Joran's struggles had lost momentum and his breathing had become labored.

The things paid her no mind. The one upon Joran's chest dipped its head and took a healthy bite of Joran's clavicle, pulling away fabric, skin, flesh, and bone.

Xiomara turned, looking for something she could use. She then paused and whirled around on tiptoe, making her way back to the front door. She skidded to a stop and looked through the doorway and out into the front yard, where she saw the old van parked at a diagonal with its front tires reaching over the cobblestone walkway and into the manicured grass. The driver's side door, from which Joran had sprung moments after Xiomara's arrival, was still open.

Glimpsing the shovel still near the doorway, Xiomara grabbed it, running back toward the hellish duo and their increasingly listless prey.

"Stop!" she commanded, wielding the shovel by the handle in a tight grip above her head. "Get away from him now!"

One monster continued playing with Joran, nipping at his chest and digging into the skin with an elongated incisor. The other seemed to take its time pulling away from Joran, fixing Xiomara with a steely, red-pupiled glare as it tilted its head. The way it looked at her, as if in recognition and acknowledgement, chilled her. She had worked with creatures like these for years, but there was never anything between them that in any way exhibited familiarity.

Riddled with grief and heartbreak, and enraged that the beasts dared to defy her, Xiomara ran at them with a scream, shovel aloft, as she first beat at the one sitting atop Joran's chest.

"Get away from him!" she screamed, punctuating each word with a blow until the thing extracted itself and skittered off with a howl. She then turned to the one that had been studying her, wild-eyed and panting, before again raising the shovel overhead.

"Do as I say," warned Xiomara, "before I summon your master."

It roared at that before scampering away in the same direction as the other. Xiomara tossed the shovel to one side with a clatter and rushed to where Joran lay battered, bloody, moaning, and mumbling incoherently.

"Find... godfind... sho... sho... run," he babbled, eyes squeezed shut in a face twisted in pain and wet with blood-tinged streaks of saliva from being licked. "Sho... run..."

Xiomara's tears ran unchecked and copious as full realization rolled over her. Joran was thinking of her and trying to save her, as though she were somewhere inside the cabin and at risk of being hurt.

"Sho... run..." he gurgled, somehow attempting to move though his eyes remained closed.

"Sssh," she reassured with a tremor. "I'm here. I'm okay."

"Xiomara!" His unfocused green eyes, when he opened them, were filling. "Those things... Go... l-leave..."

"Not without you!" she insisted, looking around for something to staunch the flow of blood from the most severe of his injuries.

Without a beast straddling him, she could see the series of jagged claw marks from sternum to hip and the bite that was concealed by the blood filling the hole. More blood on his lower abdomen looked discolored and much too dark. Unable to find anything nearby, she ripped her gold-threaded, cream-colored sweater overhead and balled it up, pressing it against Joran's shredded stomach. He groaned in renewed pain and grasped her wrist with surprising strength.

"Be still!" she said.

"'lease... go..." he rasped.

"Why are you here?" she moaned through her tears. "You were supposed to stay away! You told me!"

His breaths were coming faster, and his usual healthy pallor drained and tinged with gray. It captivated Xiomara when he blinked into focus and looked at her with sudden clarity.

"Had t'check..." he began. "Thought... Gabriel might try... Don't... be mad... I trust... I trust you... but... went to... 'partment... was no ans..."

Xiomara wailed, realizing what his last text message to her meant. He had gone to her place after his concert when she ignored his phone calls. When she did not answer, he thought the worst.

Not at all caring about what Joran was covered in, she draped her body across his as she shook with anguish. She could feel Joran's attempts to put his arms around her. At last, he grunted as his arms dropped to his sides. Xiomara then sat up.

"I have to get you out of here," she declared, running a bloodied hand through her hair.

Joran coughed in response, his lips carmine as a dark red stream trickled from the corner of his mouth. His eyes had grown distant again, and Xiomara felt panicked. She felt for a pulse, which was faint, slapped at both his cheeks, and her brow furrowed in determination. Joran emitted a deep, bubbling sigh as his eyelids fluttered and then closed.

"No! Joran! Stay with me—stay!" She snatched at the pockets of her jeans for a moment and then stopped. She did not have her phone with her. It was in her car, which was parked a mile down the road.

She slapped Joran's face again. At last, his eyes crept open, though they were even more unfocused than before. Xiomara heard a gurgling rattle deep inside his chest, and when he exhaled again, fresh blood bubbled between his lips. He was still again.

Xiomara cried out in a mixture of anguish and rage.

"Please!" she yelled. "Not him! No, no, no!" She put her hands on either side of Joran's face and stared into his lifeless eyes, speaking in rapid, tear-soaked whispers. "Come back! Joran, you can't... don't leave... you don't understand... I'll do anything! I'll do anything..." She grabbed at his tattered and gore-stained shirt as if she could throttle him awake. "You are supposed to live!" she screamed. "You deserve to have a long and happy life! I want that for you! Why did you come back for me?"

Xiomara closed her eyes and threw herself across him again, touching his face and caressing the blood-drenched curls. She wept, as this time, he did not and could not try to wrap his arms around her. Her thoughts tangled around all the things she had never told Joran and would surrender forever if only he would live. She had resigned herself to him forgetting who Xiomara Grant was. Instead, his dying moments were filled with excruciating pain, fear, and concern for her rather than for himself.

"I can't let you go like this," she said in a conversational tone. "I won't let you go like this. I refuse to let anyone find you here with them. I will get you away from here somehow, Joran. I'll fix this."

She sat up again, opening her eyes as she wiped her eyes and face. When her hand came away, though, she gasped. Aside from the obvious wetness from crying, her hand was clean. There was no blood, chips of bone, or any of the other evidence of Joran's ordeal.

Xiomara looked at him, and the cry of surprise became wedged in her throat. His shirt was still ripped. However, he had no visible wounds, and all the stains had vanished. His hair was once again golden, and Xiomara's sweater, which now lay beside him, appeared laundered and fresh. Joran looked the picture of health and, aside from the distressed nature of his clothing, seemed only to be sleeping.

"I..." Xiomara managed. "What..."

When Joran coughed, Xiomara skittered backward on her palms and heels away from him. She stared, listening to him groan as he reached out without opening his eyes. His arms fell, and he grew still again. The gentle rise and fall of his stomach told Xiomara that he was alive.

Joran was alive.

He blurred before her as she struggled to process what had taken place. "What?" she panted. "How? You were just..."

Xiomara was cautious as she crept over on her hands and knees, tucking a lock of hair behind one ear as she examined him. His breaths were steady as she reached for him before reconsidering, dropping her hand. As fresh tears spilled onto her cheeks, Xiomara heard approaching footsteps.

PART TWO

Chapter Thirty-One

The tall, hooded figure pressed against the corner of the elevator, careful not to bump into anyone as they pushed their way inside. A small child, roughly three years old, bent over at the waist in an exaggerated attempt to peer beneath the hood from far below while making comical faces. The child's mother, taking a moment to look up from the blue-hued glow of the display on her cell phone, glanced first at the still figure before reaching down to tug at a lock of the child's dark brown hair.

"Maggie!" she hissed. "Leave that woman alone. She's not trying to fool with you!"

Most of the inhabitants of the elevator alighted on the next floor, including Maggie and her mother, leaving Xiomara to continue alone. When she got off the elevator, she pushed the hood back and away from her tousled dark head, looking at the arrows on the wall that listed the range of patient room numbers in either direction. She appreciated the smell of the unit: clean, with undertones of bleach, but not overly antiseptic, and she sauntered along the blue-tiled hallway with her hands shoved into her pockets as she looked to her right to read the names on each door that she passed.

Toward the middle of the corridor, the path opened on the left side to reveal a large nurse's station, at which a young woman in colorful scrubs stood, removing what remained of the Halloween décor. She snatched at the decorations while sighing loudly.

"Shelley!" barked a larger and older nurse from her comfortable, wide-backed seat in one corner of the station. "Quit dragging tail and get those done! Halloween was over a week ago!"

"Coulda gotten off of your fat ass to do it a week ago, too, Bridget," Shelley muttered, not quietly enough to escape Xiomara's hearing. Upon seeing Xiomara, Shelley's eyes widened as if she had been caught. Xiomara peered back at her with a blank expression and then turned to the right to read the name on the door.

TALBERT, JORAN H.

Xiomara approached the door and took a breath, pushing the lever to let herself in. The room was almost dark, as they had drawn the curtains to shield the space from the bright morning light. She closed the door behind her and lingered in front of it for a time, her breaths falling into rhythm with the beeps from the machine monitoring Joran's vital signs.

She shivered, knowing it had nothing to do with the temperature of the room and everything to do with the exact reasons Joran came to be hospitalized. But it could have been worse. In fact, it was.

As her eyes adjusted, she could see Joran's outline as he slept. Though it had been only ten days, Joran was far thinner than he was when Xiomara last saw him. He was, however, still looking much better overall than when Xiomara last saw him, and Xiomara felt overwhelmed with gratitude. She was also still conflicted.

She could not resist saying goodbye, though, as Joran had been the one person in over ten years who was worthy of saving. There was more, though, much more to Joran than Xiomara would allow herself to admit. Finding him asleep was fortunate.

Xiomara crept closer to the bed, mindful of the various lines connecting Joran to the machine monitoring his oxygen level, heart rate, and blood pressure—the incessant beeping ensuring that anyone within earshot would have no doubts about how Joran was faring. An IV bag dripped steadily into a line that disappeared beneath the blankets. Xiomara jumped as someone pushed the door open and Shelley ambled in.

"Need to take his vitals and check the drip," she offered in apology, moving to look at the monitor by the bed. "I'm so glad he has a visitor—other than that wife of his."

"Ex-wife," Xiomara could not help saying.

"Probably a good thing," Shelley said, moving to the other side of the bed and pulling the covers back from Joran's chest down to his waist. "I don't think she stayed but five minutes, and she didn't even ask questions. We only called her because she was listed as an emergency contact on an old card in his wallet." As Xiomara studied Joran, she could feel Shelley studying her. "Is he your boyfriend?" Xiomara looked up at her and could not bring herself to respond. Shelley smiled. "It's the way you look at him, is all, like you're so..."

"What's that?" Xiomara interrupted.

"I'm sorry?" queried Shelley, looking confused.

"On his wrists," Xiomara said, watching Shelley's face as it first paled and then reddened before she replaced the bedclothes.

"Restraints," she answered softly.

"What for?" Xiomara asked, louder than intended.

Shelley's worried brown gaze flicked toward the doorway before she answered in a lowered tone.

"He started having these episodes a few days after they brought him in," she said.

"Nightmares?" Xiomara asked.

"Not just at night. He may be kinda skinny, but he is extraordinarily strong. So, we sometimes sedate him to keep him calm, and the restraints are there so he doesn't yank out the IV again."

Shelley went to the corner to access a portable workstation, which included a laptop anchored to a standing desk for which there was neither stool nor chair. A few keystrokes helped her bypass the login screen, and before long she was entering various bits of information taken from a piece of paper extracted from her pocket.

"How did he end up here?" Xiomara asked lightly.

"He was in a single-vehicle accident about an hour outside of town," Shelley said, folding the paper and returning it to the pocket of her scrubs. "The van he was driving was pretty banged up in front, and it was too old to have airbags. He was unconscious when they first brought him in and has been pretty out of it ever since aside from the dreams."

"Poor guy," Xiomara muttered.

"Tell me about it. He's pretty scraped up from the accident, and there's no doubt that he's experienced some trauma, but there's no internal bleeding and he didn't sustain a head injury. Makes me wonder what was going on at the time of the crash, though, given all the weird things he's been saying in his sleep."

"Weird things?" Xiomara asked with interest.

"I don't know," Shelley said, moving over to the drawn curtains and opening them a few inches to let more light into the room. "It's mostly gibberish, even though one time he mumbled something about running the show... Or run show... Show run... I don't know. Made no sense to me at all."

"Xiomara," she said to herself. "Run, Xiomara..."

"Anyway," Shelley went on, oblivious, "he remembers none of it during the times he's awake. Hasn't asked for anyone or said much of anything, and we're lucky if we can get him to eat something at least once a day. Seems like he's still in some kind of shock or just numb. I'm really glad someone else came to see him, though." She went back to the doorway and then turned to look back at Xiomara with a smile. "I need to check on my other patients," she said. "But, you make yourself comfortable. Could be that seeing a friendly face when he wakes up is what he needs to help him recover faster."

Xiomara turned back to face Joran as the door clicked shut behind her, and the monitor continued to beep. He groaned in his sleep but did not stir. She could see the rapid side-to-side darting of his eyes behind the closed lids, and she knew he was dreaming. She reached out, first caressing his forehead and then the left side of his face.

"I wish things could be different," she whispered. "I never counted on this. I never counted on you. You are owed so much better than what I could give, but how could I tell you? Nothing is as you thought, and this was not supposed to happen. I've done all I can to give your life back to you, even though I don't understand how. But, I'm glad because you've earned that and so much more."

She leaned closer as he sighed, and his pupils ceased their dance. Her face hovered inches from his. He needed only to open his eyes to find her looking down at him. But he didn't.

Xiomara's eyes filled with tears as she took him in for what she was sure was the last time, and the hand nestled in his curls trembled. She sniffled.

"You'll be all right," she assured him in a shaky whisper that increased to a hitching gasp as she spoke. "Sleep... for a bit, okay? And... and then you'll forget... all about me... You won't hurt anymore... No more bad dreams."

"Sho..." Joran groaned in his sleep.

"Ssssh," she said, as first one and then another of her tears fell and landed on his cheek. She brushed them away with her thumb and straightened up to wipe at her own face with both hands. Wiping the moisture onto a corner of the sheet, she placed a steadier hand on Joran's chest. "Goodbye. I'm so, so grateful to have met you, and I'll never forget you, Joran Hoffman Talbert." Xiomara then turned away and walked to the door, pulling the hood back up to cover her head.

"N-no," Joran whispered. Xiomara paused, but did not turn around. The monitor attached to Joran signaled an increasing heart rate as Xiomara reached for the door. "Don't... Sh-sho..."

She went out into the hallway, walking past the empty nurse's station and toward the elevators as the beeping increased, echoing behind her.

"What happened?" she heard Shelley say, while hurried footsteps resonated along the hall towards Joran's room. "What's going on—hey!"

Xiomara reached the elevator as a duo of doctors were getting off, slipping inside and blindly pressing L to take her down to the lobby as the tears returned and flowed unchecked down her face. As the doors closed, she heard Joran's unmistakable and agonizing cry of pain, frustration, and fear.

"XIOMARAAAAA!"

Xiomara walked on unsteady legs through the hospital's parking garage and to her car, leaning against the driver's side door as she pushed the hood back and ran both hands through her hair. She sniffled, having done little else since leaving Joran, and did not bother to wipe at the tears staining her face, since they would not stop soon. She got into the car, hiccuping as she activated the push-button, keyless start to the ignition.

"Stop," she whispered to herself. "He'll be fine. Just let it go. Everything will be okay." Taking a deep breath, she fastened her seatbelt before sniffling again. "Find out where you're going next and leave... that's all you have to do... is get away from here and start again, like always. He'll forget, and everything will be done."

She sighed and sat back, catching sight of her reflection in the rear-view mirror. She made note of the reddened hazel eyes shining with fresh tears and pondered their meaning. Her reflection blurred before she leaned forward and rested her head against the steering wheel.

Chapter Thirty-Two

Xiomara pushed through heavy glass double doors, the buckles on her knee-high boots jingling merrily as she walked across the silver-veined, white marble flooring toward a large desk. Behind the desk sat a middle-aged, bespectacled woman with reddish-brown hair scraped back into a bun. She regarded Xiomara, skepticism plain in her dark brown eyes.

"Marjorie," Xiomara greeted coolly, as ebony brows arched behind dark glasses. "I didn't realize you'd be here."

"That time again, is it?" Marjorie responded with an equal lack of fondness. "Run out of permission slips already? You might be more than a bit overzealous in your efforts, don't you think?"

"Where have you been spending your Friday nights, Marjorie?" Xiomara asked in a honeyed tone as she removed the glasses, folded them, and helped herself to a blue cellophane-wrapped butter mint settled among others in an etched crystal dish.

Marjorie blanched in response, turning an unbecoming shade that resembled spoiled milk. "Keep that up and I'll be seeing you about much more than a mere... permission slip."

Still staring at Marjorie, she unwrapped the mint and tucked it into her cheek. "I'll be waiting," she threatened before smiling, "over there."

Moving to the nearby reception area, she glanced over to treat Marjorie to another winning smile. As she turned back to the sitting area, however, she collided with someone.

"Oh, I'm sorry!" she said.

"Please excuse me!" he said at the same time.

Their eyes met, locked, and Xiomara took a step back as she narrowed her gaze. She found herself unable to look away from the tall man of indeterminable age as he looked down at her with a bewildered expression, through warm hazel eyes set in a tanned face and topped with a shock of thick silver hair.

Xiomara felt warm, taking another step back on shaky legs as her eyes filled with tears. Through blurred vision, she could see him reaching out to her, moving toward her, and she could not understand why she was torn between not wanting him near her and wanting very much to hold on to him.

"Khinayda, what on earth are you doing here?" he asked. "Are you all right?"

"Khinayda," she replied in a whisper, her cheeks warm with the tears spilling onto them. "How do you... how do you know my name? Who are you?"

Xiomara moved away, stumbling as the heel of her boot knocked against something. He wrapped his arms around her to steady her, and their gazes locked. There was something about his eyes—not that they were a shade of hazel that almost matched her own—but a depth and attractiveness that felt familiar in other ways.

Everything inside her lurched, and she felt herself become lightheaded as the room went dark.

The thing was outside the closet door, having made quick work of her friend, Josie. Josie had cried and begged for Khinayda to open the door, allowing her a place in the closet Khinayda had fled to. Khinayda refused. She did not know what those things were that had hunted down and eviscerated her friends. She knew only that she did not want it to happen to her as well.

Why had she come back to the cabin? She should have heeded the advice given to her just the other day by Gianni.

"You shouldn't go, Khin," he cautioned her, speaking in the slow Southern drawl she had grown fond of.

"What do you mean?" Xiomara, then known as Khinayda, had asked.

"You're not... like them. I've seen that. You have to know that."

"They're my friends," she told him, and he shook his head. His hair was longer then, curling over the collar of his shirt, and his white-blond mane was enhanced by threads of silver rather than filled with them.

"No, sweetheart," he countered. "They're just the people you settled for while you tried to find your way. You found it, though. I know you have. There's no need..." He shook his head again. "Don't come this weekend, Khinayda. I'm beggin' you."

"Won't you be there, though?" she asked, and their gazes locked. He closed his eyes, leaning toward her ever so slightly before straightening and looking away.

"Don't," he cautioned.

"Will you?" she insisted. "I don't want to be alone with them. Rebecca is so full of herself, thinking that she's doing me such a huge favor. I don't know what's gotten into her. Since her brother died last summer, she's been doing all sorts of crazy things."

"I know," he said. "This is one of them. What she's plannin' is dangerous, not to mention misguided."

"I want to talk to my mother again," Khinayda explained. "That's the only reason I'm going. The last time we got together, the spell worked. Rebecca was able to bring her back, even if for a few minutes..."

"Khinayda..."

"Stephen says that if we do... the other stuff, too... then that'll give the spell more power and my mother will stay longer."

"That wasn't your mother, Khin!" Gianni turned to her, putting his hands on her shoulders. "I know you miss her, hon', but this is not the way to go about it. Rebecca doesn't know what she's doin', Stephen's an outright moron, and they're both meddlin' in things that are way above their heads. You're never prepared for what comes back at you once you put it out there."

Khinayda shook her head. "It's not bad, though. It's white magick, good magick. Maybe just one more time..."

"Khinayda, magick has no color," Gianni stressed. "There is no white or black; it's all in the heart of the user, and Rebecca has one of the darkest hearts of anyone I've ever known. I may not have been around her as long as you have, but I definitely know her better."

"So, you're saying it's all pointless," she said.

Gianni dropped his hands, running one of them through his hair.

"I'm sayin' don't come," he said. "Stay away. Go home n'see your dad. It's about all you've been talkin' about for the last few months. The time would be better spent with him—trust me—an' I know he'll be glad to see you. This... this isn't somethin' you wanna be a part of. You don't deserve it."

"I understand what you mean about my mom," Khinayda insisted. "Who knows if it was really her, or if this is something Rebecca and Stephen cooked up. But, you're making it sound as though there's more to this, and I don't understand why you won't tell me what it is. You're going to be there. Why can't I? I'd feel better with you there, Gianni."

"Khinayda, do you trust me?" he asked.

Half a dozen ways in which she could answer that question flashed through her mind. In the end, she selected the response that was safest.

"Of course I do, Gianni."

"Good." He got to his feet, wiping his palms against his denim-clad hips. "Go see your dad. Enjoy the memories of your mom with him. That's what you should hold on to because that's what's real."

"All right, Gianni," she conceded with a sigh. "I'll go see my dad and spend the weekend with him. I'll see you when I get back though... right?"

It was the look he gave her then that worried her. For months, he had been her best friend; her confidant. He took the time to listen to her and made her feel as though he valued her as a person, and not as the convenient recipient of a trust fund provided by the old name of a distant family. Now, when she felt ready to tell him how much she appreciated him and the light he brought to her life, he stood there looking at her as though for the last time.

She was still thinking of that look later the following night as she sat in traffic on her way to the airport; that and the fact that all he would say was that everything would be okay, without answering the question she had asked. Khinayda had already ignored nineteen telephone calls and almost three dozen text messages from her so-called friends over the last twenty-four hours; teasing her about the decision to not join them—but not one text or call from the person who mattered most.

As soon as she was able, Khinayda exited the freeway and headed to the cabin owned by the maiden aunt of her friend, Rebecca. When she entered, the festivities were in full swing. Various books were strewn about the floor, some of them opened to reveal diagrams of varying configurations. The living room furniture had been shoved in every direction to make room for a variety of sketches and symbols drawn upon the dark hardwood floor in white wax.

There were also pizza boxes, opened containers of Chinese food, and bottles of expensive alcohol scattered about. The walls were vibrating from the tribal music pounding in repetitive choruses from the surround sound speakers.

Though there were no visible signs of the rest of the group, they were still inside the cabin. The music in no way drowned out the sounds of energetic group activities emanating from one bedroom. Khinayda shook her head in disgust and opened her backpack to retrieve her phone. She stared at the most recent text from Josie, Rebecca, and Stephen that promised, "You don't know what you're missing!" along with the photo of the half-dressed trio, sent half an hour before her arrival. Rolling her eyes, she browsed her contacts list, selected one, opened a new text, and began typing with her thumbs.

I know you said not to come. I really need to talk with you.

Deciding that she did not want to be around when any of the tipsy trio emerged, Khinayda instead went into the bedroom she often stayed in during cabin visits, settling on the luxurious queen-sized canopy bed as she stared at the display on her phone's screen, willing it to show a response. At some point, the ruckus died down at the end of the hall, and the music was blessedly silenced. Khinayda, phone still clutched in her hand, fell asleep.

A few hours had elapsed when Khinayda was startled awake by the sound of breaking glass and splintering wood. Her breath caught as her eyes adjusted to the darkness of the room, and she jumped at the sound of another crash that was followed by what seemed to be the guttural roar of a large and very agitated lion.

Creeping from the bed, Khinayda spied her car keys sitting atop the bedside table. Carefully pocketing them, she wondered if something was truly amiss. Perhaps the trio was enjoying a horror movie marathon and left the television on full blast. The surround sound system had cost maiden aunt Sylvia a pretty penny, to hear Rebecca tell it.

There was another roar, this time accompanied by a piercing scream. It was not a movie. The scream had come from one of the girls, followed by an exclamation from Stephen. Sounds of a scuffle and another scream—Rebecca?—forced Khinayda into a crouched position as her eyes sought another way out of the bedroom other than through the door.

171

Stephen yelled, sounding as though in extreme pain. Rebecca—she was certain now—was still screaming; the sounds frenzied as the bellowing turned into a high-pitched, keening giggle.

Khinayda raced to the window, forcing the vertical blinds in varying directions. Her trembling fingers struggled with the latch, but no matter how she twisted it and then pushed at the frame, the window would not budge. Nothing Khinayda did; grunting, pounding, heaving with all her strength, made any difference at all.

She caught sight of something large flitting past the window from the outside, and she gasped, jumping back. There was not just an intruder inside the house. There seemed to be another one outside. How many others were there? As she fled from the window, she thought she caught sight of a flash of silver in the moonlight, but she could not be certain and had no desire to check again.

Something large and heavy was thrown against the closed door to Khinayda's bedroom, causing her to jump and whirl around, a hand upon her heaving chest. Before she could respond further, the door exploded inward, and a battered and very bloody Stephen toppled through the shattered opening, grappling with something on top of him. It was unlike anything Khinayda could have imagined: compact yet thickly muscled.

Covered in coarse dark red hair that glistened with what seemed to be a combination of blood and a slimy substance that Khinayda did not recognize, the thing was a massive canine-human hybrid. It was large-headed, with a barrel-like chest and three elongated talons on each of its forefeet that pierced and then ripped at Stephen's skin and flesh. The beast looked as though it could kill Stephen at any minute and was toying with him.

"Khin!" Stephen rasped, having spotted her through the one swollen and misshapen bright blue eye he had left. "Help... me!"

The creature dipped its head, and though Khinayda could not quite see what was going on, there was no mistaking what she heard. The crunch was unmistakable, as were the rattling noises Stephen made as blood from his torn throat entered his lungs with his final breaths.

Khinayda scurried through what remained of the door and into the hallway, tripping over the prone form of Rebecca who, by her wheezing breaths, was still alive despite various deep lacerations covering her semi-nude body. Khinayda bit her lip hard to keep from screaming, the taste of her own blood bitter in her mouth as she shuffled backward on her palms and heels of her feet. She then realized that she was heading in the opposite direction of the front door to the cabin and got to her feet, intent on doubling back so that she could get free.

She had barely gone a few steps before she hit the floor again, her bare left foot caught on something. With an involuntary cry of frustration, she tried to kick herself free, looking back over her shoulder and catching the terrified glance of Rebecca, who was holding on to Khinayda's foot with what was most likely the last of her strength. Rebecca opened her mouth to speak, but could not quite manage it. Tears threatened to obscure her vision as Khinayda removed her foot from Rebecca's bloodied grip.

"I'm sorry," Khinayda mouthed, unsure if Rebecca was even aware of her words.

Rebecca opened her mouth again, as if to say more. Her eyes widened as her face twisted before exploding outward, spraying Khinayda in blood, bone fragments, and gore as the canine beast from the bedroom, having finished with Stephen, had crept up behind Rebecca, making quick work of her with a vicious punch through the back of the skull. It did not seem to be done, though, as it crouched over her with its maw dripping, lowering its head once again to dine.

Though it seemed preoccupied, Khinayda knew she would not survive if she tried running past it to the front door. Trying with all her might to drown out the slurping and crunching noises, Khinayda steeled herself and made a dash in the other direction, along the hall and into the only shelter she could find—the closet.

"I didn't want you to be there for that," the man said. Xiomara had come out of her faint to find him beside her on the plush blue sofa in the waiting area, worry apparent in his eyes. Through tears, she had confronted him with what she recalled, and he sighed in resignation. "You didn't deserve it, and when I found you..."

"...it was you outside," Xiomara interrupted shakily. "When I tried to get out of the window... It was you... Gianni."

"It broke my heart to see you there," Gianni admitted, his brow wrinkled. "Had I known what your message meant I could have stopped it."

"That... thing..." Xiomara interrupted again. "It grabbed me from the closet after it killed Josie." She got to her feet and paced in front of the sofa. Her brow furrowed. "But then the next thing I knew, I woke up in the hospital and it was weeks later... and somehow I had no injuries." She turned to look at him, and he returned the look for a moment before averting his eyes.

Xiomara sank back down onto the sofa, her legs not quite able to bear weight as realization dawned. "I didn't get hurt, did I? That is how this whole thing started. I wasn't just hurt. I... died?"

Her thoughts turned to Joran and how he, much like she had years ago, defied what he had been told and showed up at the cabin. He, too, was caught between worlds as Gabriel was claimed for his misdeeds. She had been desperate to save Joran, promising anything if she could bring him back.

"Please! Not her! I did not mean for her to be taken! I'll do anything to bring her back!"

"It was you," she said again.

"It was not supposed to happen!" Gianni insisted. "That was why I needed to save you!"

"That's not all," Xiomara said. "That's not all you did, Gianni."

He sat back and shook his head, sighing. "No," he said. "It would seem that you're right."

"It's because you saved me, isn't it?" she asked. "That's why I'm like this. Something you did changed me."

"Yes," Gianni admitted. "I mean, it has to be."

"It was because of Rebecca, wasn't it?" Xiomara asked. "She introduced you to us. She was the reason you were there."

"Yes," Gianni said. "They sent me to collect her."

"But, why?" Xiomara wondered. "You said she had a black heart. Just for helping me try to contact my mother? How was she alone to blame for that?"

"Khinayda... that wasn't all. She was responsible for what happened to Andrew."

Xiomara blinked and then stared at him for a moment.

"Her brother?" she said. "Rebecca couldn't have, Gianni. That makes no sense! He loved her, he was crazy about her, he would follow her everywhere!"

"She wasn't the person you thought you knew," he explained. "She intentionally killed the person who loved her most, her eight-year-old brother, and staged it to look as though he took his own life. His blood called me."

"Josie and Stephen?" she whispered, wide-eyed.

"They had no part in killing Andrew," Gianni said. "They didn't even know she did it. Their transgressions were light in comparison. Stephen's love for Rebecca was genuine. He was blinded by her and would have done anything she asked. Josie was acting out of loneliness. I tried to save them. I warned them not to show up, as I did with you."

"And, like me, they didn't listen," Xiomara finished and then looked at Gianni. "But, you didn't save them."

"I said that their transgressions were light. I did not say that they were nonexistent. You should not have died."

"Gianni, I finally woke up after over a month... and I was alone in a hospital two hours away from where I lived. They had brought in no one else. No one knew anything about Rebecca, Stephen, and Josie. And I..." She looked at him again, her eyes narrowing. "I didn't remember you."

"As intended," he said. "Just as no one you've encountered during your travels will remember you. They might have a vague feeling, or a lingering tug at the back of their minds. Some may even recall someone else in your place. We're meant to fade."

"Meant to fade!?" she snapped at him, uncaring that they were being stared at, even by Marjorie. "You didn't fade, Gianni! You were always there! There was no lingering tug or vague feeling! I might not have remembered everything, but I remembered enough to break my heart for fourteen years! I dreamed of you! I drew a picture of... of... You had to know the effect this would have on me!"

"No," he said with another shake of his head. "All I wanted was to bring you back! I thought you would wake up and think that you had been in an accident on your way to the airport to see your father. That is how it was supposed to work."

"It worked at first," Xiomara said. "I didn't remember. Not really. There were dreams... but, nothing I could ever fully recall after waking up." She frowned, trying to sift through the rush of memories. "I was told about an accident and that I'd been badly hurt. Over time, I didn't hear from Rebecca, Stephen, or Josie, and couldn't get in touch with them when I tried. They were gone." She looked at him. "Why? Why did you do this?"

"You have to understand," he began, staring at her, "in all of my years of collecting... you were the very first one that I brought back. You made a different choice, and their fate was not yours to share. You were... are... special. And I was supposed to leave, while you forgot all about me."

"But, I didn't, did I? I had dreams—horrible dreams of watching my friends die, screaming for help before being bitten and clawed to shreds and chewed up! And mixed in with nightmares of my mouth filling with blood that was not all mine, were visions of a face and the sound of a voice that felt so close yet was always outside of my reach."

"It wasn't supposed to be that way!" he pleaded.

"A few weeks after they released me from the hospital, I was sitting in a park," Xiomara sniffled. "There was a family there... the mom and dad and four kids... and I caught myself staring at one. She was a beautiful little girl with creamy cocoa skin, wearing a pink cotton romper and hopping around barefoot on the grass with her siblings. She wore her hair in two tight bunches and had the biggest dark brown eyes I had ever seen.

"But, as I kept looking at her, she changed. She went from a six-year-old child to a young woman of about nineteen or twenty... and she seemed to split into two. The halves loomed behind her; attached to one another, but also connected to her through these tendrils that looked like umbilical cords.

"One half of her adult being seemed clean, hardworking, considerate, respectful... But, the other half was so different. She was filthy and feral. She seemed manipulative. I saw her covered in blood; sinking to her haunches like an animal, with her head cocked to the side and staring right back at me.

"I suddenly heard baying, scratching, and heavy breathing. A thick stench that smelled like old chicken and rotting eggs overwhelmed me. It made me so sick that I started puking my guts out right at that park bench. Those parents got the kids out of there real fast, but I looked up in time to see her looking back at me. She was just a little girl again."

"I'm sorry," he said.

"You're sorry," Xiomara scoffed. "Couldn't you let me die?"

"No," he said, his face twisting into a scowl. "I couldn't ever do that! I told you. You're special."

"That certainly seems to be the case, doesn't it?" she said, snatching at the tears that spilled onto her cheeks. "I certainly am special now, aren't I? You saw to that."

"I didn't know what saving you would do," Gianni said, "to you or to me."

"To you?" Xiomara sneered. "What could it have possibly done to you? I haven't seen or heard from you in fourteen years, Gianni, so stop acting like you ever cared."

"I cared!" Gianni exploded. "That's what I'm trying to get you to understand! Leaving was difficult. You are not the only one who has been thinking about a face or a voice all this time, Khinayda, and I didn't have the luxury of an impaired memory.

"I don't... I don't have any answers for you. I do not have a ready-made speech to address an issue I never expected to face. But, you need to know that what I did wasn't malicious. Giving you back your life thrilled me, if only because of the light you brought to mine."

Divested of her anger, Xiomara leaned forward, cradling her head in her hands with a shuddering sigh. She then paused, lifted her head, and focused on Gianni.

"Your accent," she said after a moment. Gianni did not respond, reddening as Xiomara shook her head. "Your accent's gone. Either you've somehow lost it since I saw you last... or it wasn't ever real to begin with."

"Khinayda..."

"Was anything about you real?" she asked.

"With you," he began, "the deepest essence of who I am was very real."

Xiomara sighed, covering her face again and taking another shivering breath.

"So, is this what happened to you?" she asked from behind her hands. "Someone saved you once, too?"

She cast a sidelong glance at him as the silver-topped head shook again. "I started out like this," he revealed. "It was my life's work, and all I knew how to do... or so I thought. But, I couldn't anymore—not after you." He turned to face her, taking one of her hands in both of his. "You don't have to do this, Khinayda."

"My name is Xiomara now. As I'm sure you're aware, we have to change things up occasionally. Khinayda Hastings would be forty years old, and I certainly don't look it." She peered at him. He also had not changed since she last saw him, except for the color and length of his hair.

"Fine, I don't care what you want me to call you! I don't think it's possible for me to care less about that. I'm worried about you!"

"Worried for what?" Xiomara said with a dry laugh, extracting her hand. "Don't I look the picture of health?"

"I know you're upset by all of this," Gianni said.

"Upset," Xiomara mumbled. "He thinks I'm upset..."

"Disappointed? Confused? Hurt?"

"You're getting there," she encouraged smugly.

He shook his head and looked away. "Don't go in for your appointment. Walk away. Leave that life. It can be done. I can show you."

Xiomara once again thought of Joran and sighed, getting up again and turning her back to Gianni. She thought of how Joran looked at the hospital, the things Shelley told her about what he had said, and the dreams he was having. As she slunk from his room like a defeated coward, taking shelter within the departing elevator, he had called out for her, and she kept walking away.

What had she done? Better yet, what had she started by going to visit him in the first place? Gianni was right. It was meant for anyone who had come across those like him and Xiomara to be rendered unable to recall details of their likeness, or to forget they had existed altogether. Xiomara had been counting on it, which was why, on the night Joran confronted her at her apartment, she begged him to wait. Once Gabriel and Diana had gone, things should have been resolved.

The travels of a collector did not weave throughout the same circles as someone they were acquainted with before. Xiomara had only been to the same city on two occasions in a dozen years, and under such varied circumstances, it was impossible for the worlds to meet. However, seeing Gianni again after all this time opened the floodgates of her protected memories. Xiomara realized that visiting Joran might have done the same.

She could feel Gianni behind her, smell his once-again-familiar scent, and remembered with bitter joy how his nearness used to make her feel. He placed a hand on her shoulder, forcing her to turn to face him again.

"What is it?" he asked.

"I can't," she admitted.

"You can't what?" he intoned.

"I can't leave. I can't let it go."

"Why not?" he asked with a frown. "The flashes in your dreams should no longer be an issue now that your memory is coming back."

"Because it's not about me anymore." Silence hung between them, and then his eyes widened.

"Who else?" he asked.

"Doesn't matter. He's none of your concern."

"He? What do you mean? He, who?"

"As if you have a right to ask me *anything*!"

"Khinayda!"

"I didn't know what could happen!" she blurted out. "I should have left it alone, but I couldn't—I had to go see him!"

"Should have left what alone? What are you saying?" He put both hands on her shoulders and stared at her. "Did you bring someone back?"

"He should have been!" Xiomara shouted at him. "How could I have known what I can do? You left me—with no reason or explanation—and he was like me, all those years ago… showing up for someone he cared about." She shook him off and turned away again.

"I did not know!" he stressed, shifting to stand in front of her.

"I know that," she said between clenched teeth. "But, now I *do* have an idea, and… I can't go through with it. I cannot abandon him now when I'm the one who got him into this. He needed to be brought back, but he doesn't need what's coming next."

"Khinayda," Gianni whispered.

She moved back to the sofa and took a seat. Gianni followed and took her hand again.

"You were right," she continued with a sniffle. "I should have gone to see my dad that weekend, instead of heading to that cabin. It might have been the last chance I got." She looked up at Gianni, and it surprised her to see that his eyes were glistening with moisture. "He had a heart attack while waiting for me to wake up. He never got over my mother's death, and then the stress of what he thought was my illness... He was all I had left." Gianni opened his mouth to speak, and Xiomara shook her head. "Don't. Just... don't, Gianni. You didn't know what would happen. But I do.

"Things will be vastly different for Joran now. He'll feel the same thing I felt in the park that day... a pull toward certain people and places... and he won't understand the hunger. He will not understand that some people he meets will face a choice in life, and the result will determine which half will reign. He'll have a compelling need to take certain people from this world, a few souls at a time." She shook her head. "Do you know how terrifying that was for me? It was like a craving... I couldn't eat, I couldn't sleep, I was jumping at anything that moved. I thought I was going crazy, and I started drinking to drown it out and that only made it worse... because when you're in a dead drunk, you can't exactly rouse yourself from a nightmare."

"What will you do?" Gianni interjected. "What will you say to him?"

"I have absolutely no idea," Xiomara admitted. "But, I need to be the one to do it whenever I figure it out. He deserves so much more than to be enlightened as to the uniqueness of his existence by Kushiel." Gianni paused and then groaned, running a hand through his hair. She chuckled again. "You know him, then?"

"We've met," was all he said.

"One night, I awoke to find the bedroom window of my fifth story apartment wide open, and someone standing at the foot of my bed. Not standing on the floor, mind you, but perched on the edge of the footboard like some avian lunatic."

"Sounds like Kushiel," Gianni muttered.

"And since you've met him, I'm sure you understand why I can't leave Joran to face that alone."

Gianni nodded. Xiomara got up, preparing to leave, when he caught the sleeve of her leather coat. She did not turn back to look at him, but neither did she remove herself from his grasp.

"Khinayda, I don't want to lose you," he said. "Not again."

"You didn't lose me," she said. "You gave me up."

"I'm here now, and I have to believe that we've met again for a reason." He moved to face her again. "I thought about you, Khinayda, all the time. Like I said—you are why I stopped. I didn't know what would happen. I have missed you, okay? I've missed you very much."

"Look," Xiomara began, "who you've missed is not who is standing in front of you now. I can't go back fourteen years—neither of us can."

"Don't punish me as though I set out to hurt you! All I wanted was for you to be okay."

"And I want him to be okay," Xiomara said. "I'm almost certain that when he wakes up again, if he hasn't already, he's going to remember everything. There will not be over a decade of periodic dreams about a face and a voice and wondering if the feeling of being ripped open is a persistent terror or something else. He will remember that he is alive, but his friends are gone. He'll know what killed them and be burdened with the knowledge because no one would ever believe him if he told."

"I need to know something," Gianni said, to which Xiomara responded by arching a brow. "What did Kushiel tell you during that first visit when he showed up at your apartment?"

Xiomara snickered.

"That I had been awakened… and was a different person than before the accident," she said. "But, he had the answers. He could explain what it was I had been going through and show me what I needed to find a balance. He knew about what happened in the park. He replayed the encounter for me and explained what I saw and why."

"Nothing about how you were transformed," Gianni said.

"Nothing," Xiomara answered.

"Nothing about me?"

"Obviously."

"And nothing about the fact that he was sending you out with the same type of monsters that killed you!?"

"Funny you should mention that," Xiomara said. "I would swear that one of them recognized me on this last assignment. I couldn't quite understand then what was going on, and certainly didn't have time to reflect upon it while in the moment, but there was something in how the thing looked at me. Now I know why."

Gianni shook his head in disbelief. "There's apparently no limit to the depths of Kushiel's recklessness..."

"Plenty of that to go around, I'd say!" Xiomara said with mock cheerfulness. "I think I will skip the appointment. I have to get back to the hospital." She side-stepped around Gianni and prepared to walk away, but he put himself in her way again.

"What about after that?" he asked. "Where will you go?" She shot him a look. "Come on, Khinayda!"

"Xiomara!" she snapped.

"For now," he countered, and then took a breath. "Just... just think about this. You don't have to do this by yourself!"

"I won't be," she replied. "I won't shirk my responsibility to him." Her hazel gaze flicked over him. "Take care of yourself, Gianni. It's been... interesting seeing you again."

He stiffened. "Interesting? That's all you have to say?"

Xiomara slipped a hand into one of her pockets, extracting a small cellophane bag containing a circular green puff. She watched as Gianni's eyes widened and then warmed with fond recognition.

"Cotton candy," he said with a gentle smile. "My favorite."

"And apparently mine," she revealed, returning it to her pocket. "It would seem that you've had quite the influence, even when I didn't realize it."

"Xiomara," he said, "will you stay? I'm... asking you."

She felt transported back in time to the question she had asked him years ago, when she was desperate to know whether she could count on him to be at the cabin on what turned out to be a life-altering weekend. As he could not answer then, Xiomara found herself unable to now.

When she would only look at him without responding, he walked over to Marjorie, who seemed to have missed nothing, and they began speaking in rushed whispers. Xiomara removed the dark glasses from her other pocket and slipped them into place before leaving the reception area, foregoing the elevator and instead heading for the stairs.

In minutes, she was coasting through traffic on instinct, scarcely seeing where she was going, though she maneuvered with expert precision. She thought of her discussion with Gianni and wondered if she could as easily walk away from the life she had embraced. For years, she had met and mingled with people—with the assignation of judge, jury, and executioner. She had lost count of the number of souls she collected during that time, and though she was affected by loss when each ultimately remained on the path that doomed them, she had eventually considered it a hazard of the job before leaving it behind her.

The few friends she had made had long since forgotten her. The fewer dalliances she indulged in were meaningless. For Xiomara, any feelings of affinity never lasted and were a part of her work, and any feelings of loneliness were soothed away by a random night here or there. Joran, however, had made an indelible mark for reasons Xiomara had not expected and was not prepared for. Walking away from him in the hospital ranked among the hardest things she had ever done.

She was so entangled in her thoughts that the ringing of her cell phone caught her off-guard. She blinked, pulling herself out of her reverie to glance at the dashboard's display to see who the caller was. Her eyes widened, and she slammed on the brakes. Ignoring the torrent of blaring horns from the other drivers, and the cacophony of profanity to her right and left as they moved around her, Xiomara pressed a button on the steering wheel and took a shuddering breath.

"H-hello?" she ventured.

"Hello!?" a female voice said, barely audible over the sounds of commotion in the background. Xiomara recognized the rapid beeping of the hospital monitor and the voice yelling over a chorus of others.

"Yes?"

"Is this Xiomara Grant!?"

"Yes!"

"This is Shelley Haas—the nurse from Adventist Hospital—we met earlier this morning!"

"Let me talk to her! Give me my phone!" Xiomara heard Joran demand between grunting breaths.

"He's awake?" Xiomara said, almost to herself, since she managed the words aloud.

"I don't know what happened this morning," Shelley said in a rush, "but, you need to get here right away."

Cars continued to honk as they passed on either side of Xiomara, but she did not care.

"I said give me my phone!" Joran demanded in the background. "Xiomara—can you hear me!?"

"I hear you," she whispered, her mind racing.

"My charge nurse is after the attending fellow to have him sedated, and I mean totally knocked out!" Shelley whispered into the phone. "I don't want to—not if you can come help. But, I can't delay it for too much longer. Miss Grant, are you still there? Please!"

"Yes," Xiomara said. "I'm still here. I'm on my way."

Chapter Thirty-Three

Xiomara bypassed the bank of elevators and bounded up the stairs, taking two at a time until she reached the eighth floor. Catching her breath as she rounded the corner after exiting the stairwell, she could hear distant commotion as she entered the main hall and approached the nurse's station. She saw Shelley lingering near the door to Joran's room while Bridget, the charge nurse, gestured wildly and spoke with a pair of officers near the main desk.

"Miss Grant!" Shelley cried in relief when she spotted Xiomara and approached her. Three other pairs of eyes shifted until they, too, focused on Xiomara, and the conversation ceased between Bridget and the officers.

"Did I make it in time?" Xiomara asked Shelley under her breath.

"Barely," Shelley whispered, glancing back at the trio. "I've had a hell of a time stalling. She's about to get the cops involved in another minute."

They were both startled when Joran cried out, though what he said was incomprehensible through the closed door.

"She called the police over a patient who's basically shackled to the bed?" Xiomara said in surprise.

"No," Shelley said, as she reddened and bit her lower lip. She tugged at Xiomara's leather-clad arm until they had both advanced a little further down the hall and out of earshot of the others. "She got the order for the sedative, but the vial came up missing before she could administer it."

Xiomara's eyes widened as realization hit.

"Shelley, you didn't."

"Don't worry about that," Shelley said quickly. "I can fix that—but, I needed to make sure you could get here first."

"What happened?"

"He yelled your name when you left. He wanted us to find you and get you to come back. He was totally panicked, and we couldn't get him to calm

185

down, and he's refused to tell us what's wrong, so I told him I'd find you even though I did not know how to do that. It worked for a while, though, but as time went on and you didn't come back, he lost it."

"Oh, God," Xiomara sighed.

"Then I remembered what he was brought in with, and he had a cell phone on him. Obviously, it was dead, so I had to charge it up. I heard what name he used when he called you, so I figured I could find you in his contacts and quietly get you to agree to come back here."

"That was quiet?" Xiomara said, remembering the ruckus during the call.

"That was because some big-mouthed tech who thought she was helping told Mr. Talbert that we had his phone... and thought it was his ex-wife he wanted to see... and said that we were going to call her to come back and see him again. He freaked out, demanded the phone, and was still going off about it during the call to you."

Another outcry from the room caused them both to jump. Xiomara then placed a hand on Shelley's shoulder and nodded.

"Thank you," she told the young nurse. "I'll make sure he's okay, and this time I won't leave until he is."

"Is there a problem over here?" one officer asked as he approached. Xiomara's hazel gaze examined him, and her instincts told her he was more concerned with Joran's well-being rather than any issue regarding a missing vial of medication.

"I was just getting a status update, Officer," she replied. "I'm on my way in to see Joran now."

"He's about to be sedated!" Bridget interjected, shuffling over. "And I'm not sure you should be able to see him again since he got so upset after you left earlier!"

"He was asleep when I came in this morning," Xiomara explained in an even tone, keeping her focus on the officer. "I had no way of knowing that leaving would have the effect that it did."

"I don't think there's any harm in it," the officer said, smiling at Xiomara before turning to Bridget. "If she's the one he's been calling for, we could all end up being able to get back to work once he calms down." He looked at Xiomara again. "Until we know for sure, though, my partner and I are going to stay right here—do you understand?"

"Perfectly!" Xiomara said before Bridget could comment, returning the officer's smile. At his nod, she walked alone toward Joran's room and took a breath before opening the door.

She stood framed in the doorway, watching as a red-faced Joran bucked and strained at the restraints on his wrists and the new ones strapped across his chest and legs, holding him against the mangled sheets.

His hair, darkened from sweat, was plastered to his forehead and limp around his ears. The light blue hospital gown was wet around the neck, chest, and armpits. The monitor, now unplugged and silent, was shoved into a far corner.

"Get out!" Joran rasped, his voice the result of continual yelling. "All of you, stay out! Don't come in here until you get Xiomara back!"

"I am back, Joran," she said, her voice catching as she spoke.

He gasped, turning his head toward the door.

"Xiomara!?"

She rushed to the bed, brushing the hair back from his forehead as she looked down at him, feeling a deep ache within her chest as he pushed against the bonds while trying to reach for her.

"Don't, don't!" she whispered, babbling. "You'll hurt yourself. I'm so sorry that I left. I promise I'll explain everything. Be still for one more minute! I'll get someone to let you out." She turned toward the hallway, keeping a hand on his chest. "Shelley!" The nurse rushed in, followed closely by Bridget and the officers. "Get him out of this right now!"

"I don't think that's a good idea," Bridget cautioned as Shelley moved toward the bed.

"There's no reason for it!" Xiomara countered. "You know he's not a danger to anyone! He wanted me and now I'm here!"

"Officer?" Bridget asked, looking at the one who'd been speaking with Xiomara earlier. Xiomara also looked at him as her eyes filled again.

"Please!" Joran added from the bed, his hands reaching for Xiomara.

The police officer nodded at Shelley, whose nimble fingers moved deftly over each section of the restraints until Joran could pull Xiomara into an embrace. He trembled and clung to her; his entire body wracked with sobs as she whispered reassurances into his ear.

Chapter Thirty-Four

"I can't thank you enough," Xiomara said to Shelley as she packed Joran's few belongings into a dark blue duffel bag.

Joran was sitting on the hospital bed, his curls dull and in great need of thorough washing, as Shelley used a bit of cotton soaked with rubbing alcohol to dab away patches of adhesive left on Joran's arms. He turned his head away as he yawned, and Shelley sighed.

"No need to thank me," the young nurse said with a shake of her head. "I just wanted everything to turn out okay, and I'm so glad that it has." She appeared to study a rough patch on Joran's right bicep, wiping at it with the cotton. "Mr. Talbert improved so much once you came back, and especially when you started staying overnight. I know that cot isn't comfortable on the best day, especially not every night for three weeks."

Xiomara zipped the duffel bag shut and then smirked.

"My kinks have kinks," she admitted, "but we'll be fine from here. I've spent some time over the last few afternoons making arrangements." Her eyes met Joran's, and they smiled at each other before Xiomara turned to Shelley again. "I also had a meeting with the unit manager, Shelley. I needed to make sure that she knew how amazing you've been. Really, thank you."

Shelley blushed. "I'm glad to help. I just wish I could do more about the marks on these arms."

"They'll fade," Joran said with another yawn, examining the array of splotches on his limbs as Shelley moved away and tossed the cotton into a nearby trash can.

"I hope you'll be able to rest once you're out of here," Shelley commented.

"That's definitely the primary aim," Xiomara said, handing Joran a jacket.

"No nosy charge nurse and no cops," Shelley said with authority.

"They got what they needed," Xiomara said, hoisting the strap of the duffel bag onto one shoulder. "They won't be bothering you again... or us."

"Does that mean they found your friends?" Shelley asked Joran with a hopeful smile.

Xiomara watched as Joran paused for a moment before treating Shelley to a gentle smile.

"No," he said as he shook his head, "and the investigation is still open. But I'm sure it'll all work out."

"It's just so weird!" Shelley insisted. "How do two people just up and disappear like that? Were you on your way to see them when you got into that accident?"

"Shelley, you have been in here for almost an hour!" Bridget said from the doorway, accompanied by a young man in standard-issue hospital scrubs pushing a large wheelchair. "I'm sure that Mr. Talbert would love to be on his way and leave this place far behind him."

Shelley looked at Xiomara and crossed her eyes. Xiomara responded with a wink as the younger nurse smiled at Joran before leaving the room, followed by Bridget.

"I think that was probably the one time I was glad to see that woman," Joran commented to Xiomara in an undertone before glancing at the young man and the wheelchair. "Oh, no!"

"Oh, yes," Xiomara countered, smiling at the man. "Hospital policy, right?"

"Yes, ma'am," he replied with a smile. Xiomara turned to Joran, her expression leaving no room for argument.

"Hospital policy," she repeated with an arched brow.

"We're so glad to have you with us, Miss Grant."

An older woman greeted Xiomara and Joran as they entered the lobby of the hotel. Joran, sitting in a hotel-issued wheelchair, was leaning to one side with his eyes half-closed. He had fallen asleep on the way from the hospital, and Xiomara wanted nothing more than to tuck him into a soft, warm bed as soon as possible.

The woman greeting them wore a tailored black suit and a soft lilac blouse. Her blonde hair had been slicked back into a chignon, and oversized horn-rimmed glasses perched on the end of her upturned nose. The gold nametag she wore read: 'Lily T.' in black block letters.

"Thank you," Xiomara whispered, in part to keep from disturbing Joran. "Thank you for being able to accommodate us on such short notice."

"Not at all, we're happy to!" the woman beamed before extending a manicured hand. "I'm Ileana Tescadero—but please call me Lily. I'm one of the Hospitality Coordinators."

"I'm glad to meet you, Lily," Xiomara said, taking the proffered hand and giving it a shake.

"Everything's ready for you both," Lily assured Xiomara, her bright cornflower eyes taking in Joran's exhausted state before she looked at Xiomara again and nodded. "I have your key. Let's get you to the suite right away."

Lily smiled and turned away to walk through the lobby and toward the massive bank of elevators, Xiomara not too far behind along with Joran and the valet maneuvering the wheelchair.

"We want to make certain that you enjoy your time here," Lily said a short while later, standing outside the double doors marked "1520" in gold script lettering after they had arrived via private elevator. "I wanted to remind you, though: the kitchen is fully stocked with everything you've requested, but we haven't yet received your order for the selection of complimentary hors d'oeuvres or a schedule for the in-suite bartender. Please don't forget that these amenities are at your disposal—as is a deluxe breakfast for every morning of your stay. You also have open access to our Executive Lounge."

"Thank you, Lily," Xiomara said. "I don't think we'll be needing the bartender, but I trust you can come up with a wonderful mix of treats for tonight's hors d'oeuvres? I can manage the schedule for the rest."

"It would be my pleasure," Lily returned brightly. "I'll put an order in right away, and have it brought up within the hour."

Ileana "Lily" Tescadero handed Xiomara a keycard so heavy it felt made of brass, briefly inclined her head again in farewell, and returned to the private elevator with the smile never leaving her face. Xiomara watched until the doors closed and then turned back to face the valet and a now-sleeping Joran.

"Let's get him inside," Xiomara said.

Chapter Thirty-Five

She heard him.

Xiomara rushed from the bed, doing nothing to smooth her tousled, berry-black mane of hair as she moved across the suite to Joran's bedroom. She found him folded over the toilet in his private bathroom, being quite sick.

Brow furrowed, she went to the sink and ran a clean washcloth under the stream of warm water, wringing it out before approaching him. He groaned, leaning his forehead against the porcelain before closing his eyes and coughing. Draping the washcloth across the back of his neck, Xiomara rubbed Joran's back in a gentle, circular motion.

"Wasn't trying to wake you," he managed.

"Stop it," she chided, reaching over him to flush the toilet. "What's got you sick?"

"Nightmare," he sighed, sitting up and focusing a weary green gaze upon Xiomara.

The way he looked struck Xiomara. He'd lost weight during his time in the hospital, and though he performed well during regular visits from an inpatient physical therapist, it would be weeks before he was back to full strength.

Though the full extent of his injuries had never been visible to those treating him, the trauma of dying and being forced back among the living was harrowing. Xiomara knew that what he would need most was time.

"You had a nightmare?" she asked, willing the apprehension she felt to stay out of her tone.

"Or something like that," Joran said. "It was weird. Maybe it was more of a reenactment. It was the cabin all over again." He sighed. "You said you had nightmares, too, right?"

Xiomara nodded. "But I never knew that they were actually memories and not just bad dreams."

"Kushiel kept it from you," he commented. "The reasons and origin behind them..."

"He did," she said.

"Didn't you ever wonder if there was something more that he wasn't telling you?" Joran asked, taking the washcloth from his neck and using it to wipe his face and mouth.

"There wasn't ever a reason to question anything he said," Xiomara said honestly, though her jaw was tight. "I could remember nothing between being on my way to go visit my father and then waking up in the hospital." She got up from where she kneeled on the floor, moving back to the sink to study her reflection in the mirror above it. "When Kushiel came to see me the first time, I was ready to hear almost anything to explain what I could suddenly see."

"And ready to believe that a car accident was the reason you became a harbinger?"

She turned to him again, leaning her backside against the countertop.

"What's wrong, Joran? This isn't about a nightmare."

He paused, and she watched as emotion flitted across his gaunt yet handsome face.

"What are we?" he asked, his tone hushed. "Are we demons? Those things... the things that killed us... the things you command..."

"...are not exactly saintly," Xiomara finished, going back over to where Joran sat and again taking the spot beside him. "But we're not demons, Joran. We're not angels, either."

"So, you punish people that go against... who?"

"I don't punish people, Joran," she sighed, shaking her head. "I am just a facilitator of certain consequences. The choice is always theirs."

"Like the little girl in the park that you told me about," he said, yawning. Xiomara nodded. "And when it's time to find her... when she reaches the age that she was in your vision... you'll see what choice she ended up making?"

She paused before answering, measuring her words.

"If she chooses a certain path... her name will be placed among others for those seeking an assignment," she said. "If I am the one chosen to find her again, I'll become a part of her life, and pray that my vision all those years ago was wrong and that I can make a difference."

"Are your visions ever wrong? Is the choice ever different?"

Xiomara heard Joran's heavy sigh after she averted her eyes and did not respond. The room was silent, except for the humming of the bathroom's air filtration system.

"There's so much that I don't know," he said after a long pause. She tilted her head and continued to wait, her stomach knotting up at the sight of the building moisture in his eyes. "I feel like I'm waiting for something... and jumping at every little thing. When the server comes to deliver meals, I wonder if this is when I'll see something... see the path. Will I run into someone here at the hotel that I'll eventually have to hunt down in ten years?"

"You can't think like that," Xiomara cautioned. "You can't let thoughts like that cloud your judgement."

"It's got to be so hard, though," he said. "I mean, are we doomed as a people?"

"Joran..."

"You can't even look me in the eye and tell me that when the time comes, when it's Zero Hour, someone makes the choice that will save their soul. Don't you tire of the same result, time after time?"

"Stop," she said, placing a hand on his shoulder. "There's nothing to be gained by this, Joran. You don't need to worry right now. You need rest. We've been lucky enough to not be bothered here at the hotel by anyone trying to find you. This is the best chance for you to recover, and then we can move on."

"Will you help me?" Joran asked, sniffling. Xiomara watched as he drew the washcloth across drowsy and reddening eyes.

"Of course," she assured him, getting up again. "Ready to head back to bed?"

Joran got to his feet and then looked down at her.

"I don't mean that," he said, wiping his face again. "I mean help me with this... this life... this new world that I'm now a part of. Will you help me, Xiomara?"

She paused, shifting her weight from one foot to the other.

"Kushiel," she began, "I... I'm sure that he'll..."

"I don't want Kushiel!" he said, tossing the cloth onto the vanity. "He didn't exactly do too well by you, did he? You think I want to trust my care to HIM? I don't even know what I'll do when I see him, after the way he's lied and kept things from you for all this time! But I trust you!"

"Joran," Xiomara said, looking up at him, "it hasn't even been twelve hours since they released you from the hospital. You're trying to take on too much, too soon, and you're already sick over it. I need you to calm down, and let's get you back into bed."

"We couldn't talk about this at the hospital! We couldn't risk being overheard, and my mind won't stop now that we're alone."

"We'll talk," she promised. "But, there's time."

"I need a drink," Joran said.

"No, you don't," she said quickly. "You do, however, need something to settle your stomach and maybe help you rest."

"I keep thinking I'll wake up and find you gone," Joran blurted. Xiomara took a step back, stunned. He gazed at her and then shrugged as he sniffled again. "How can I rest? I'm just waiting... to see when the other shoe drops."

He turned away from her then, making his unsteady way from the bathroom and back to the adjoining bedroom. Xiomara walked over to the vanity, absently turning the water on in the basin to rinse the washcloth that Joran had discarded. Wringing it out, she draped it over the nearby towel rack, turning the bathroom light off as she exited.

She stood there for a moment, her eyes adjusting to the darkness and focusing on his still form on the bed. He had pulled the blankets over his head, and the knots returned to her stomach when she heard a periodic sniffle coming from beneath the bedclothes. She stood rigid, fighting the desire to go to him and give him the reassurance that he needed more than anything.

Wringing her hands together, Xiomara approached the bed. She then froze, wrapping her arms around her midsection before turning on her heels toward the door and taking a few hesitant steps. She then straightened, dropped her arms, and continued walking.

"Good night, Xiomara," came Joran's tired voice from the bed.

She turned back. He had partially emerged and was watching her.

"Good night, Joran," she returned. "I'll see you in the morning."

He nodded, turning his back to her as he settled beneath the covers again.

Xiomara left the room and closed the door behind her with a soft click.

Chapter Thirty-Six

Xiomara awoke with a sighing groan, slowly turning over onto her back as her eyes opened. She blinked the room into focus, concentrating on the intricate weaving of diamond shapes overhead on the ceiling before rubbing her eyes.

Turning to the left, she made a note of the time displayed on the brightly lit digital clock, and it surprised her to see that for the first time in years she had slept past eight o'clock in the morning.

Xiomara sat up, pushing a curtain of hair from her face with a puzzled expression. The unspoken question was answered when an elasticized bundle of burgundy fabric fell from her heavy tangle of hair and into her lap. She chuckled, running both hands through her hair as she pulled it back into a ponytail and returned the burgundy scrunchie to its place.

A short while later, Xiomara emerged through a cloud of steam from the adjoining bathroom, running a brush through her long hair as she padded past the ornate, oval-shaped brass mirror toward the window. She opened the curtains, peering out into the grayness of the day as the brush whispered through her wet locks.

She noted her reflection in the window: the soft pink T-shirt she wore with lacy white ruffles at the hem, and the pink cotton shorts dotted with small, embroidered strawberries. Her eyes were no longer rimmed with red, and the darkness beneath them had faded days ago. She could not remember the last time she'd had so many consecutive nights of sound sleep.

Xiomara moved out of the bedroom and through the spacious suite, placing the hairbrush atop an accent table and approaching the other bedroom. She pressed an ear against the closed door, and hearing nothing, quietly let herself in. The bedroom curtains were drawn, shielding the room from any semblance of light except for the illuminated face of the bedside clock and the stream of light trickling in through the open door.

Curled up on his side, his lanky body almost arched into a crescent shape, lay Joran. Xiomara noticed he had kicked the bedclothes to the floor and was fully clothed yet wearing one sock. But she did not want to risk disturbing his sleep by lingering for too long.

Closing the door with a soft click, she retreated to the living room and walked over to the sofa, in front of which sat a brass-legged, glass-topped, oval-shaped coffee table with a wireless keyboard and mouse on top of it. The 52-inch flat-screen television, mounted high upon the wall across from where she sat, blinked to life at the touch of a button on the remote control sitting beside her on the sofa.

Xiomara pressed another button, lowering the volume so as not to make too much noise. A somber-looking, middle-aged television news reporter appearing on-screen greeted her beside—of all things—a photo of a smiling Diana dressed in her chef's jacket and posing with a whisk in her right hand.

"What in cat spit hell is this?" Xiomara muttered, increasing the volume again enough so that she could hear what was being said.

"The shocking and sudden disappearance of local chef Diana Watley-Sinclair has producers of the online show, 'Bootleg Chef,' scrambling to pick through dozens of hours of taped footage from the still-ongoing competition to give the culinary nonentity more exposure while hoping to create buzz."

"Nonentity," Xiomara sighed. "Not quite what you were shooting for, was it, Diana?"

"Her downtown eatery, La Bonne Vie, has seen quite a boon in business as of late because of the mystery surrounding her absence." The station switched the picture of Diana to one of a smiling Gabriel, who was holding an engraved plaque in his hands. "This would interest the owner of the building housing the restaurant, Gabriel Q. Matheson, except he has also vanished. David Sinclair, husband of Diana, issued this cryptic statement..."

The picture shifted once more to a video of an attractive man who looked in his early forties, with closely cropped dark red hair and very direct green eyes.

"This is just like her, you know," David said through a tightened jaw, his face flushed. "She's wanted for years to be so much bigger than what she was. She refused to allow herself to be content with the limits of her abilities. I may not know where she is right now, but I would say it's pretty obvious who she's with, and this time she's gone too far. This isn't a coincidence, not by any means."

"You do not know how right you are," Xiomara said, as the camera switched back to the news anchor.

"Sources tell us that contracts reflecting the merger between Matheson Media and EJB Advertising have been signed but not yet formally filed. With the disappearance of Gabriel Matheson, however, circumstances could now end up differently." Xiomara's gaze softened as Edmund Blake appeared on-screen, looking thinner than when she last saw him, though his face was still kind.

"This is definitely an unexpected event," Blake was saying. "I've returned early from a trip out of the country because I'm committed to making sure that both Matheson Media and EJB Advertising remain strong so that, in the event of Gabriel's return, he can once again assume the helm."

"Will you be trying to take your company back now, Mr. Blake?" an offscreen reporter asked.

Blake shook his head. "It's much too soon to even think about anything like that, and it might never be necessary. But, as my people at EJB were always cared for while under my wing, those at Matheson will be, too. I've been working closely with Gabriel's assistant, Ruby Cunningham. She was an integral part of assisting with the merger and she'll continue to be of great help as we go through this trial."

Xiomara's smile was wistful as she changed the channel, this time to display the hotel directory. Though she felt a bit of sadness that Edmund Blake would no longer remember her, she was glad that Ruby was finally getting her due. Xiomara knew Ruby would be fine with Blake's tutelage.

Putting the remote control down, she retrieved the wireless keyboard and entered some information. Smiling as the room service menu appeared on-screen, she typed.

"How much longer am I going to feel like this?" Joran asked a short time later as they sat across from each other in the suite's cozy breakfast nook, indulging in the morning selection. "I'm so tired all the time."

Though some of his color had returned, his eyes still seemed a bit too large for his face, and there were blemishes beneath them. He slept through the night, but he still looked exhausted.

"Hard to say," Xiomara told him, reaching into the breadbasket to place a plump blueberry muffin beside the scrambled eggs, sliced tomatoes, and potatoes already heaped onto his plate. "I imagine it's different for everyone. I was in the hospital for over two months, and I spent most of that in a coma. Even once I got out, I still didn't feel like myself for ages. My behavior certainly didn't help, though."

"What do you mean?" Joran asked, also reaching into the breadbasket to grab a large croissant, which he placed on Xiomara's plate beside a modest serving of Eggs Florentine and two slices of ham. He then took up his cup of black coffee and sipped it.

Xiomara smirked and grabbed the croissant, smearing it with soft butter. "Alcohol," she said simply.

Joran blinked at her. "What?"

"I was a drunk," she said, taking one bite of the pastry before putting it back onto her plate. "Mind-numbingly, excessively, arrested-for-unlawful-entry-after-falling-asleep-in-someone-else's-apartment drunk."

"But, there was always wine served at Diana's dinners," he said.

"Yes," Xiomara replied with a smirk.

He frowned in remembrance and then sighed. "You never touched yours. You touched none of the alcoholic drinks offered."

"No."

"And you turned down the in-suite bartender," he mentioned. "Plus, the whiskey that I brought over that night."

"Yes," Xiomara said again.

"But, you said nothing."

"No," she replied.

"What about Gabriel?"

"What about him?"

"Did he know?" Joran asked.

"No," Xiomara snickered, reaching for her mug of hot tea.

"About Gabriel..." Joran began with hesitation, swallowing hard. Xiomara looked at him, blowing at the steam wafting from her mug. "He kissed you that night, the night of the funeral."

Xiomara placed the mug on the table with a sigh. "He did," she responded.

"Couldn't you... couldn't you have saved him, like you did me?"

"What do you mean?" she asked with a slight frown.

"I mean that I'm still here... and he isn't."

"Joran, your situation differs from his. He made a choice."

"Yeah, he did," Joran agreed. "But, that choice was you."

Xiomara blinked and then folded her arms across her chest, sitting back in her chair.

"I don't understand, Joran," she admitted.

"He obviously felt something for you," he said, his face flushed. "We've talked about it. Did you ever consider maybe influencing him against what he was doing?"

"I tried. I told Gabriel that he needed to think about the way he handled business and how he was living his life."

"I don't mean that," Joran said with a shake of his head. "Did you ever think of talking to him as the person he'd developed feelings for, and using that to keep him from what ended up happening?"

"No, Joran," Xiomara said. "That would have been taking advantage, and that's not how free will works. Besides, to what end? That would have set up an expectation that I wasn't prepared to fulfill. It wasn't Gabriel that I cared about."

Xiomara turned back to her mug and picked it up again, warming her hands against the sides as she took a sip. She could feel Joran still watching her, and she felt her face grow warm as well, though she knew it had nothing at all to do with the cup she was holding. She tilted her head forward so that her hair would shift and cover parts of her face, and she was thankful that none of the strands landed in her tea.

"I swear that I'll tie all that hair up into knots if you don't stop using it to hide from me," Joran said, not entirely joking. Xiomara looked up, startled, as he pointed a finger at her. "You care for me? You were going to leave me at that hospital and never come back, and because of it, I spent our first week here scared to death I'd wake up to find you gone again."

"Probably because it's what I do, Joran," Xiomara admitted with a shrug. "I show up, I fit in, I make my assessment so that I can collect what I came for, and then I leave."

"But?"

"But," she repeated, "when I came to see you at the hospital the first time, I negated whatever was supposed to make you forget, according to what I figured out after talking with Gianni. I couldn't leave after that. It wouldn't have been right."

"I don't think that's it," Joran revealed, putting his cup down and focusing on her. "I don't think that's right."

"You don't think that's why I came back?" Xiomara said, puzzled.

"I don't think that I would have ever forgotten about you," he said, leaning across the table to take the mug from her hands before setting it beside his. "I understand your nightmares better now, and why you kept seeing Gianni's face. But, the same thing would have happened to me even if you never came back to the hospital that day. Plus, I don't believe that's the sole reason you came back for me." Xiomara felt her face grow warm again, and she averted her eyes. "Why do you always do that?"

"I don't know what you mean," she lied, keeping her gaze locked on the view outside the nearby window.

"You keep trying to avoid talking about this," he said, "and I'm tired of dancing around it. I saw you. I remember the look on your face in the hospital that day. I know what I felt when you held me. I dream about the things you said to me when you finally let your guard down.

"The first night we were here, and you found me in the bathroom puking up my guts because of that nightmare, you stayed with me. Even though you left at first, you came back to my room. You sat with me all night, and you didn't move once. You thought I'd fallen asleep, but I knew.

"Each time I woke up feeling afraid and thought I was alone, you were still there, and you comforted me. But, it seems like ever since then you're trying to pretend like none of those things happened, and that's what had me so freaked out because I know I didn't imagine any of it."

"No, I guess you didn't," she said, looking at him again.

"So, what changed? Is it because you've had more time to think about Gianni and what you had with him?"

"I never 'had' anything with Gianni. I was an infatuated kid, living off a distorted memory disguised as dreams. As angry as I was when the memories first came flooding back, I realized rather quickly that he was right to leave."

"And you were right to stay, Xiomara," Joran replied, shifting his chair around the table until he was sitting beside her. "And you don't have to downplay your history with him. I'm a big boy."

"Joran," Xiomara said, holding up one hand to keep him from advancing further, "Gianni has nothing to do with any of this."

"Then what is it?" he insisted. "Why do you keep throwing up roadblocks? We seem to get so far, and then you back away from me."

"I've told you how I live... the existence I've had for over ten years now. It's difficult and can affect the way you think and feel about things. I've had to meet people, settle into their lives, gain their trust, and ultimately aid in their destruction..."

"I know that!" Joran exclaimed. "You've told me that! Tell me something that I haven't already heard."

"Like what?" Xiomara asked.

"Is there anyone else?" Joran asked. "Anyone else like me, I mean?"

Xiomara's brow furrowed. "Of course," she said. "We've talked about that before. We're all over the world..."

"No," Joran said, shaking his head. "I don't mean that. I mean, is there anyone else like me for you?"

Xiomara blinked. "Wait a minute. Are you trying to ask me, if things were different, whether there'd be a you and I?"

"No," he said again. "I'm asking if there's a you and I now."

Xiomara knew he was studying the rapid succession of emotions dancing across her face. She could hear her heart pounding, accompanied by the sound of the nearby clock ticking away each second it took for her brain to sift through myriad emotions, grasping for words that could even describe the conflict she had been feeling for weeks. She finally locked eyes with him and shrugged, shaking her head as she lowered her hand.

"Joran," she said, unable to contain the tremor in her voice, "what do you want to hear? I hated leaving you at that hospital, but at the time, I thought it was for the best. I heard you call out for me. I felt your pain because it was also my own, yet I thought that you'd be better off without me and that all you needed was to forget that I ever existed.

"Even when I saw Gianni, and I remembered I loved him a long time ago, I still couldn't think of anything but the fact that I needed to get back to you. I didn't think about what could happen after that, or what it meant. All I knew was that there was nothing more important to me at that moment.

"I came back for you, Joran. I came back more than once, and I know you've been scared, but I have not left you. I can't tell you anything that means more than that."

He smiled at her then, taking her hand. She studied how small it looked when compared with his. Small, but safe.

"You just did," he revealed with a soft chuckle as he, too, looked at their hands, "and I'm sorry, Xiomara. This isn't easy for me, either, and I don't mean to make you try to prove anything to me." He frowned a bit, focusing on her neat manicure. "Gabriel talked about you all the time before the night I met you at Diana's, but I was still unprepared—for that meeting and everything that followed.

"I wasn't ready for how the first glimpse of you would make me feel... how easy it would be to talk with you... how your smile and laugh would eventually set the tone for my day... and I tried not to care for you because I knew Gabriel had plans of his own.

"I had never seen him as adamant or as determined about anyone the way he was with you," Joran continued, his green eyes narrowing as he looked at Xiomara. "It wasn't just that you didn't dote on him as so many others seemed to. It was almost as if the challenge was deeper. Maybe it was the opinion you shared the night Diana brought up wanting his help with that cooking show. Something about you set him off, maybe on a spiritual level, and he needed to win to prove that his way was better."

"I don't think he knew what it was," Xiomara said with a shake of her head before looking closely at Joran. "And, I'm sorry that you felt caught in the middle."

"Any amount of time with you was better than the thought of none," he admitted, studying their hands again. "The night you called when you had that nightmare... was the happiest night of my life in a long time. That's why I came over. I didn't want to let that feeling go, or have it written off by you as a mistake. I needed you to want me there as much as I needed to be there.

"And on the nights leading up to when Gabriel wanted all of us to get together, I was terrified. I thought... maybe I could lose you to him and to what he would have offered you. All I could do was pray that you'd be stronger than that. Yet, I couldn't tell you about that fear. Didn't feel I had a right to."

"Joran..."

"I want to know you, Xiomara," he continued. "I want to know Khinayda Hastings."

"I've told you some things about me," Xiomara said. "It's not a cheerful story, Joran."

"But, it's yours," he said, "and that makes it important to me. You know everything about me, Xiomara. I've shared more with you than I have with anyone—ever—and that includes both Gabriel and my ex-wife."

"I don't even know where to start," she laughed, all thoughts of food pushed from her mind.

"Wherever is most comfortable," Joran said, sitting back in his chair, though he held onto her hand.

"Comfortable," she repeated with a sigh before focusing on him. "No, that would be too easy, and... not entirely fair, since there are some things you should know. And... I promised that day at the hospital to tell you everything."

Joran shifted in his chair, staring at her.

"All right, Xiomara," he said at last.

"I've been doing this for about twelve years," she began. "I didn't go into it right away. I've told you about the issues I had with adjusting... and once I did, I wanted time to tie up some loose ends in my old life and try to figure out a plan for my future."

She got up, releasing his hand as she walked around the table, wringing her hands together. She felt Joran's eyes following her, and his concern comforted yet made her anxious at the same time.

"There was a lot to do," she continued. "I initially left Daddy's business dealings in the hands of the board of directors until we could sell things off, and my interests were more personal. Daddy kept the house I grew up in. He hadn't lived there in a while... he couldn't without Mama... but he made sure that it was cleaned regularly, and they tended the gardens. He wanted it to be ready for whenever I came home.

"So, the first thing I did was have he and Mama taken out of that awful mausoleum they were buried in and placed together beneath an enormous magnolia tree on the property. Mama loved that tree... so much. When I was little, and the weather was nice, we'd sit underneath it. She'd read to me or sing... we'd have picnics and she'd braid the magnolia blossoms into my hair."

She stopped walking, her eyes filling with tears as the warm memories flooded through her. Then she chuckled, turned to Joran, and took a deep breath.

"The second thing I did was purchase the cabin I died in."

Chapter Thirty-Seven

Joran stared at Xiomara, and neither spoke for a long moment. He got up, ran a hand through his hair, and then scratched at the scruff on his cheeks and neck.

"You offered a cabin for Gabriel to use," he said.

"Yes," she answered.

"It's the same place?"

"Yes," she said again.

"Where I also died!?" he demanded.

She nodded. "Yes, Joran."

"Why?" he asked. "Why there?"

"I felt drawn to it, Joran," she explained. "I didn't remember that I died there, and even though I never paid it much attention on the occasions I'd been there before, something about that place made it hard to let go.

"An investigator got around to contacting me months after everything happened, and the timing couldn't have been better. He was hired by Rebecca's aunt, Sylvia, after they realized that Josie, Stephen, and Rebecca had disappeared and weren't on some wild binge, but the police had already closed the case."

"Just like now," Joran surmised.

"Now and every other time before with these specific circumstances," Xiomara confirmed. "They were three adults that knew each other. To the cops, it seemed less like foul play and more that they didn't want to be found and would probably end up coming back on their own."

"Like Gabriel and Diana."

"Yes," she said. "I found out that Rebecca's aunt was debating selling the cabin and the surrounding property. She knew that Rebecca always used that place for parties, and it was too much for her to deal with when she realized Rebecca wasn't coming back."

"Because they killed her in that cabin," he interjected.

"Sylvia didn't know that," Xiomara reminded him. "All she knew was that Rebecca disappeared. The investigator gave me Sylvia's contact information in case I ever heard from Rebecca, and when I sent an offer to buy the lot, she was glad to be rid of it. She even offered to sell it cheaply, but I wouldn't allow that. I think she hoped I would preserve it in the eventuality that Rebecca returned."

"Why did you offer the cabin to Gabriel?"

"He was planning to have the ritual at his usual place," she said. "I didn't know where that place was, but I couldn't allow it. I knew what was coming for him and had to get him to a place far from other people—innocent people. The cabin wasn't that far outside of the city, and I already knew that no one lived close enough to it to happen by at the wrong time."

"Diana," Joran whispered.

"I tried talking her out of it!" Xiomara insisted. "She wouldn't listen. She thought I was planning a double cross and wanted her away from Gabriel. As much as I was trying to get her not to go, he was obviously filling her head with promises of what she could gain if she did."

His face reddened, and he stared at her.

"Do you think that he would have hurt you had you shown up when he wanted?"

Xiomara couldn't help shuddering as she shook her head.

"No, Joran," she said. "He was very adamant about arranging the times for us to get there. He specifically wanted Diana there early, and she was more than happy to oblige. I was to come much later, and they did not expect you at all."

"That makes little sense, though. He had to know that you'd notice Diana wasn't there. What was he going to do, lie and say she never showed up?"

"That's probably it exactly. He didn't know that she and I talked outside those dinners, or that she was texting me.

"She had already messaged me to say he'd been checking on her to make sure she was on the way... but then I received a message from him a short while after she told me she'd arrived, saying he was planning to make sure she was still coming."

"So, he meant to take care of her and destroy the evidence before you got there."

"There was a shovel near the front porch," Xiomara revealed. "At first, I didn't understand why it was there or where it came from." She paused and took another breath. "I also found something else later, after... well, after you were taken. Gabriel left a bag in one bedroom. There was a debris tarp inside of it—a big one."

"What the hell would he need with a..." Joran began with a grimace, trailing off. She watched as understanding dawned and he gasped. "To wrap her body in?" he said, aghast.

"Couldn't have been anything else," Xiomara answered. "And she was in an Uber he'd ordered for her, so that she wouldn't drive her own car."

"He thought of everything," he mused.

"Almost."

"Why would he do it, though? What could he hope to gain by killing Diana? She adored him. She would have done anything for him..." He then stared at Xiomara. "The comment you made at dinner that night... about one day offering the heart of the one that loved you the most."

She nodded. "Gabriel had a painting in his apartment of a young woman that seemed to have done the same thing. It must have been his plan the entire time."

"If only she'd been paying closer attention to what you were trying to warn her about." He sat down again, and Xiomara joined him. "And, the way you found them... he certainly covered all his bases. Diana's love... the sex..."

"He wanted to put a mark on the world unlike anything ever seen," she commented. "I'm sure he thought this would help him reach that goal. He hadn't gotten around to removing her heart before he was taken."

"You should have left them there," Joran said through clenched teeth. "You should have let everyone see what he was. Getting rid of everything makes it feel like he still won somehow."

"And, then what?" she asked. "It would turn into a circus—one you're tied to. It would be attached to you wherever you go."

"I had nothing to do with it!"

"You think that would matter? You already have a following, Joran. This would increase it in ways you do not need and probably aren't prepared for. A mysterious disappearance is easier to sweep under the rug than ritualistic murder."

Joran looked over at Xiomara, reaching out to brush the hair from her shoulder before tracing her right brow with a fingertip.

"I'm sorry," he said. "I know this wasn't easy for you. You had to somehow get me out of that place so that I could be found and taken to a hospital. None of how you've lived for the last fourteen years could have been easy. I hope to have half your resilience."

"You don't have to," Xiomara said.

He lowered his hand, his eyes narrowing.

"Don't start that," he warned, getting up and walking to the kitchen.

Xiomara sighed, listening to the sound of the refrigerator door being yanked open, followed by clattering and the sound of the door being slammed shut. Joran then returned, a cold bottle of water in each hand, one of which he handed to her. She cradled it in her lap, watching as he wrenched his bottle open and drank half the contents in a few swallows. Lowering the bottle, he shook his head.

"I thought we were making progress just now," he commented without looking at her. "I thought we were past the point of you trying to get rid of me."

"I wasn't," she countered.

"You were about to say that I don't have to do this, and that I can choose differently."

"You don't... and you can."

"Xiomara, don't do that!" he exploded, staring down at where she sat in the chair. "I'm not playing these word games with you. You will not talk to me in circles or ever get me to agree to walk away from you."

"Not from me," she interjected.

"To walk away from this new life would be to walk away from you, unless you decided you were walking away, too," he insisted. "Look, I will not pretend that there wasn't anyone else in your life from the time Gianni left you until we met. But, you're here now—with me. I want to stay—with you. You are strong, Xiomara, and you have strengthened me these last few weeks. We can be strong together."

She studied him, taking in the rounded green eyes, the tangle of curls, the charcoal gray T-shirt hanging from his lanky frame, and the baggy black cargo shorts. As she looked him over, the thought crept into her mind that she might consider asking him to keep the scruff.

She got up from the chair before placing the bottle of water atop the table as she approached him. He looked down at her, and she could hear the rapid thudding of his heart as he waited.

She smiled.

"Okay," she said, resting her head against his chest.

His embrace lifted Xiomara off the floor with ease. She nuzzled her face against the roughness of his neck, indulging in the feel and smell of him as the weight on her heart finally lifted.

Chapter Thirty-Eight

Xiomara awoke with a start, drenched in sweat. With a trembling hand on her chest, she willed her heart to steady itself as she took deep breaths and wiped the dampness from her forehead. Her eyes burned, and she knew from the wetness on her cheeks that she had been crying.

A quick glance toward the window gave her a hint of the time, confirmed by the bedside clock. It was a few minutes past one in the morning. She had been asleep for less than an hour and had the worst nightmare she had ever experienced.

Untangling herself from the twisted sheets, Xiomara swung her legs over the side of the bed as her breathing settled. The knot in her stomach hadn't, and she fought a wave of nausea.

Nightmares were not new to Xiomara by any means. The repeated images of being torn apart by hell hounds—some of which were now at her disposal—had plagued her occasionally for years, well before she understood why. The latest one, however, was more troubling than anything she had experienced. In it, she watched as those hounds hunted and disemboweled Joran, while a grinning Gabriel pinned her to the floor, forcing her to watch.

Xiomara shuddered and got up from the bed, entering the adjoining bathroom and reaching into the shower to turn the water on. After adjusting the temperature to her liking, she stripped away her wet clothes and stepped into the steady stream of very warm water.

Twenty minutes later, she emerged wrapped in an oversized white towel and with her hair oiled and pulled back into two thick braids hanging past her shoulders. She walked through the room toward the bureau and then paused. Tilting her head, she realized she could hear music.

Though the wonderfully comfortable hotel suite had an intricate sound system, it had gone unused since she and Joran checked in, and what she heard was not coming from the sound system.

Joran was playing the cello.

Xiomara could not resist a smile, as it was the first time she'd heard him play since the funeral of Lavinia Blake. Though Joran's life was forever altered since then, she hoped it was a sign that he would be okay.

He was still playing when she came out of her bedroom a short time later, dressed in a red Chicago Blackhawks nightshirt and matching socks. He smiled upon seeing her, but finished the melodic piece, his large hands moving along the strings as he commanded the bow. When he finished, Xiomara clapped.

"You're filled with surprises," she told him. "Thank you. That was beautiful."

"I didn't know what else to do," Joran said softly, leaning the cello against one knee as he rested the bow across his lap.

"What do you mean?" Xiomara asked, her smile fading.

"Sometimes, when I can't sleep, I'll come out here to sit," he explained, his face flaming up to his hairline. "I guess I got used to it from those first nights here when I was having trouble sleeping and you were always nearby."

Xiomara glanced over at the sofa, which was against the wall shared by her bedroom. She looked at him and understood.

"You heard me have the nightmare," she said.

"Is that what it was?" he blurted. "You were crying and talking... and I couldn't be sure because I couldn't make out what you were saying."

"Yeah, that's what it was," she admitted, moving over to the sofa to take a seat.

"I didn't know if I could come in... I couldn't think of what to do... So, I thought that maybe if I sat outside your room and played something for you... maybe... maybe you could go back to sleep. I honestly wasn't trying to disturb you."

With her hair pulled back and away from her face, Xiomara was neither able to hide the look on her face in response to Joran's words, nor the tears building in her eyes because of them. When she turned away, she could hear Joran shifting in the chair.

Then he was there; large and lanky, smelling of soap and fabric softener, with bright green eyes full of concern. The tension in his body was palpable, and she knew he wanted to hold her. Doing what she could to put him at ease, she leaned her still-damp head against his arm, hearing him exhale as he wrapped his arms around her.

"Stop trying to do everything on your own," Joran murmured in her ear as he rubbed her back. "You can talk to me. Haven't we been doing okay by talking to each other?"

"Yes," Xiomara said, sniffling.

"Was it the nightmare from your life before? I thought those had stopped."

Not wanting to think about the sounds of Joran's screams and the gleeful chitters from the hounds, Xiomara buried her face in Joran's chest and quickly shook her head as fresh tears burned behind her lids. In response, his arms tightened around her.

"Okay, okay," he assured her in a whisper. "You don't have to. I'll change the subject." Xiomara's reply was a nod and another sniffle. "How about I teach you some of the finer basics of cello playing?"

She looked up at him, brows raised. She figured she must look a fright from doing all she could to stifle her tears. But Joran seemed to take no notice as he smiled down at her and wiped away the errant wetness caught in her long lashes.

"What?" she asked, watching as Joran got up and returned to the chair, cello, and bow. He stood beside the former and held the latter as he smiled at her.

"Come and sit," he said.

"Why?"

Joran laughed. "How else can I show you?"

Xiomara got to her feet, smoothed down the hem of her nightshirt.

"There are certain types of movies with a scene that begins very much like this," she said casually, laughing as Joran's face reddened again. Not wanting to prolong his discomfort, she walked over and took a seat. Balancing the cello upright, he got to his knees beside her and affectionately tugged at a braid with the hand holding the bow.

"I'll teach you how to play 'sidesaddle' to ease any concerns," he offered with a smirk.

Xiomara considered this. Finally, she smiled and slid the bow from his hand, her eyes not leaving his.

"Spoilsport," she countered.

Chapter Thirty-Nine

Xiomara crept from the bed, pulling one of Joran's blue T-shirts from the bundle of clothing on the floor. She moved through the room, pulling it overhead as she walked to the door before exiting. Crossing the living room with a yawn, she entered her own room across the way and closed the door behind her.

A short while later, she emerged, bathed and clad in a light blue cotton tank top and matching pinstriped pajama bottoms. Rather than returning to the room to rouse Joran, she walked toward the double doors leading to the balcony.

Xiomara stepped outside, inhaling the crisp December air, paying no attention to how inadequately dressed she was for the elements. The air felt wonderful against her skin, though, and she enjoyed the breeze that played with her damp hair. Closing her eyes, she drew in a deep breath and could not resist a smile.

"You're going to catch a deathly cold, young lady," chided a singsong voice to her left. Xiomara sighed and opened her eyes again, casting a wary glance in the interloper's direction.

At five-foot ten, he was the same height as Xiomara, aided by the ridiculous four-inch platform heels of his black alligator boots, to which silver spurs were attached. His dark red jeans were snug, but his long-sleeved black shirt was loose and rippled in the breeze, twisting the hem around his slender hips.

An unlit cigarette dangled from the corner of his smiling, generous mouth, and the chilled environment had infused his cappuccino-hued skin with a rosy tint. Running his long fingers through silver-tipped, spiked black hair, he peered at Xiomara through a pair of antique black pince-nez.

"Kushiel," Xiomara greeted in a monotone, rolling her eyes.

"Khinayda," he returned with a titter. She looked at where he sat, balanced upon the ledge of the balcony with his back to what would be a drop of about 150 feet. "You're looking a tidbit nipply this morning."

Xiomara crossed her arms in front of her chest, glaring at the still-smiling visitor. "What do you want?" she demanded.

Kushiel removed the pince-nez, polishing them upon the hem of his shirt. When he looked up at Xiomara, she did not flinch—long used to the pure whiteness of his eyes.

"How's he doing?" Kushiel asked, jerking his head in the suite's direction.

"He's finally sleeping at night," Xiomara answered.

"Alone?" he queried, though the smile had not left his face. Xiomara glared at him.

He sniggered, replacing the eyewear. "You're such a heartbreaker, Khinayda Hastings."

"Xiomara Grant," she said acidly.

"Not to me," Kushiel shrugged, hopping from the edge and landing on the balcony with a light bounce. He stood beside Xiomara, looking out at the skyline. "You're being introspective again, I can tell."

"Can't help it," Xiomara said.

"You do this at the end of every assignment," Kushiel mentioned. "Doesn't it ever get old?"

She glanced over at him. "Does it ever for you?"

"Time isn't the same creature for me as for you," he replied. "I was never human. I've always been an objective observer."

"Objective!" Xiomara snorted. "You?"

"Yes, me!" Kushiel squealed. "I've watched this world for many, many years, and I've always seen it for what it is and not what I hoped it would be."

"No rose-colored pince-nez for you, then?"

Kushiel grinned at her.

"I've always liked you, Hastings," he revealed. "You're one of very few able to keep up with me."

"I'm unsure of whether that's a compliment," Xiomara mused.

"Of course, it is!" Kushiel responded. "I'm fabulous! You should be so lucky."

"Objectively speaking, of course," she countered, widening his impossible grin.

"Cheeky," he praised. "That's another reason I like you. Snap out of it, though. This isn't the time to get mucked down by thoughts of what could have been." He considered her. "Go ahead. You won't feel right until you say it."

"Sometimes I wonder why we have to do this," Xiomara murmured.

"And there it is," Kushiel chuckled. "The answer hasn't changed in the dozen years since you've asked, you know. It won't change after another dozen."

"I could have more influence," she mused.

"That train of thought is destined for derailment, Khinayda Hastings. The moment you think you can assume dominion over Man is when you lean too far toward the other side."

"I'm not trying to do that!" Xiomara insisted.

"It's a slippery slope," Kushiel said. "Sure, you might start out with the best of intentions, but then what? What if your charge rebukes your influence? You push a little harder, all in the name of guidance... and then turn out no better than our competitor."

"Competitor," Xiomara snorted again. "Some game we're playing."

"The biggest game there is!" Kushiel said, the grin returning to his handsome face.

"Why are we still playing it?"

"He's got you questioning your work now?"

"This isn't about Joran," Xiomara stressed. "It's not the first time I've asked the question."

"Yes, but I thought I'd broken you of the habit!" Kushiel said. "Now, look!" He peered out at the skyline again. "I'll tell you why we play this game, and the reason is the same no matter which side of the field you favor.

"Collusion is sweet... but Conversion is SO much more delicious. Take your average unhappily married man... with a wife of twenty years who has not truly satisfied him for at least eighteen. So, he takes a lover—not necessarily younger, but more willing—and he can indulge in her in ways dear wifey routinely rebelled against.

"As sweet as the lover is... as complicit as she is... as much as he enjoys every aspect of her in the two or three years they have together... and as much as he might actually come to truly love her… nothing she does for him can ever compare to that moment when the wife—with her position threatened by what's become much more than a casual dalliance—finally succumbs to his whims. Conversion is like the Holy Grail."

Kushiel turned to look at Xiomara.

"We do this for the chance to save that one soul that would have been lost to us otherwise," he continued. "I would raze ten thousand eager co-conspirators for that."

"Not very saint-like," Xiomara commented.

"I was never a saint," Kushiel returned, tittering as he licked the tip of his pinky and then smoothed his right eyebrow with it. Xiomara watched him; taking in the almost exaggerated bravado, flamboyance, and aura of confidence that he always displayed, and then smirked.

"Unhappily married man?" she queried.

"Mind your business," he chided, returning the smirk.

"As you like," she said in her lazy drawl, turning back once more to enjoy the view.

"Heading back to the office soon for your next assignment?" Kushiel asked after a moment.

Xiomara's thoughts settled upon Gianni and running into him that day.

"No," she said, choosing to keep her reasoning private. "I'm thinking of taking Joran west. I can always get work from the office out there."

"He's not there anymore," Kushiel told her. Xiomara remained focused on the view ahead of her, rather than turning to face him. "No sense in hiding—since he resigned on the afternoon of your visit." He snickered again. "Heartbreaker."

"Shut up."

"Manners!" Kushiel gasped in a falsetto, clutching at his slender throat as if at a delicate strand of pearls.

"What Gianni did or whether he did has nothing at all to do with me," she insisted.

"As you like," he drawled in a mocking tone.

"And thanks for warning me, by the way, that he was going to be there."

"Who knew?" Kushiel said in his normal tone as he shrugged slender shoulders. "Keeping track of John's whereabouts wasn't my job at the time."

Xiomara paused, her brow furrowing at the use of a name she had not heard before. She wondered if Kushiel's insistence upon referring to his associates by their birth names meant that Gianni's given name was John.

"You and I have a lot to talk about," Xiomara told him. "You have quite the talent for concealment."

"Never intending to harm, Khinayda," Kushiel replied.

"You didn't tell me about Gianni, and you didn't tell me I could make another like me. You obviously failed to inform Gianni about this little trick, too. He thought I'd traipsed off somewhere and was living the idyllic dream."

"Our numbers are dwindling, Khinayda," he said, "and they have blessed not all in my employ with the trait of immortality. We must ensure that our numbers grow. Besides, only those who are truly special can become one of us. You're among a very select group."

"So, you knew... you knew what Gianni could do, and you kept both of us in the dark," she said, shaking her head. "You should have told me about him."

"What would you have done had I told you the truth about John, hmm? Or the truth about any of it? If I confessed what really happened to you and how you came to be, you would have tried to run off and find him... and then what? Your inexperience would have made you stick out like a sore thumb, ripe for being picked off by the other side. Or, you would have gotten yourself killed a second time. Then where would we be?"

He giggled, and Xiomara glared at him.

"Joran's not too happy with you," she said.

"Oooooh!" Kushiel sang with glee. "Maybe you should tell him I'm the one who helped get him out of that cabin and staged his minor mishap." Xiomara turned away from him with a roll of her eyes. "And, while you're at it, tell him how much of a pain it was to do so in that horrible van he borrowed. Manual transmission, indeed! Felt like being back in the Dark Ages. I could have dusted off my old chariot and done better."

"Kushiel—what do you want?" she asked again, irritated.

He grinned, reaching up to caress a silver spike.

"Is that all you're planning for now—to go west?"

"Yes," Xiomara said.

"With our little friend in there?"

Xiomara turned to face him, leaning against the ledge. "What else would you have me do?"

"Hide out for a while," he suggested with a shrug. "You and the Pocket Rocket can lie low as you have been."

"Why would we do that?" Xiomara could not help snorting at the reference. At six-foot four inches, Joran was hardly petite.

"He's not exactly an unknown, Khinayda," Kushiel remarked. "Lots of activity around this one: headlines, publicity, questions... You've gotten lucky so far, but it probably won't last."

"Not the first time you've dealt with it," she said.

"He needs training," Kushiel cautioned.

"I can train him," Xiomara said. "I planned to do just that once we get to where we're going. I'm more than capable."

He nodded. "Indeed, you are... though your methods on this last sojourn were a tad sloppy." He leered at her. "A shovel... really? Where were your elite skills then?"

"They were killing him," Xiomara returned through clenched teeth.

"As they're meant to do," Kushiel shrugged yet again. "But, I forgive you. Sure hope that they can, though. Centuries of teaching; combat of every kind, only to be felled by a lusty woman wielding a gardening tool... how mortifying!"

"It was less than what they were owed!" Xiomara shot back. "And, that's another thing I have to thank you for—sending the beast that killed me on this assignment? Really, Kushiel?"

Kushiel looked chagrined. "I'll give you that," he admitted. "But, I didn't expect the thing to remember, let alone to get sassy about it." He sighed. "I hope you know what you're doing, though, keeping him with you."

"I learned from you, didn't I?" Xiomara said, ignoring the rest. "And I'm sure you'll step in if you feel Joran needs it."

"I think he'll be fine under your tutelage," Kushiel said carefully before the smile dropped. "That's not what I'm referring to."

"Then what's the problem?" Xiomara asked. "You've been hedging since you got here. What aren't you telling me?"

"It's not the norm to partner up."

"I'm not the norm," she countered, "and I won't leave him to do this alone."

"You don't owe him anything, Khinayda!" Kushiel said in a tone more serious than he had used throughout their entire exchange.

"It's not about owing him," Xiomara sighed. He studied her for a moment before nodding.

"Perhaps it's for the best," Kushiel said, grinning again. "You've attracted quite a bit of attention."

"So, you've hinted."

"Everyone's talking about it..."

"That issue at the office was not my doing," Xiomara contested. "And if Marjorie has been running her mouth, especially considering the fact that..."

"I'm not talking about that," he interrupted. "I'm talking about this last assignment."

Xiomara turned to him again, giving her full attention. "What about it?" she wanted to know.

"One soul you collected... greatly interests the competition."

"What? In what way?"

"Caused quite a stir when you claimed it. Its ownership is... under debate. Might be a bit of a problem."

Xiomara shook her head, feeling Kushiel's pupil-less eyes upon her through the pince-nez. "There's nothing to debate," she maintained. "I did exactly what I was meant to do and overstepped no boundaries."

"No one's questioning your methods. That's not what's under debate; but, if the question of having to... relinquish this particular trophy is broached, it will mean trouble for you. He might hold a grudge."

"How? What kind of trouble?"

Kushiel would only smile as he toyed with his spiked hair again. "Hopefully, we won't have to find out," was all he'd say, turning to walk away.

"Wait!" Xiomara called out to him. "You have to tell me more than that! There were two on this last assignment. Which one of them is under debate?" Then she paused as realization hit. "You said that 'he' might hold a grudge? Kushiel!"

"I'm sure that, between the three of you, you'll be fine," Kushiel tossed over his shoulder.

She stopped at that. "The three of us? What are you talking about? Talk to me!"

"What's going on?" said a voice from behind Xiomara, causing her to jump before whirling around. Joran, his halo of curls scattered about his head from recent sleep, was stepping through the open doors from inside the suite. He looked groggy, though better rested. "Who are you talking to?"

Xiomara did not need to look back over her shoulder to know that Kushiel had gone; over the balcony of the fifteenth floor in a way he alone could manage. She shook her head, tucking a lock of hair behind one ear as she forced a smile.

"Hey," she managed, walking over to Joran and looking up at him. "You look a lot better. How do you feel?"

"Still a little tired," Joran admitted. "But, I thought it was time to get up, anyway."

"Nightmares?" Xiomara asked gently. Joran reached out to touch Xiomara's hair. She thought perhaps he wanted to extract something that had become entangled in it, but when he withdrew his hand, it was empty.

"No," he said. "Not really. I mean, I had a dream about Gabriel, but this one was different."

Xiomara stiffened, recalling her nightmare from the evening before. "What do you mean?"

"I don't know," he shrugged. "Nothing happened in it. He was just... watching me." He smiled down at her. "I'd say that's an improvement over the ones where I watch myself be torn to shreds, wouldn't you?" When she did not respond, his smile faded. This time, when he touched her hair, he let his hand linger as his fingertips settled within the thick locks. "Your hair's still wet."

"Never mind that," Xiomara said, grabbing his hand and shifting it away, their fingers entwining briefly before parting. "I just came out for a bit."

"You'll catch cold," Joran chided, to which Xiomara could not resist a chuckle.

"That seems to be the consensus," she smirked.

"Why didn't you wake me?" he asked with a yawn. "It's after eleven."

"Because you needed to sleep," Xiomara answered, going through the doors and back inside.

"I'm not the only one who should sleep," Joran countered as he followed her in and closed the doors behind them, "especially since we were both up pretty late last night."

"I slept late enough as it is," she countered.

"Who was outside with you?" he asked. "I heard you talking with someone."

"Kushiel," Xiomara responded.

Joran paused, looking through the doors leading to the balcony, and then at Xiomara again. "What'd he do, backflip off the side?"

"Probably!" she answered, retrieving her hairbrush and pulling it through her locks a few times.

"Xiomara, are you okay?" Joran asked.

"Yeah," she said after a moment, and then looked up at him. She tapped the broad, flat end of the brush against her other palm. "How are you feeling?"

"Pretty good," he replied. "Better than longer than I can remember."

"Good enough for a road trip?"

"Sure!" Joran said, his brows raised in surprise as he studied her. "I thought we were driving out to Portland in a few days."

"We were," Xiomara said, tucking a lock of curling hair behind one ear. "But, now that you're feeling better, it might be a good idea to head out earlier than planned."

"What's going on?" he asked, eyes narrowing. "This is really strange, even for you. What did Kushiel say?"

"It's more what he left out," Xiomara admitted. "You know how Kushiel talks in riddles."

"Yeah, I'd say I'm fairly familiar with that," Joran said with a straight face. "So, what didn't he say?"

"I'll tell you all about it during the drive. For now, we should get moving."

"Fifteen minutes if all I have time to do is pack," Joran said.

"Fine," she said. "I'll get us checked out and then start on my stuff."

As Joran returned to the bedroom, Xiomara reached for the phone sitting atop one of the end tables in the living room, pressed 'O' for the operator, and waited. As someone answered, there was a knock at the door.

"I'm sorry," Xiomara said into the receiver, "I'll call you right back." Hanging up, she walked over to the door and opened it. Before she could respond, Gianni brushed past her and entered the suite. "What the hell!?" Slamming the door, she turned to face him, her expression less than pleased. "What are you doing here? Who told you how to find me?"

Gianni ran a hand through his silver hair and shook his head, his hazel eyes shifting from Xiomara to Joran, who had returned with a puzzled expression. The two men studied each other in silence and then turned to Xiomara.

"Did you tell him?" Gianni asked her.

"How is that any of your business?" Xiomara demanded. "How do you even know?"

"You can speak to me directly, you know," Joran said from the doorway of the bedroom.

"Suit yourself," Gianni returned, looking at Joran. "Did she tell you about Gabriel?"

"Gianni—seriously!?" Xiomara said through clenched teeth.

Joran looked at Xiomara. "What about Gabriel?" he asked. "Does he have something to do with what you wanted to talk to me about?"

Xiomara glared at Gianni, shaking her head. Gianni sighed and then shrugged.

"It's probably a good idea for you to pack," he answered.

"What do you think we were doing when you barged in here?" Joran said, with an edge of temper Xiomara had not heard from him before. Gianni chuckled, fixing Xiomara in his amused gaze.

"All right, sweetheart," he said, returning to the familiar drawl that Xiomara remembered, "looks like we're about to have ourselves a li'l fun!"

Epilogue

They packed into the elevator, ignoring all written warnings regarding occupancy and weight. As the vessel ascended from the lobby, stopping every few floors along the way, it became less cluttered as the number of floors grew higher. By the time it reached the 45th floor, only two occupants remained, including a young man clad in an expensive three-piece suit.

He glanced at the young woman, appraising her beauty while critiquing her attire. The uppermost floors held the offices of some of the most prestigious companies in the country, and here she was—dressed from tousled head to steeled toe in black leather: buckled knee-length coat, tight pants, and wedge heeled boots glittering with buckles and studs. Her creamy caramel-colored skin was devoid of makeup—a miracle in this age—and a pair of dark glasses hid her eyes.

"Beautiful morning, isn't it?" he heard himself say. How stupid. The sky was a dreary gray, and it was going to rain again at any moment.

As he mentally berated himself for behaving like a preteen at his first co-ed function, the young woman turned to look at him, removing her glasses. His breath caught at the clarity and directness of her thickly lashed hazel eyes.

She seemed to take him all in at once, the dark lashes sweeping her cheeks as her gaze washed over him from top to toe. In a moment that seemed all at once to be both too long and too short, she released him from her gaze and slid her glasses back on.

"Always," the young woman said at last, turning back to face the elevator doors.

"Don't think I've seen you here before," the young man went on in a rush, as if seeing an opening and charging through before it was lost.

"Can't imagine why you would," she told him. "My business has never brought me here before."

"Oh… I guess that does explain it." He noticed her leather satchel. "Are you a courier from one of the local companies?"

He so hoped that she was. He would get the name of the company she worked for and ensure that he would get to lay eyes on her again—soon. He could see the curve of her smile, and it made his breath catch. She tucked a lock of hair behind one ear using her left hand—upon which she wore no ring, he noted with happiness—and gently nodded.

"I am indeed a courier of sorts," she admitted. "But my employer is not just local. He is worldwide."

"Ah… perhaps then I could…"

The elevator dinged, interrupting him as the doors opened. It dismayed him to see his vision in black shift before moving toward and then through the doors. He opened his mouth to speak and then lunged for the control panel, pressing the button marked "Open."

She turned to face him and blessed him with another smile. In that moment, he forgot what it was he wanted to say to her.

"Not to worry," she assured him. "We may see one another again… in about four years."

He froze and gaped at her, not understanding. But his finger slipped from the button he had been holding, and the closing doors separated the two. He was quick to select the number of the next floor on the panel, intending to seek her out, yet in the seconds it took to go up a single floor, not only had the desire to find the mysterious beauty faded, but so had any memory that she had existed at all.

Puzzled and wondering why he'd gotten off on the wrong floor, the young man shook his head as if to clear it and took the stairs.

"Excuse me!" he said after colliding with someone as he rounded a corner of the stairwell, dropping his briefcase.

"Careful," he was told.

He couldn't help noticing the delicately tapered fingers of the other man, who was looking at him with amusement in his bright blue eyes, as the briefcase was retrieved and handed to him. The businessman walked the short distance to the door leading back into the building and reached for the handle.

"See you in four years," he heard behind him.

Pausing, he turned around in confusion, his bewilderment increasing as he realized he was alone.

Bonus: Alternate Ending

Xiomara crept from the bed, pulling one of Joran's blue T-shirts from the bundle of clothing on the floor. She moved through the room, pulling it overhead as she walked to the door before exiting. Crossing the living room with a yawn, she entered her own room across the way and closed the door behind her.

A short while later, she emerged, bathed and clad in a light blue cotton tank top and matching pinstriped pajama bottoms. Rather than returning to the room to rouse Joran, she walked toward the double doors leading to the balcony.

Xiomara stepped outside, inhaling the crisp December air, paying no attention to how inadequately dressed she was for the elements. The air felt wonderful against her skin, though, and she enjoyed the breeze that played with her damp hair. Closing her eyes, she drew in a deep breath and could not resist a smile.

"You're going to catch a deathly cold, young lady," chided a singsong voice to her left. Xiomara sighed and opened her eyes again, casting a wary glance in the interloper's direction.

At five-foot ten, he was the same height as Xiomara, aided by the ridiculous four-inch platform heels of his black alligator boots, to which silver spurs were attached. His dark red jeans were snug, but his long-sleeved black shirt was loose and rippled in the breeze, twisting the hem around his slender hips.

An unlit cigarette dangled from the corner of his smiling, generous mouth, and the chilled environment had infused his cappuccino-hued skin with a rosy tint. Running his long fingers through silver-tipped, spiked black hair, he peered at Xiomara through a pair of antique black pince-nez.

"Kushiel," Xiomara greeted in a monotone, rolling her eyes.

"Khinayda," he returned with a titter. She looked at where he sat, balanced upon the ledge of the balcony with his back to what would be a drop of about 150 feet. "You're looking a tidbit nipply this morning."

Xiomara crossed her arms in front of her chest, glaring at the still-smiling visitor. "What do you want?" she demanded.

Kushiel removed the pince-nez, polishing them upon the hem of his shirt. When he looked up at Xiomara, she did not flinch—long used to the pure whiteness of his eyes.

"How's he doing?" Kushiel asked, jerking his head in the suite's direction.

"He's finally sleeping at night," Xiomara answered.

"Alone?" he queried, though the smile had not left his face. Xiomara glared at him.

He sniggered, replacing the eyewear. "You're such a heartbreaker, Khinayda Hastings."

"Xiomara Grant," she said acidly.

"Not to me," Kushiel shrugged, hopping from the edge and landing on the balcony with a light bounce. He stood beside Xiomara, looking out at the skyline. "You're being introspective again, I can tell."

"Can't help it," Xiomara said.

"You do this at the end of every assignment," Kushiel mentioned. "Doesn't it ever get old?"

She glanced over at him. "Does it ever for you?"

"Time isn't the same creature for me as for you," he replied. "I was never human. I've always been an objective observer."

"Objective!" Xiomara snorted. "You?"

"Yes, me!" Kushiel squealed. "I've watched this world for many, many years, and I've always seen it for what it is and not what I hoped it would be."

"No rose-colored pince-nez for you, then?"

Kushiel grinned at her.

"I've always liked you, Hastings," he revealed. "You're one of very few able to keep up with me."

"I'm unsure of whether that's a compliment," Xiomara mused.

"Of course, it is!" Kushiel responded. "I'm fabulous! You should be so lucky."

"Objectively speaking, of course," she countered, widening his impossible grin.

"Cheeky," he praised. "That's another reason I like you. Snap out of it, though. This isn't the time to get mucked down by thoughts of what could have been." He considered her. "Go ahead. You won't feel right until you say it."

"Sometimes I wonder why we have to do this," Xiomara murmured.

"And there it is," Kushiel chuckled. "The answer hasn't changed in the dozen years since you've asked, you know. It won't change after another dozen."

"I could have more influence," she mused.

"That train of thought is destined for derailment, Khinayda Hastings. The moment you think you can assume dominion over Man is when you lean too far toward the other side."

"I'm not trying to do that!" Xiomara insisted.

"It's a slippery slope," Kushiel said. "Sure, you might start out with the best of intentions, but then what? What if your charge rebukes your influence? You push a little harder, all in the name of guidance... and then turn out no better than our competitor."

"Competitor," Xiomara snorted again. "Some game we're playing."

"The biggest game there is!" Kushiel said, the grin returning to his handsome face.

"Why are we still playing it?"

"He's got you questioning your work now?"

"This isn't about Joran," Xiomara stressed. "It's not the first time I've asked the question."

"Yes, but I thought I'd broken you of the habit!" Kushiel said. "Now, look!" He peered out at the skyline again. "I'll tell you why we play this game, and the reason is the same no matter which side of the field you favor.

"Collusion is sweet... but Conversion is SO much more delicious. Take your average unhappily married man... with a wife of twenty years who has not truly satisfied him for at least eighteen. So, he takes a lover—not necessarily younger, but more willing—and he can indulge in her in ways dear wifey routinely rebelled against.

"As sweet as the lover is... as complicit as she is... as much as he enjoys every aspect of her in the two or three years they have together... and as much as he might actually come to truly love her… nothing she does for him can ever compare to that moment when the wife—with her position threatened by what's become much more than a casual dalliance—finally succumbs to his whims. Conversion is like the Holy Grail."

Kushiel turned to look at Xiomara.

"We do this for the chance to save that one soul that would have been lost to us otherwise," he continued. "I would raze ten thousand eager co-conspirators for that."

"Not very saint-like," Xiomara commented.

"I was never a saint," Kushiel returned, tittering as he licked the tip of his pinky and then smoothed his right eyebrow with it. Xiomara watched him; taking in the almost exaggerated bravado, flamboyance, and aura of confidence that he always displayed, and then smirked.

"Unhappily married man?" she queried.

"Mind your business," he chided, returning the smirk.

"As you like," she said in her lazy drawl, turning back once more to enjoy the view.

"Heading back to the office soon for your next assignment?" Kushiel asked after a moment.

Xiomara's thoughts settled upon Gianni and running into him that day.

"No," she said, choosing to keep her reasoning private. "I'm thinking of taking Joran west. I can always get work from the office out there."

"He's not there anymore," Kushiel told her. Xiomara remained focused on the view ahead of her, rather than turning to face him. "No sense in hiding—since he resigned on the afternoon of your visit." He snickered again. "Heartbreaker."

"Shut up."

"Manners!" Kushiel gasped in a falsetto, clutching at his slender throat as if at a delicate strand of pearls.

"What Gianni did or whether he did has nothing at all to do with me," she insisted.

"As you like," he drawled in a mocking tone.

"And thanks for warning me, by the way, that he was going to be there."

"Who knew?" Kushiel said in his normal tone as he shrugged slender shoulders. "Keeping track of John's whereabouts wasn't my job at the time."

Xiomara paused, her brow furrowing at the use of a name she had not heard before. She wondered if Kushiel's insistence upon referring to his associates by their birth names meant that Gianni's given name was John.

"You and I have a lot to talk about," Xiomara told him. "You have quite the talent for concealment."

"Never intending to harm, Khinayda," Kushiel replied.

"You didn't tell me about Gianni, and you didn't tell me I could make another like me. You obviously failed to inform Gianni about this little trick, too. He thought I'd traipsed off somewhere and was living the idyllic dream."

"Our numbers are dwindling, Khinayda," he said, "and they have blessed not all in my employ with the trait of immortality. We must ensure that our numbers grow. Besides, only those who are truly special can become one of us. You're among a very select group."

"So, you knew... you knew what Gianni could do, and you kept both of us in the dark," she said, shaking her head. "You should have told me about him."

"What would you have done had I told you the truth about John, hmm? Or the truth about any of it? If I confessed what really happened to you and how you came to be, you would have tried to run off and find him... and then what? Your inexperience would have made you stick out like a sore thumb, ripe for being picked off by the other side. Or, you would have gotten yourself killed a second time. Then where would we be?"

He giggled, and Xiomara glared at him.

"Joran's not too happy with you," she said.

"Oooooh!" Kushiel sang with glee. "Maybe you should tell him I'm the one who helped get him out of that cabin and staged his minor mishap." Xiomara turned away from him with a roll of her eyes. "And, while you're at it, tell him how much of a pain it was to do so in that horrible van he borrowed. Manual transmission, indeed! Felt like being back in the Dark Ages. I could have dusted off my old chariot and done better."

"Kushiel—what do you want?" she asked again, irritated.

He grinned, reaching up to caress a silver spike.

"Is that all you're planning for now—to go west?"

"Yes," Xiomara said.

"With our little friend in there?"

Xiomara turned to face him, leaning against the ledge. "What else would you have me do?"

"Hide out for a while," he suggested with a shrug. "You and the Pocket Rocket can lie low as you have been."

"Why would we do that?" Xiomara could not help snorting at the reference. At six-foot four inches, Joran was hardly petite.

"He's not exactly an unknown, Khinayda," Kushiel remarked. "Lots of activity around this one: headlines, publicity, questions... You've gotten lucky so far, but it probably won't last."

"Not the first time you've dealt with it," she said.

"He needs training," Kushiel cautioned.

"I can train him," Xiomara said. "I planned to do just that once we get to where we're going. I'm more than capable."

He nodded. "Indeed, you are... though your methods on this last sojourn were a tad sloppy." He leered at her. "A shovel... really? Where were your elite skills then?"

"They were killing him," Xiomara returned through clenched teeth.

"As they're meant to do," Kushiel shrugged yet again. "But, I forgive you. Sure hope that they can, though. Centuries of teaching; combat of every kind, only to be felled by a lusty woman wielding a gardening tool... how mortifying!"

"It was less than what they were owed!" Xiomara shot back. "And, that's another thing I have to thank you for—sending the beast that killed me on this assignment? Really, Kushiel?"

Kushiel looked chagrined. "I'll give you that," he admitted. "But, I didn't expect the thing to remember, let alone to get sassy about it." He sighed. "I hope you know what you're doing, though, keeping him with you."

"I learned from you, didn't I?" Xiomara said, ignoring the rest. "And I'm sure you'll step in if you feel Joran needs it."

"I think he'll be fine under your tutelage," Kushiel said carefully before the smile dropped. "That's not what I'm referring to."

"Then what's the problem?" Xiomara asked. "You've been hedging since you got here. What aren't you telling me?"

"It's not the norm to partner up."

"I'm not the norm," she countered, "and I won't leave him to do this alone."

"You don't owe him anything, Khinayda!" Kushiel said in a tone more serious than he had used throughout their entire exchange.

"It's not about owing him," Xiomara sighed. He studied her for a moment before nodding.

"Perhaps it's for the best," Kushiel said, grinning again. "You've attracted quite a bit of attention."

"So, you've hinted."

"Everyone's talking about it..."

"That issue at the office was not my doing," Xiomara contested. "And if Marjorie has been running her mouth, especially considering the fact that..."

"I'm not talking about that," he interrupted. "I'm talking about this last assignment."

Xiomara turned to him again, giving her full attention. "What about it?" she wanted to know.

"One soul you collected... greatly interests the competition."

"What? In what way?"

"Caused quite a stir when you claimed it. Its ownership is... under debate. Might be a bit of a problem."

Xiomara shook her head, feeling Kushiel's pupil-less eyes upon her through the pince-nez. "There's nothing to debate," she maintained. "I did exactly what I was meant to do and overstepped no boundaries."

"No one's questioning your methods. That's not what's under debate; but, if the question of having to... relinquish this particular trophy is broached, it will mean trouble for you. He might hold a grudge."

"How? What kind of trouble?"

"Trouble that you don't need, and he can't handle just yet," Kushiel answered, indicating the absent and sleeping Joran with a nod of his head.

"Stop talking in riddles, Kushiel," Xiomara demanded.

"Leave him," Kushiel said simply. Xiomara took a step back, her brow furrowed.

"What?"

"Leave. Him."

"Leave Joran?"

"Yes," he said firmly.

"Why? What is going on?"

"As I said—nothing yet…"

"I told you to stop talking in riddles!"

"And I'm telling you that Joran is a distraction you might not be able to afford right now!" Kushiel said, raising his voice for the first time.

"But, to leave him?" Xiomara said. "Since you won't tell me what's going on, can you at least tell me if that's the only option?"

"It is the option that makes the most sense," Kushiel said in a gentle tone. "You need to trust me on this, Khinayda. If this plays out a certain way, it would do you no good to be together. He is a liability right now. Besides, he'll be in good company."

"With you?"

"For a time." The grin was back. "He'll be kept safe."

"Guarded by the very things that killed him?" Xiomara said, turning away to study the landscape again, shaking her head. "You're telling me there's no other choice?"

"You're telling me you hadn't already thought of leaving him at some point?" Kushiel countered. "I know you, Khinayda. I know better than anyone how… reluctant… you can be when someone gets close. This way you can sleep easier knowing where he is. If nothing comes of it, come back and get him. You and the Pocket Rocket can blaze your own lusty trail from here to the West Coast for all I care."

Xiomara ran both hands through her damp hair before crossing her arms tightly across her chest. She sighed.

"I've only just finally let him in… and now I have to let him go."

Kushiel watched her, careful not to acknowledge the presentation of her words as a statement rather than a question.

"How much time do you need?" he asked softly.

"Ten minutes," she answered through clenched teeth, refusing to meet his eyes. "You know I always travel light."

Kushiel continued to watch as Xiomara's jaw repeatedly tightened, sending ripples up and along the side of her face and to her temple. He saw the moisture gradually building, the shimmering landscape reflecting in her hazel eyes. Kushiel knew at that moment that the decision, though heart-wrenching for her, was for the best.

"What will you tell him?" Xiomara finally asked. The look she turned on Kushiel had hardened significantly, and he nodded in unasked approval.

"He's not stupid, Khinayda," Kushiel said with a shrug. "I won't insult him, or you, by making up stories. I'll tell him I told you to go. In the meantime, I'll have him trained. He will know... that it is his way back to you. It'll keep him focused. It may even help if it comes down to it."

"How long?"

"Khinayda..."

"How long?" Xiomara asked again. "How much time is this going to take, Kushiel?"

"Who's to say?" Kushiel said. "However long is needed."

Xiomara turned on her heel without another word, marching back inside the suite. She hurried through the living room and into her bedroom, quickly securing her hair into a low knot before packing. It took only eight minutes, not ten as she had estimated, before she was dressed and ready to leave.

Her Chicago Blackhawks nightshirt was still on Joran's bedroom floor, but she would have to leave it behind. Xiomara hoped he would cherish it much as she intended to hold dear the T-shirt of his that she wore only a short time ago, now lovingly folded inside her bag.

As Xiomara exited her bedroom, hefting both the leather satchel and its matching duffle bag, she knew without even looking that Kushiel had gone. She knew, too, that he would be back when Joran needed him. She was not entirely sure that she could trust Kushiel to tell Joran the full truth. Kushiel had a fondness for sharing only that which he felt someone needed to know for the moment, and nothing more. Besides, Xiomara was not stupid either. She had pieced together the source of Kushiel's concern.

Gabriel.

If Gabriel's was the soul under contention, and if that soul ended up being relinquished, things could get messy. Being so newly converted, Joran needed to be elsewhere... and apart from Xiomara.

Xiomara swiftly moved through the space, only stopping to close the door of the suite softly behind her before rushing to the elevator. By the time she reached the lobby, she felt dizzy, and she briefly wondered if she had held her breath the entire time.

Pausing briefly at the front desk to plan for the continued payment of the room, she declined the services of a valet and traveled alone to the parking garage.

Or at least she thought she was alone.

Leaning against the trunk of her car, a duffle bag of his own resting at his feet, was Gianni. Xiomara glared at him as she approached, but he stepped to one side and only watched as she opened the trunk, tossed her belongings inside, and then slammed it shut.

"I should have known there was a catch," she said as she walked over to the driver's side of the vehicle. She opened the door and then looked at Gianni. "I can take care of myself. You can go."

"Actually, I can't," Gianni said. "I can't let you go out there alone."

"You don't even know where I'm going."

"It doesn't matter. I already left you once when you needed me. I can't do that again."

"I don't need you," Xiomara said tightly, though her eyes were shining.

"No," Gianni agreed after a brief pause, with a sad shake of his head. "Not... not in the way I wish you did. But, you still shouldn't be alone. Obviously, I know what has happened. I also know that I've never heard of the acquisition of a soul being contested like this." He held his hands out at his sides. "Be angry with me, Khinayda. Hurl every hateful word at me you want, but... please don't leave here by yourself. Please. You need someone to help you sort this out and to confront it if need be."

They stared at one another; Gianni's soft hazel gaze meeting Xiomara's flinty one. Finally, she pressed a button on her key fob, and the trunk popped open again.

"Put your shit in and hurry up," she said before getting into the car and slamming the door.

They were on the road for roughly twenty minutes, with nothing more said between them. Gianni stole periodic glances at Xiomara, watching the cycles play out in her eyes as they went from sad and filling to glinting and sharp. Finally, he shook his head.

"Where are we going?" he asked.

"Need to swap out the car, my phone, and ID," Xiomara said. "It's about a nine-hour drive to the meet-up spot. You weren't part of the plan, so you'll have to get your own stuff."

"I've got it covered," he said.

"Bully for you."

"Okay, so then let's talk," Gianni said in an even tone after a couple more minutes of uncomfortable silence.

"I've got nothing to talk with you about."

"Khinayda, I'm only trying to help you!"

"My name is Xiomara!" she yelled, slapping her right palm against the edge of the steering wheel.

"Maybe for the next nine hours it is!" Gianni yelled back. He then sighed and ran a hand through his hair, evening his tone. "Look, we... we can't do this. We are supposed to be working together. I'm here to help you, and I need to know what we're up against." Xiomara sighed and gripped the steering wheel, but didn't answer. "Tell me what the deal is with this Gabriel Matheson. There's got to be something for the other side to want him so badly."

"That doesn't surprise me at all, considering," Xiomara said after a few moments.

"Considering what?"

"His lineage," Xiomara said. "His history. Still, despite who he was, I hoped I could change things. We're taught to hope until the very end."

"I don't think we've neared the end yet," Gianni said.

"Apparently not. But, if Gabriel does somehow get to come back, I don't think that redemption will be on his mind, anyway."

Gianni arched a sandy brow at her. "You think he hates you that much?"

"I think he loves me that much."

Gianni's eyes widened as he studied Xiomara. His gaze then shifted as he peered through the passenger-side window, absently making note of the information on a passing road marker as his thoughts churned.

"Well," he finally said, returning to the familiar drawl that Xiomara remembered, "I guess we're about to have ourselves a li'l fun..."

Acknowledgements

The publication of this novel results from many years of self-doubt and longing, surmounted by determination and fiery resolve. I've been able to keep my head up because of the support of an amazing group of family, friends, and loved ones who have rallied around me to make sure that I didn't falter.

The brilliant artist Jason Elizaldi did the drawing at the beginning of the novel. He conceptualized the core theme of Duality in a picture that means approximately 75,000 words.

Suanne Fried-Goodman shared her wisdom and love of character study to help me bring out the best qualities in some of the worst people. I am in awe of her eye for detail and hope someday to acquire it as I continue my journey as a published author.

Very special thanks to David Mitchum, my beautiful baby sister, my remarkable mother—to whom this novel is dedicated—and other family and friends too many to name individually. You have each been part of my own dualities and, therefore, a part of the creation of this book. I love all of you.

Ametra

The Fractured Soul Saga continues with Book Two...

Hey, Roomie!

In the cold grip of a Portland winter, Chelsia Toussaint is trying to build something stable. A quiet job. A steady relationship. A future that finally feels within reach.

But when a sudden death shatters that fragile life, everything she thought she understood begins to unravel.

Drawn into a web of quiet tensions and unspoken truths, Chelsia finds herself surrounded by people who do not quite add up. A detective watches her too closely. A new "roomie" greets her with effortless charm but keeps too many secrets. Beneath it all, a growing sense takes hold that nothing and no one is what they seem.

As suspicion deepens and the past refuses to stay buried, Chelsia must decide how far she is willing to go to protect what little remains of her life.

Because the greatest danger might not be what she is running from.

It might be what has been following her all along.

Available at your favorite online retailers in e-book or paperback.

Ask at your local bookstore.

ARRAYED FORMATS
PUBLISHING

www.ingramcontent.com/pod-product-compliance
Lightning Source LLC
Chambersburg PA
CBHW060631260626
47161CB00008B/2863